SMOKE AND MIRRORS

A Miss Barnum Mystery

Casey Daniels

This first world edition published 2017
in Great Britain and the USA by
SEVERN HOUSE PUBLISHERS LTD of
Eardley House, 4 Uxbridge Street, London W8 7SY.
Trade paperback edition first published
in Great Britain and the USA 2018 by
SEVERN HOUSE PUBLISHERS LTD.

British Library Cataloguing in Publication Data
A CIP catalogue record for this title is available from the British Library.

ISBN-13: 978-0-7278-8725-2 (cased)
ISBN-13: 978-1-84751-830-9 (trade paper)
ISBN-13: 978-1-78010-900-8 (e-book)

Typeset by Palimpsest Book Production Ltd.,
Falkirk, Stirlingshire, Scotland.

*The first book of a new series
is always for
David.
This one is no exception.*

ACKNOWLEDGMENTS

The best advice I've ever heard regarding research came from none other than the great mystery writer Elizabeth Peters (if you haven't read her Amelia Peabody books, don't delay). We were discussing a problem I had with a Victorian-era book I was writing. A fabulous diamond figured into the plot and I wanted it to tie into ancient Egypt, only I found out the Egyptians didn't mine diamonds.

Her response was priceless—

'That's when you say, it was a *rare* example of an Egyptian diamond!'

I kept that wisdom in mind as I was writing *Smoke and Mirrors*. Yes, I researched the heck out of New York in 1842, the American Museum, the Barnum family, and a host of other details. But I fudged a little, too, for the sake of the story. I took the biggest liberty with P.T. Barnum's family. He did have sisters, but not one named Evangeline.

The details of the museum itself are true and yes, it was an amazing place. Live animals (including a whale!), strange displays, a wax museum . . . the list of wonders and curiosities goes on. Once I read about the American Museum, I couldn't resist setting a mystery there.

As always, I need to thank a host of people for their help and support including Gail Fortune, my agent, and the members of my wonderful brainstorming group: Shelley Costa, Serena Miller and Emilie Richards, all great writers. Their books are well worth reading.

And of course, a big thank you to my family. My husband, David, is always there for me. Ernie, the Airedale, is ever at my side, even though he's usually sleeping. Just as I finished this book, we welcomed a new addition, Lucy, the big, mixed breed . . . er . . . well, Lucy is every much an oddity as those in the American Museum.

ONE

September, 1842

They came in droves, the gullible and the curious, the naïve and the trusting and those who wanted so badly to believe they were willing to deny their suspicions and abandon their common sense. Some arrived at the urging of their neighbors who had already seen what the journalists – bought and paid for by my brother, Phineas T. Barnum – called an exhibit of wonder and astonishment. Others yielded their twenty-five cents for more prurient reasons: they were eager to see in person the glorious maiden pictured in newspaper woodcuts, hair loose around her shoulders and her breasts bare.

They stood in long lines out on Broadway, and when the doors of Barnum's American Museum opened at eight each morning, many of them ignored the exhibits downstairs and hurried here to the second floor. I had seen it a thousand times in the months I had been in the employ of my brother; no sooner were their feet off the stairs than their voices became hushed and their breaths suspended, as if they were entering a church.

'And it is all because of you.'

Alone in the Picture Gallery at this early hour, I looked toward the exhibit that stood behind glass in front of me and, for a moment, saw only my own knowing smile reflected back in the soft glow of the whale oil lamps.

'The Feejee Mermaid.' I exhaled the words written on the nearby placard as I had heard so many of our patrons do.

She was surely a fantastical creature, or so my brother had led the world to believe. A freak of nature similar to those living human oddities who were also exhibited at the museum. But rather than a giantess, like our seven-foot-tall Rebecca Cromwell, or a diminutive genius, like Phin's newly discovered sensation, General Tom Thumb, the Feejee Mermaid was neither fish nor human being. She was, in all fact, a strange combination of both, and according to the stories my brother had put forth, she had been captured in the Pacific near the island of Feejee many years previously.

She was no more than three-feet long, a blackened, dried-up specimen whose ribs showed one after another beneath her desiccated skin. Her mouth was open in what always seemed to me a silent scream. Her tail was luxurious and covered with fish scales. Her arms were thrown over her head, and though Phin had told me time and again that I was altogether too imaginative, I was convinced she had the appearance of having died in great agony.

She was surely astounding.

And, it is only fair to report, a complete humbug – the product of a taxidermist of some great skill who had managed to create a flawless compound of the tail of a fish, the head of a monkey and the body of an orangutan.

The Feejee Mermaid had created quite the sensation here in New York City and, as a result, she had made my brother very rich.

I did not hold this against him, no more than I looked down on those who were credulous enough to believe such a creature might actually exist and pay their hard-earned money to see it. But being a more practical person than my brother, more orderly in mind and habit, or so he says, I was more inclined to take a pragmatic approach to the exhibit. As I did every morning, I made sure it was clean and neat and that the light shone upon it just right, so that when the crowds gathered the Feejee Mermaid would be ready to receive them.

Thus satisfied, I made my way toward the Waxworks Room just beyond the Portrait Gallery. I was nearly there when a man's voice called out from the stairway.

'Miss Barnum!'

For one terrifying second, I imagined I recognized the voice and froze.

It was one second too long.

'Miss Barnum, it is you! I did not think I could be so fortunate to locate you so quickly.'

I swallowed hard and turned to face my old friend, Andrew Emerson.

Was my smile enough to convince him that I was pleased by the chance meeting? I couldn't be sure, but I kept it in place and raised my chin. 'Mr Emerson. What on earth are you doing—'

'I must apologize for arriving unannounced, and so early in the morning, too.' Andrew raced up the last of the stairs at the same time he swept his tall top hat off his head. He closed in on me, his blue eyes ablaze with excitement.

'But how did you—' As if it might explain my confusion, I glanced at the stairway.

'I know it's early and the museum doesn't open for another twenty minutes. I hope I haven't caused trouble for the man at the door. I explained that I am an old friend of your family, that we were all acquainted back in Bethel, Connecticut.'

Bethel.

The one topic above all others I did not wish to discuss.

To be sure I would not have to, I lifted the skirts of my brown dress, the better to sail into the Waxworks Room and the refuge of my office beyond. 'It's very nice seeing you again. But I really must be going, Mr Emerson. I have duties to attend to and—'

'I understand. Truly, I do. I have much news of home to share.' He dangled the words like a fat worm on a fishhook, and when I did not respond because all I could feel was panic and all I could think was that I needed to get away, he presumed I was interested. 'Abigail Ross – you remember her, the girl with the squint eyes – married Parson Thompson's son, Ezra, in the spring. And the mill burned just a month ago. Did you hear the story? No one could talk of another thing for weeks after.'

'That is . . . thank you.' I stepped back. 'Perhaps we might meet another time and chat about it all. But for now—'

'Please, Miss Barnum. Evangeline. Please. I have come the seventy miles from Bethel, and I would not think to bother you if it wasn't essential. It is why I went to your home in Bethel and talked to your mother and—'

'My mother?' Even to my own ears, my words sounded as if they had been formed of ice. I thought to clear the chill away with a cough but decided against it. Andrew and I had known each other since childhood. He was not the type who would notice the coldness of my words, or if he did, he would be too polite to mention it. And I was not the type who could so easily put so raw a wound behind me.

'What exactly was it my mother told you?' I asked him.

'Well, that's the deuce of it, isn't it? If you'll pardon the expression, dear Evangeline. You left Bethel so quickly two years ago, and I didn't know how I might get in touch with you again, so I went to see Mrs Barnum to inquire after you. I thought she would surely help me, knowing that we have long been friends. But your mother—'

'My mother?' Tears sprang to my eyes, and I blinked rapidly to hide them while at the same time cursing myself for my weakness.

'Your mother told me she had absolutely no idea where you'd gone! It made no sense to me. No sense at all. You have always been a loving and devoted daughter and your mother—'

When Andrew shook his head in wonder, his coppery hair – combed slightly forward and long over his ears as was the fashion for young men – fell against his brow. He pushed it back with one well-shaped hand. Since his father's death, Andrew had taken over the running of *The Intelligencer*, the newspaper in Bethel, and he was a reliable, steady sort of fellow with a gentle nature and a generous heart. He believed the best of people. Even when they didn't deserve it.

'Your mother must have been having a turn of some sort. I thought it was important for you to know. Perhaps she needs the services of a doctor.'

I exhaled a breath of relief. If all Andrew wanted was to tell me my mother's mind was not as clear as it once had been, then our business was concluded. 'Thank you,' I said and turned away.

'But Evie!'

The childhood name brought a wave of memories crashing over me, and for the sake of our long friendship, I paused.

'I've come all this way,' Andrew said, his words spilling out, one over top of the other. 'I took the chance of coming here to New York City, thinking I might speak to your brother of your whereabouts, but now that I've found you, well, it really is a miracle. I must talk to you, Evie. I haven't been able to eat. I haven't been able to sleep. I will not be able to, not until we talk. Not until you help me.'

I looked over my shoulder at him and knew he was telling the truth. On close inspection, I saw there were smudges of sleeplessness under Andrew's eyes that looked particularly gray against his white linen shirt and especially ghastly considering he was wearing a gay charcoal, red and cream bow tie. He wore tan sit-down-upons (even here in the city, no one dared be so libertine as to use the word *trousers*), a black, calf-length frock coat and, even as I turned to him, his fingers worked over the brim of his stovepipe hat.

'I . . . I can't help you,' I told him.

'But you can. I am certain of it!' There was a catch in his voice. 'You're the only one who can, Evie. Please. If you'll give me just a minute or two—'

'I wish I could, but I have my duties. The museum is about to open, and when it does there will be hundreds of people here in the gallery in a matter of moments.'

'Then we must talk quickly.'

'No. I wish I could, but I can't. I must . . .' I fingered the white silk reticule I'd brought with me that morning from the home I shared with Phin and his wife, Charity, and was grateful I needn't lie. 'I must pay our human oddities their weekly wages,' I told Andrew without bothering to add I had planned to do it that afternoon, not that morning. 'It would be rude of me to keep them waiting. In fact . . .' From habit, I glanced over my shoulder toward the Waxworks Room. I knew that often, Jeffrey Hollister, the man we were so bold as to advertise as the Lizard Man of Borneo, spent his free hours there because the light was good for reading and he invariably had a book with him. 'They are waiting for me. I must . . . Really, Andrew, it has been wonderful to see you but I must be going.'

I cannot say what happened first, or how it happened at all, seeing as I didn't realize Jeffrey Hollister was at that moment in the Waxworks Room. But when Andrew stepped forward yet one more time, clapped a hand on my arm and said, 'Evie, please, I beg you,' Jeffrey flew out of the shadows and, like the half-man half-beast we purported him to be, he went straight for Andrew's throat.

For a moment, I was unable to do anything but watch in horror as Jeffrey's hands closed over Andrew's windpipe. In keeping with his wild-man persona, Jeffrey's fingernails were grotesquely long and his skin was a dull green thanks to the combination of ground coffee, henna and spinach he rubbed over it each morning, the better to fascinate the adults who came to observe him and to frighten their children. The color added a gruesome accent to the natural texture of his skin, coarse and scabrous from birth, as did the fact that he wore nothing more than a loincloth and roughly made sandals.

There was a cage nearby, an exhibit my brother liked to call the 'Happy Family,' and the animals in it did not take kindly to the commotion. The dogs barked. The hawk wheeled through the cage and screeched. The seven monkeys that lived therein flung themselves at the steel bars, screaming.

Through it all and the ferocious racket of my pounding heart, I heard Jeffrey grunt and growl and saw Andrew's eyes goggle out of his head, and I knew I had to do something quickly.

'Mr Hollister! No!' I raced forward and put a hand on Jeffrey's bare shoulder. In my time at the museum I had seen him nearly every day and, as with all the other oddities, I had become immune to the freakishness of his physical qualities. But I had never, of course, touched him, and the texture of his skin – like that of sand – repelled me. Taken aback, I dropped my hand and pulled away. That is, before I realized I did not have a moment to lose. Not if I was going to save Andrew, who was now backed against the glass case that contained the Feejee Mermaid and whose cheeks were a particularly horrifying shade of maroon.

I rushed forward and closed a hand on each of Jeffrey's shoulders, pulling him as firmly as I could to my side, and by the time I was done the ringlets that cascaded down from the central part of my hair hung in loose spirals.

'Mr Hollister, it's fine. Really.' I hauled in a breath and steadied myself, the better – I hoped – to calm Jeffrey when I wrapped an unyielding arm around his waist. 'Mr Emerson is an old friend. He meant me no harm.'

Jeffrey tore himself out of my grasp but, fortunately, when he scuttled away it was toward the Waxworks Room and away from Andrew. 'He touched you, he did.' His eyes were small and dark and they shot a look of pure hatred at Andrew. 'I saw it myself. I saw Miss was in trouble. He . . . he shouldn't have done that.'

'I didn't mean . . .' Andrew pulled in a breath and steadied himself, one hand flat against the mermaid exhibit. He tugged his waistcoat back into place. 'I'm sorry, Evie. I didn't mean to . . .'

'No need,' I told him and, with one hand out – stained with the green color that dyed Jeffrey's skin – I stopped him when he tried to step nearer. Though I thought Jeffrey had possession of his temper, it was difficult to say for sure. Of all our oddities, he was the most likely to lash out when provoked, and he was often provoked for very little reason. Though I could not in any way approve, I did understand. He had spent his life as an outcast and a misfit. He had endured years of mistreatment and abuse simply because he looked peculiar. Before my brother discovered him and paid him more than a living wage to be part of the museum, poor Jeffrey had performed in the circus and lived on the streets. He was a bitter man and unpredictable, though he had proven himself a quick study when it came to learning to read and had demonstrated – surely not in quite the right way this time – that he had a noble heart and a courageous nature.

'Mr Hollister thought I might be in danger.' I smiled at our Lizard Man as a way of conveying my thanks. Later, when he was calm and when my lungs weren't on fire and my blood wasn't racing, I would remind him that though I appreciated him coming to what he thought was my rescue, violence would not be tolerated inside the walls of the museum. 'I am very fortunate, indeed, to have him here looking after me.'

Just as I'd hoped, this comment elicited a small smile from my protector.

'Thank you very much, Mr Hollister,' I told him and stepped back so he might return to the Waxworks Room. 'I am grateful for your care and concern.'

Jeffrey mumbled something that might have been 'You're welcome,' and disappeared back into the room from which he had come.

Andrew's stovepipe hat was on the floor and, gulping down breath after breath, he bent to retrieve it. 'You know I didn't mean anything of it, Evie. You know I would never hurt you.'

There was no truth to the rumor that I had once given Andrew Emerson the mitten. We were never engaged to be married and, had we been, I never would have broken it off. I wasn't in love with Andrew. I never had been. But he was a good man and there was honor in him. For all the world, I could not have broken my promise to him and risked breaking his heart.

Just because I did not love him did not mean I wasn't moved by the softness of his smile.

Drat it all, he saw the softening of my resolve and his eyes pleaded with me. 'Please give me a few moments. For the sake of the friendship we shared. For the sake of everything that happened back in Bethel.'

If only he knew! It was what had happened back in Bethel that worried me so, and what would happen – to me and to my family – if the truth of the matter became public. Two years previously, I had convinced myself the only way to assure secrecy was to never let down my guard and to never reveal my secrets.

I had never loved Andrew Emerson, but I valued our friendship.

I knew if I took the time to talk to him, both my safety and those secrets might be put at risk.

I inched my shoulders back. 'I am grateful Mr Hollister didn't injure you and I hope you will forgive him. As you might imagine, he has not had an easy life. He is well-intentioned in spite of his temper. For reasons I cannot explain, he feels proprietary when it comes to me.'

'Perhaps he recognizes the goodness that has always been inside you, dear Evie.' I thought Andrew might take my hand, but one look over my shoulder toward the Waxworks Room and he changed his mind. 'I recognize the strength of your character, too. That's why I've come to see you. Evie, please listen.' He reached into the pocket of his frock coat and pulled out a single piece of paper, folded in half. 'Let me show you something. Just so you might read it. Just so you might understand. Then you'll surely see why I need your help.'

He was so sincere and I was terrified I might be convinced. Panic spread through my bloodstream and quickened my pulse. My stomach clutched. 'I wish I could, Andrew. But no matter what you think I can do for you, I cannot.'

The pain of his expression was too much to bear, so I refused to look him in the face.

'But for the sake of our friendship!' He made to press the

paper into my hand, but I closed my fingers tight over my palm and refused to yield. 'Please, Evie.'

I shook my head. 'I am not the girl you knew back in Bethel.'

Before he could question my statement or once again pull me in with reminders of our long acquaintance, I turned on my heel and swept into the Waxworks Room.

Andrew came as far as the doorway, his voice rough with emotion and touched with desperation.

'Please, Evie, please,' he called after me. 'Don't you see? I need your help. She . . . she needs your help!'

I need your help.

She needs your help.

The words echoed through my mind all morning, shaming me for my callousness. They did not, however, change my heart or dampen my resolve. That day, I kept myself safely behind the closed door of my office, coming out only once at two and only because every Friday at that time I shared a meal with Madame Chantilly DePris (who was, in reality, a woman named Bess Buttle), our most current Bearded Lady. I will admit that while it was off-putting at first, after these few months, I hardly noticed Bess's full growth of facial hair and was, in fact, more interested in the amusing stories she told of her life back in London and her time on the road in freak shows and circuses both in this country and abroad. Not only would I miss seeing Bess this Friday, but she would not easily forgive me if I cancelled.

With Bess and luncheon in mind and, feeling very much like the coward I was, I inched open my office door and peeked outside. The room where I looked over the ledgers and handled other portions of the administrative duties that kept the museum operating smoothly was directly beyond the Waxworks Room and, from there, I could see the knots of people gathered in front of our exhibits, engaged in lively conversation. There were more patrons in the Portrait Gallery, I could hear their voices and, when I stepped outside the office, I saw what I expected – most of them were gathered around the mermaid, their mouths open in wonder, their eyes wide with amazement. Still more of them tramped up the steps to visit our Feejee beauty.

I was relieved to see that none of these was Andrew Emerson.

After luncheon I handed out wages to our oddities, then I returned to my office and spent the rest of the day closed in there. At dinnertime, I might have called for a carriage to take me to Castle Garden and – thanks to the largesse of my brother – paid five dollars to stroll the grounds, relax and sip a mint julep. Or I might have gone to Delmonico's, where the same amount of money would have bought me dinner, including a slice of oyster pie.

But that day I did none of those things. I stayed in my office, the door closed against old friends and the memories of my past.

By nine, I was sorely tired of looking through the ledgers, and though I knew Phin would be pleased I had accomplished so much that day in terms of examining our incoming funds (colossal, indeed!) and our outgoing expenses, after so many hours the figures swam before my eyes. Another hour and the museum would close. Surely, after all this time, Andrew Emerson would no longer be lying in wait for me.

My neck ached and I rubbed it with one hand, gathered my reticule and left my office. I would stop on the first floor and tell Mr Dewey, the assistant manager of the museum, that I was leaving early, and I knew he would not mind. I had put in a full day's work, and besides, Mr Dewey was always obliging. The fact that I was P.T. Barnum's sister might have had something to do with it.

The Waxworks Room was empty of patrons and, as I did each night, I strolled through it to make sure all was in order, stopping for a moment to look at the wax miniatures of thirty eminent Mexican generals and statesmen. Though I was not especially fond of the exhibit, finding no interest in the colorful and rich costumes of the figures, the nearby placard declared it of 'universal interest.' Since, at the moment, I was the only one in the Waxworks Room, this might not have been completely true.

The thought amused me, and for the first time in the hours since I'd seen Andrew Emerson, I found myself smiling. I completed my circuit of the Waxworks Room and proceeded on to the Portrait Gallery. It, too, appeared to be empty at this late hour, and I could only imagine that our patrons, so eager to see the mermaid when they first arrived, had proceeded on to the other exhibits: live animals and stuffed specimens, mummies and statues that had been carved in antiquity, recreated scenes of the great cities of the world and, of course, those poor souls, our human oddities.

No sooner had the thought crossed my mind than I swore I saw a flash of dull green somewhere to my left. I turned that way and called out, 'Mr Hollister, is that you?' but I must surely have been mistaken. Though Jeffrey Hollister could be sullen, he was never impolite, and he did not respond. Or perhaps I simply did not hear him thanks to the lively chatter of our Happy Family monkeys.

Eager to get home, to put up my feet and to eat whatever might be left from Phin and Charity's dinner, I hurried to the stairway but stopped at the top of the steps. There was a curious and unfamiliar aroma in the room, the faintest smell of rusting metal that mingled with the slightly fishy odor of the burning whale oil lamps and the scent of joss sticks that wafted from a nearby exhibit of Oriental wonders.

Curious, I turned and glanced toward the mermaid and, when I did, my heart banged against my ribs then stopped, its beat frozen, as was my breath.

Tan sit-down-upons. A black frock coat. A stovepipe hat beneath the glass case that contained the mermaid.

And Andrew Emerson's body sprawled on the floor, his arms flung out at his sides, his legs twisted at an unnatural angle and those genial blue eyes of his open and staring. A river of blood bubbled from the open wound at the top of his head, and there were bits of skull and brain matter splattered on the floor and the glass case where the mermaid watched the scene, her mouth open in a silent scream.

TWO

As soon as I was able to swallow my horror and find my voice, I summoned an attendant and told him to find Mr Dewey, who in turn sent for another attendant and instructed him to usher our patrons out of the building by way of a back staircase so they would not catch sight of the gruesome scene there in the Portrait Gallery. A third attendant, one who usually sat near the front door so he might answer visitors' questions, was sent in search of a constable. As he was assistant manager of the museum and it was his place to convey the terrible news, Mr Dewey himself, visibly shaken though he was, departed to fetch my brother.

That left me alone with Andrew Emerson's body.

His body and my stinging conscience.

'You said you needed my help. You said she . . . she needed my help, though I cannot imagine who you were talking about. Andrew . . .' I stared at Andrew's lifeless body and pictured in my mind's eye the energetic and able-bodied young man who had always had an ear for my troubles and an arm to steady me when we walked together through Bethel. Though the scene before my eyes repulsed me, I was powerless to fight against its lodestone strength. I stepped nearer to the body.

Might I have changed the outcome to that tragic day if I had taken the time to listen to Andrew?

In answer to my own question, I shook my head and stared at Andrew and the ever-growing pool of blood that flowed around him, reaching its red tentacles across the floor, soaking into the spaces between the boards.

My palms were hot and moist and I scraped them against the skirt of my gown. I had never been particularly queasy when it came to things like injuries or blood, but I had never before seen a murder victim. And surely poor Andrew had been murdered, for there was nothing in the vicinity that could have injured him so grievously by accident and nothing else that could explain what happened.

But who?

I had never been one to panic, either, yet I could not help myself. I glanced around, examining the shadows, peering into the Waxworks Room and reflexively moving toward the stairway when I thought I heard the creak of a floorboard when I should have been the only person about. There were attendants still downstairs near the front door, and I had no doubt they had their heads together, discussing the tragedy. I would be safe with them until Phin arrived, I told myself, and I would find comfort in their company.

Safety and comfort, yes, but downstairs I would not find the answers to the questions that pounded through my brain.

'Why?' My voice was small and lost in the gray shadows that seemed to have grown ever deeper in each corner of the gallery. 'Who would do this, Andrew? And why? And how . . .' When I swallowed, my throat ached. 'How did you think I might help you?'

As far as I could see, there was only one way to find out.

I peered down the stairway to be sure none of the staff was anywhere near and, my resolution more steady than my shaking hands, I lifted my skirts to keep them out of the blood and closed in on Andrew's body.

'Ooh, do be careful there, Miss Barnum!'

At the sound of Bess Buttle's high-pitched voice, I clutched a hand to my heart and spun around.

'Sorry, didn't mean to startle you like that.' A smile showed through the four-inch growth of dark whiskers that covered Bess's chin. 'Just didn't want you getting your skirts all soaked up in the blood.' Her eyes wide and her cheeks shot through with color, she scooted closer. 'Is that him? Well, of course it is, ain't it? There can't be two dead bodies in the museum. They're talking about this one downstairs. Talking about some man who went and got himself killed. Well, if that don't cap the climax! So that's him?'

'Andrew Emerson, yes.' Bess's chattering had given my heart a moment to settle and I released a long breath. 'He was a friend of mine. In fact, he stopped earlier today and we chatted.'

'I'm sorry. Truly.' In spite of the beard as bushy as any man's, Bess was a woman through and through. She had dainty hands and a compact, curved figure. She took a lace-edged handkerchief from her sleeve and touched it to her eyes. 'It's an awful thing, ain't it, and I can understand how you would want to pay your respects and all, but really, should you be here? I mean, begging your pardon, Miss Barnum, but the man's been hatcheted in the head, if I'm any judge. Should you be here? Alone?'

'I'm perfectly safe,' I told her, hoping I sounded as confident as I wanted her – and myself – to believe I was. 'There are attendants downstairs should I need assistance.'

'There were attendants down there a while ago, too.' Beneath the whiskers that matched the inky color of her hair, Bess's face paled to a shade not unlike her dove-gray gown. 'That didn't do him no good, did it?'

It went without saying.

And made me think.

'He must have been come upon unawares,' I told Bess. 'Otherwise, as you say, he would have cried out and someone would have heard him. He would have fought back and there would be some evidence of the ensuing scuffle.' I craned my neck, trying for a better look at Andrew but, from this distance, it was impossible so, once again, I lifted my skirts and moved closer to the body.

'You're not going to—' Bess clapped a hand on my arm. 'You don't mean to get nearer to him, do you?'

'That is exactly what I mean to do.' I shook off her ministering touch. 'Do you mean to fetch an attendant to stop me?'

Bess chewed her lower lip but it took her only a moment to make up her mind. 'Here, then.' She scooted behind me, reached down and gathered my skirts and petticoats into her hands then, with one swift motion, raised them all above my knees. 'If you're going to take a close look you don't want to end up covered with blood. I'll hang on. You be careful.'

Careful, indeed, for if anyone came upon us they would see not only my chemise but my ankles where they showed above the tops of my boots!

The thought encouraged me to move quickly and, with Bess

trailing behind and tugging at my skirts, I bent to study the wound at the top of Andrew's head.

'The wound is perfectly round,' I pointed out, in case Bess could not so easily see it from her vantage point. 'It is perhaps three inches in circumference. It looks as if . . .' I stood so quickly to demonstrate that Bess nearly lost her footing and her hold on my skirts. She grabbed them up before they could sink into the stream of blood near my feet and, once she'd gotten a good grip, I demonstrated, using some invisible weapon in my right hand as if to attack her.

'It looks as if his skull has been pierced by a sharp object applied quickly and with great force,' I said, acting out the motion before bringing my hand back to my side. 'It takes little imagination to think what would have happened after that. His skull gave way; his brain was punctured. I know very little about anatomy or science but I believe death would have come very quickly.'

'Thank goodness,' she muttered, looking down at the corpse.

Wondering what the murder weapon might be, I glanced around the area but saw nothing with so singular a shape. 'He took it with him,' I muttered, then added for Bess's benefit, 'Whatever caused the wound, the killer took it with him. I see nothing like it here.'

Done scanning the scene, I turned my attention back to Andrew and thought of what I'd told Bess earlier. Had he been surprised? Had Andrew fought back? I bent closer still and, this time, lifted Andrew's left hand in mine.

He was still warm, and his fingers were as supple as I remembered them when he had laid his hand on my arm earlier in the day. The skin of his hand was the same ashen color as his face. This close, I saw that his pupils were dilated, his jaw had fallen open and his skin sagged. His bow tie was slightly askew and, beneath it, I saw the purple bruising on his neck.

'Looks as if someone likely tried to choke the life out of him first. What does that tell you, Miss Barnum?' As if afraid to speak the words outright, Bess whispered the question.

'The marks on his neck are not from the attack that killed him,' I told her, though I didn't bother to explain how I knew. 'But look at his hands. You see here, there are no bruises on his knuckles, no cuts or scratches. I do believe it is as we said earlier – Mr Emerson was come upon unawares.'

Just as he was earlier today, I reminded myself, *when Jeffrey Hollister leapt out of the shadows and went for his throat so quickly and with such force that Andrew did not have time to defend himself.*

'So what do you think, then?' Bess, too, had bent over, the better to peer at Andrew, and her beard scratched my ear. 'Done in by some heartless ruffian, no doubt. It's a shame, isn't it, Miss Barnum, what some will do to get their hands on other people's money.'

It was, indeed, yet something told me this was not the case.

To prove it to myself, I laid Andrew's hand aside and fingered the silver watch tucked into a pocket in his waistcoat. 'The assailant didn't take this,' I pointed out to Bess.

'Could be he didn't have time. How about money?'

It was a legitimate question. Feeling a ghoul, I put my hand in the pocket of Andrew's sit-down-upons and came out with a small stack of coins. 'I can't believe they would have taken the rest and not this, too.'

'Then not robbed.' Bess thought this over. 'Was he the type of man someone might want to kill? By which I mean, was he a rogue? Or dishonest? Was there maliciousness in the man?'

When I shook my head, my curls brushed my cheeks. 'Andrew was kind and thoughtful, a real gentleman.'

'Yet real gentlemen . . .' Bess gulped. 'I cannot say, for I do not know for sure, Miss Barnum, but I'm thinking a real gentleman does not usually find himself set upon and murdered in a public place.'

She had a point.

Thinking it all through, I went over the scene that had unfolded earlier in the day. 'There was something he tried to show me earlier,' I told Bess, because as my confidante in this matter I thought it only fair for her to know my thought processes. 'He took a paper from his pocket and made to press it into my hand.'

Once again, I was obliged to bend nearer and, as she had so favorably done before, Bess held onto my skirts. I had just reached into the pocket of Andrew's coat when I heard a commotion from downstairs in the direction of the front door. My head came up; my heartbeat raced.

'My brother? So quickly?'

I did not need Bess to answer. I knew better than to think any mortal could have made the trip all the way from Fifth Avenue here to the corner of Broadway and Ann Street so swiftly. But then, if there was anything my brother had shown the world in the thirty-two years he had been on it, it was that he was not just any mortal.

No sooner had I had the thought than I heard the pounding of footsteps on the stairs, and that's when I made up my mind.

I had not given Andrew Emerson time to tell me what he wanted or how I might help him when he was alive. I would not let the opportunity pass again.

Swiftly and efficiently, I went through Andrew's pockets and found not one but two pieces of paper. I closed my fingers over both and stood and, in unison, Bess and I stepped away from the body. She had just finished smoothing my skirts back into place when my brother appeared at the top of the stairs.

'Evie! And Miss Buttle! What idiot left you two here all by yourselves? And . . . my goodness!' Phin had a high, sloping forehead and apple-round cheeks that gave some people the mistaken impression that he was perpetually cheerful. His halo of curly hair was the same indeterminate color between brown and honey as mine. When he spied Andrew's body in the sea of blood, his jaw slackened and his blue eyes popped.

'This is awful. It's terrible.' Mr Dewey was behind Phin on the stairs and my brother shot a look his way. 'We must get poor Mr Emerson removed as quickly as possible. Why isn't that being taken care of? Where is the night watch?'

'Mr Gable has gone for the constable, Mr Barnum,' Dewey told him.

'That's good. That's very good. And Miss Buttle . . .' He turned her way. 'What are you doing here?'

'Consoling me,' I broke in, because I knew Phin did not cotton to the thought of the oddities having free rein of the museum. If patrons thought they might see our human oddities walking freely through the building, they might be equally inclined to think they might bump into them strolling the streets of New York. And if that were to happen, or so Phin thought, why would anyone pay the admission price to look at them here?

'Miss Buttle has been so kind as to keep me company while I waited for you,' I told Phin. 'She saw I was upset and has provided me much comfort.'

'That's good. That's very good.' Phin made a quick bow in Bess's direction, effectively dismissing her. 'Thank you, Miss Buttle. You may leave us now.'

'Yes, thank you.' The look I sent Bess spoke volumes. 'Good night.'

Our Bearded Lady disappeared the way she'd come, into the Waxworks Room, and Phin slipped an arm through mine and marched me past a display of butterflies under glass and toward the skeleton of a horse displayed not far from where Bess had accessed a stairway to take her to her room.

'You should not have had to see this,' he said.

'I could hardly help it since I found poor Andrew.'

Phin's gaze flitted again to the terrible scene. 'What does it mean? How could it have happened? And why?'

I had no answers for him, or any to satisfy myself for that matter and, until I did, I knew better than to speculate. My brother was older than me by eight years and, since the death of our father when I was but seven, he saw himself as a paternal figure in my life. This was surely to be commended and I have been perpetually grateful for his charity. Phin was the one who took me in when I had no place else to go. He was the one who, over the objections of everyone from Mr Dewey to Charity, his own wife, insisted on giving me the opportunity to work at the museum and earn my own keep.

Still, I had no illusions. As kind-hearted as he might be, Phin was still Phin and always would be. He was mercurial and he could be frenetic. He was so quick-thinking that often those of us who were not so intellectually well-endowed were left scrambling to keep up with his thought processes. Phin was loud, he was charismatic and he was a wizard when it came to attracting – and keeping – the public's attention. Yet he could be overblown and so quick to jump from one idea to another that he often left me shaking my head in wonder.

Any mention of Andrew's plea for help would have surely

sent him on a tear to discover the source of Andrew's distress and I wasn't ready for that. Not until I had more information.

To that end, I made a show of getting my handkerchief from my reticule and, at the same time, tucked away the papers I had purloined from Andrew's pocket.

'He was here earlier today,' I told Phin because I knew he would hear the same report from the man who had been at the door that morning and I did not want it to look as if I had any reason to keep Andrew's visit a secret. 'Mr Emerson stopped to see me.'

'Did he?' Phin considered this. 'Came all the way from Bethel? Just to see you? What did he want?'

'Just to catch up on old times,' I said, and really, I wasn't surprised at how easily the lie fell from my lips. I had, after all, been lying to the world for some time now. 'The mill burned, you know. Just last month. Mr Emerson and I chatted for a bit, then he went on his way.'

'Much alive, it is to be presumed.'

'Certainly.'

'He seems to have returned.'

I, too, had thought of this but, unlike Phin, I reasoned I knew why: Andrew was waiting to see me. He hoped to ambush me a second time so that he might once again plead for my help.

He never had the chance.

'Perhaps he hoped to see you,' I told my brother. 'As a courtesy.'

'Or because he had something to ask me!' Phin's eyes sparked. 'To ask for your hand, perhaps.'

'No.' This was one thing I could not lie about. 'Put it out of your mind, Phin, for there is no chance of it. There was never more than friendship between Andrew and myself.'

'But you never know, eh?' When Phin tried to get me to smile, he was never shy of a tease. His look was sly. 'You might grow to love a man like Andrew Emerson.'

I let my gaze wander again to the terrible scene. 'Not any longer.'

'No. No. Of course not.' Phin's expression sobered. 'I am sorry, Evie.' He patted my arm. 'I know he was a dear friend and—'

A racket from downstairs cut short Phin's words and he raced to the stairway and peered over the bannister. 'It's the constable,' he said. 'He'll want to hear what you have to say, I believe, for it may have some bearing on Mr Emerson's last hours.'

The constable in question was a man named Slater whose waistcoat was a bit too snug over his round belly and whose shoes looked to need a good cleaning. Though he had certainly been told why he had been summoned to the museum, all thoughts of corpses and murders and mysterious circumstances seemed to fly out of his head the moment he was introduced to my brother.

'Marvelous place!' Slater had small, dark eyes and they darted over the exhibits surrounding us at the same time as he pumped Phin's hand. 'Been meaning to bring the missus, but what with the cost and all . . .' He looked imploringly at my brother and I knew what was bound to happen.

Phin has a charitable soul.

And I – or so I have been told – have less than I should of womanly patience.

'We would appreciate your help in the matter of Mr Emerson's death,' I told Slater, stepping forward. 'Surely there is something you can do to find his murderer.'

Slater's dark brows slid slowly up his forehead. 'And what's a woman to do with this matter?' As if I were invisible, he addressed this question to Phin. 'Surely she cannot be involved in either your astonishing establishment, Mr Barnum, or in the unfortunate circumstances that have befallen this young man.'

'Ah, but you're wrong there.' Phin stepped to my side and slipped an arm through mine. 'This is my sister, Miss Evangeline Barnum; she is as intelligent as any man in the room and more commonsensical than half of New York. She does have an interest in this matter, sir, as she is my aide-de-camp, so to speak. She was also a friend of Mr Emerson and the one who discovered his body.'

'You don't say!' Slater's gaze slid from my brother to me. 'You saw what happened?'

'No. I came from my office and walked here to the Portrait Gallery and—'

'So there was no one who saw what became of this young man.' Slater swept past us and studied Andrew's body, but not before he took a gander at the mermaid and chuckled with delight at having the opportunity for a private audience.

When he was done, he whirled to face us. 'Must have been an accident,' he announced. 'For surely there's no other explanation.'

'If so, what caused the peculiar wound?' I asked, going to the constable's side so that I could point out the injury. 'And why is there no trace of the weapon anywhere at hand?'

As if he would surely find it if he looked long enough, Slater did a quick turn around the area.

The monkeys in the Happy Family cage did not take kindly to a disturbance at so late an hour and, as they had when I left my office, screeched and jumped to the front of the cage. Slater leapt back.

'Well, how about those critters, then?' he asked no one in particular. 'Seems to me they're vicious, and no doubt, this man here—'

'Andrew Emerson,' I told him.

'This Andrew Emerson here, he got too close, and one of these wild creatures became aroused at the intrusion. Animals such as this are unpredictable.'

'They are, indeed,' I told him. 'And as far as we have been able to ascertain, they are far more intelligent than most give them credit for. But they are not devious. Not as a human being might be devious. And they are not malicious. They do not use weapons, and if they did, they would not be so duplicitous as to hide them after.'

It took Slater a minute to work through my logic. One minute is generally all Phin gives anyone to catch up with what's happening around him.

'You need to find the perpetrator,' he told Slater. 'Get a move on, man. We cannot have people think the museum is dangerous.'

'Ah, well, as for that.' Slater's beady eyes lit up and he walked around the body, peering at it but not getting too near. 'We might certainly be able to keep the word from traveling about, if you get what I'm saying, Mr Barnum. There's none need to know what happened here. Not the newspapers or the public, if you get my meaning.'

Oh, Phin got his meaning, to be sure, and I already knew what my brother was thinking. A murder would add to the notoriety of the establishment. The news would bring even more crowds. If Slater thought to keep it secret at the cost of admission for him and his missus, he had a great deal to learn about P.T. Barnum.

'What's this, do you suppose?' Slater asked, forgetting his dreams of free admission when he saw the bruising on Andrew's neck. 'It looks as if someone tried to strangle him before he knocked Mr Emerson on the head.'

Drat it all. I was counting on Slater not to notice and, now that he had, I had no choice but to speak the truth.

'The injury has nothing to do with Mr Emerson's murder,' I told the constable. 'It happened earlier today. You see, Mr Emerson had an encounter with Jeffrey Hollister and—'

'Hollister!' Phin's eyes flashed lightning. 'I will not tolerate the man causing dissension here. If he attacked Mr Emerson—'

'He thought he was defending me,' I told Phin. 'And he did no real harm.'

'No real harm, eh?' Squint-eyed, Slater did another turn around the body. 'So you say someone here at the museum—'

'Jeffrey Hollister,' Phin said. 'Our Lizard Man from Borneo.'

Such appellations are usually enough to take a person aback, and Slater was no exception. He chewed over the thought for a moment before he said, 'And this Lizard Man, he attacked our victim?'

'He did.' I tried to wave away the implications of Slater's question, but it was clear he would not listen. 'He meant no harm.'

'But he did harm, didn't he? Or Mr Emerson here would not be bruised and battered. And if I am any judge . . .' Thinking, Slater pressed his lips together. 'It looks to me as if this Hollister fellow came back to finish the fight.'

'But there is no proof of that.' I did not know how I could be clearer but, as it turned out, it didn't matter. Before I could explain, Slater asked Phin where to find Jeffrey and Phin sent an attendant up to the fifth floor of the building where our oddities had their rooms.

Waiting, I hugged my arms around myself and fought to control my rising panic. 'Mr Hollister can get angry,' I felt obliged to point out. 'But he calms quickly enough. You cannot think—'

'I'll be the judge of what I can and cannot think, Miss Barnum,' the constable told me. 'We will need your testimony, of course. What you saw this morning. How this Hollister fellow tried to kill Mr Emerson.'

'But he didn't!' I stomped one foot. Surely it was a childish way to draw attention, but since Slater wasn't listening anyway, it hardly mattered. 'Mr Hollister—'

'Is gone, sir.' The attendant was back from upstairs, breathing hard when he reported the news to Phin. 'He isn't in his room, and his few things are packed and taken.'

'Aha!' Slater swept toward the stairway. 'Absquatulated, has he? We have our man, if I'm not mistaken, and this proves it. We will find him, Mr Barnum. I swear to you, we will find this Jeffrey Hollister and we will bring him to justice.'

THREE

When our father, Philo Barnum died, my brother, though he was but fifteen years of age, was charged with the difficult task of providing for the family – my mother, my four sisters, and me in addition to himself. It should come as no surprise that Phin was a clever boy just as it is no revelation to those of us who know him well that he has never been fond of physical labor. Faced with putting food on the table, he worked with his head, not his hands. He ran a lottery scheme and sold cherry rum to soldiers. He eventually owned a newspaper, a boarding house and a book-auctioning business.

Still, opportunities came slowly. That is, until the year 1835, when at the age of twenty-five he was apprised of a woman named Joice Heth, a slave who not only claimed to be one-hundred-and-sixty years old but who told the story of how she had once been the nursemaid of none other than the infant who grew to be General George Washington. Like all right-thinking people, my brother is firmly against the abomination that is slavery. He does, however, have an unerring sense of what the public not only wants but what it is willing to pay to see. He purchased the services of Joice Heth, advertised her as, 'the most astonishing and interesting curiosity in the world,' and put her on display at the theater Niblo's Garden in New York City. Just as with the Feejee Mermaid, the curious arrived by the thousands.

And they made my brother very rich.

So it was that six years later, when Phin purchased the five-story building that housed Scudder's American Museum along with its contents, I was not surprised. He reopened the establishment and added his own flair to the more mundane displays of rocks and gems and shells and fossils – his human oddities, mummies, Ned the Performing Seal, a loom run by a dog, the trunk of a tree under which the disciples of Jesus had once gathered.

The museum was a wonder, to be sure, and its glories were not merely confined to inside its walls.

The exterior of the building was painted with gigantic portraits of some of the animals that lived inside – lions and bears and elephants. Banners and flags fluttered in the breeze, the worst musicians Phin could find played on a balcony above the front entrance (so as to encourage people to go inside and so escape the disharmonies, he said), and the entire building was illuminated with the new and amazing limelight that was impossible to ignore or resist.

Indeed, Barnum's American Museum glowed like a beacon there at the southern end of Manhattan, and it drew guests by the thousands.

And they made my brother even richer.

As worried and weary as I was, as much as the weight of sorrow sat on my shoulders and bunched in my stomach, I couldn't help but consider these facts when my brother's carriage turned into the drive that led to Phin's house on Fifth Avenue.

'It's a long way from Bethel.'

He must have been thinking exactly the same, for next to me on the leather seat, Phin put a hand on mine and gave it a squeeze even as he looked beyond me toward the house he'd just had built. It was a sprawling brick mansion made to look, as was the current fashion, like an Italian Renaissance villa with porches and balconies, wide eaves and a square tower that rose above it all, even taller than the cupola in the center of the roof.

'It is a lovely place,' I told him, though he surely knew it and did not need to hear it from me.

Still, Phin chuckled. 'It will be lovelier and I will surely be poorer by the time Charity is done choosing the furnishings. She was looking at wallpaper for the dining room when I was called away this evening. Artichokes.' He didn't so much sniff at the word as he gave it a curious twist. 'Why the deuce would I want to look at artichokes on my walls when I am eating them on my plate?'

'Charity has excellent taste.' This was something else I didn't need to point out, but it seemed the polite response. 'The house will be as lovely inside as it is out.'

'And, dash it all, I suppose once it is I will be required to invite the neighbors in.' Since Phin is the most amiable and social person I know, I knew the protest was for show, but then I could hardly blame him if he were nervous about the reception he might get from the people whose grand houses surrounded his. They were bankers and merchants and politicians, and an upstart showman with a penchant for the bizarre and an uncanny knack of turning other people's taste for the fantastical into dollars made Phin something of an oddity himself.

When the carriage stopped outside the front door, he didn't wait for the coachman but jumped out and handed me down himself. Before either of us could say another word, the front door opened and light spilled onto the steps.

'Portman.' Phin nodded and handed his hat to the man who waited inside. I did not bother with my cloak or bonnet but headed directly for the stairs.

'I'll just say goodnight to the children,' I told my brother. 'Then I'll be back down again.'

'It is very late.' Charity's voice drifted from the parlor on the other side of the broad marble hallway. Her words were not light and airy, more like a cloud that foretells a coming rain: not so threatening in and of itself – not at that moment – but simply a reminder that there is a chance there are darker things to come. 'The children have been asleep for hours.'

I paused, my hand on the bannister and one foot already on the bottommost step, and I would have looked my brother's way if I knew I would find any support there. It was not that Phin was cowed by his wife, it was just that he knew she was usually right. As she was this time. With a sigh, I turned away from the stairway.

'Of course.' I made sure I spoke loud enough for Charity to hear and looked toward the parlor, but the door was partially closed and I knew that, from where she sat, my sister-in-law could not see me. That allowed me to take a moment to swallow my disappointment. Phin and Charity's daughters, Caroline, Helen and Frances, along with dear little Walter, were the joys of my life and, if I was early enough, I always visited the nursery when I returned from the museum.

'You did hear me, didn't you?' Charity's voice might have been muffled by the half-closed door but there was no mistaking the fact she would brook no argument. 'The girls and my son have been asleep these few hours already.'

'Yes, of course.' I pulled off my bonnet and cloak and handed them to Portman who, ever capable, stood nearby, and by the time I entered the parlor I'd already smoothed my gown, touched a hand to my hair and wiped any trace of emotion from my face.

Because it was at the center of the family's life – for receiving friends and for those business appointments Phin chose to make away from the museum – the parlor was one of the rooms Charity had made sure was finished soonest and, just as I'd mentioned to Phin in the carriage, she had done it with a sense of taste and refinement which I am told is unusual for the newly wealthy. The walls were papered in tasteful cream and maroon and the draperies were of the same colors. Thanks to Portman and a staff that included Cook, a housekeeper, a nursery maid and two young girls who did not live in but came each day to handle the cleaning, every inch of the place gleamed, from the white marble fireplace to the mahogany table where Charity sat in a chair with an elaborate scrollwork back and upholstery that matched exactly the color of the draperies. Otherwise, she would not have purchased them.

My sister-in-law did not look up when I walked in. She was too busy studying a piece of wallpaper that featured a riot of foliage on a yellow background along with those artichokes – very large, very green artichokes – that Phin had noted earlier. They must have been interesting artichokes, indeed, for she still didn't look my way even when I said, 'I'd forgotten how late it was.'

Charity Hallet Barnum was two years my brother's senior, a small woman with dark hair which she wore in ringlets that bobbed over her ears from beneath her lace cap. She had a thin face and a long nose and, though she was but thirty-four and her skin was smooth and her eyes yet bright, I often found myself thinking that, when she was elderly, she would have the narrow, pinched look of a weasel. It was unkind of me, not to mention small-minded, and this time, like all the other times the thought struck, I firmly set it aside.

'It is unseemly for a woman to be out at such late hours.' Charity set aside the piece of wallpaper, the better to skewer me with a look. 'At least you had Phin with you tonight to accompany you home. If you were alone—'

'I am often alone when I travel home from the museum.' I sat down on the opposite side of the table from her and wondered who had convinced her that these chairs had been made for comfort. My shoulders are wide for a woman's and my legs are long, and I squirmed to settle myself. 'I was grateful to have Phin with me tonight.'

'Yes. Tonight.' Charity folded her hands together on the table in front of her. 'There is talk of unpleasantness.'

Thinking of the events of the evening as no more than unpleasantness rather deadened the impact of murder, but before I had the opportunity to point this out Phin sailed into the room and gave Charity a peck on the cheek. When her hands fluttered as if she would have liked to do nothing more than push him away, I pretended not to notice.

'You must be especially kind to our dear Evie tonight,' he told his wife. 'She has had a shock.'

Charity's brows rose a fraction of an inch and I knew I had her permission to explain. 'It was Andrew,' I said. 'Andrew Emerson.'

'From Bethel?'

I couldn't tell if she was surprised or if she thought all along that being from Bethel made Andrew somehow more likely to be murdered than if he had been, say, from Bridgeport.

'What is he doing in New York?'

'He is . . . he was . . .' I adjusted to this new way of speaking about Andrew and lied with far more ease than I would have thought myself capable of but a few years earlier. 'He had business to attend to here in the city,' I told Charity. 'At least, that is what he told me when we spoke this morning.'

'You spoke to him? A man who was set upon and murdered?'

'She obviously spoke to him before he was murdered,' her husband reminded her. 'And they were dear friends, were they not, back home? Our Evie has had a shock, finding Andrew Emerson like that.'

Charity's face paled to the color of the lace at her collar and her blue eyes goggled as surely as they would have had Phin announced that I was the one who'd hatcheted Andrew. 'You? You found him?'

I couldn't help but think that, for once, my sister-in-law might live up to her name. 'I am fine,' I told her. 'Though I am grateful for your concern. It was a terrible—'

'It is unacceptable, to be sure.' Charity rose and swept toward the door. 'It is unacceptable and unseemly and I . . .' She paused and put a hand to her cheek before she stepped into the hallway. 'It is late and hearing that you have again been involved in something so inappropriate, it is . . . it is . . . I must lie down. Good night.'

I waited until I heard her footsteps on the stairs before I dared speak a word. 'You'd think she was the one who'd found a man with his brains bashed in.' Instantly, I held up a hand to stop the protest I knew would come from my brother. He might have agreed with me, but he was a loyal husband and I did not want to put him in an awkward position. 'I know, I know, she is of a delicate nature and I shouldn't be so unkind. Still . . .'

'Still, I was right when I said you've had a shock.' Phin went to a sideboard, filled two glasses from a crystal decanter then handed one to me. 'Sherry,' he said, 'and if anyone deserves a drink tonight, it is you.'

I couldn't have agreed more. I took a sip of sherry and closed my eyes, refusing to concentrate on the picture of Andrew's body that materialized in my mind and, instead, allowing myself the luxury of enjoying the sensation of warmth that traveled down my throat and thawed some of the ice that had built inside me in the hours since I'd walked out of my office and into the horror that awaited me in front of our mermaid. Another taste of sherry and I felt more capable of rational conversation.

'Who would do such a thing?' I asked my brother. 'And why?'

He downed half the sherry in his glass. 'You heard what the constable said. Jeffrey Hollister—'

'Is not a killer. You and I both know that.'

'We do.' Phin acknowledged the rightness of my statement with a nod. 'And yet, he's gone.'

'Yes.' I shook my shoulders to be rid of the chill that had settled there and wished it had helped. 'I'm worried about him.'

'Jeffrey can take care of himself.'

'That is exactly what I'm worried about. He was on display

today. His skin was dyed that bilious green. If he's seen on the streets—'

'Good heavens! Let us hope not. If people think our oddities can be seen about town—'

'I am not talking about business now, Phin. I'm talking about Jeffrey. He is surely quick to anger, and if someone taunts him—'

'Do you think Andrew Emerson might have done as much?'

In spite of everything that had happened that night, and everything I'd seen, this was one thought that had not crossed my mind. 'Andrew was not unkind,' I reminded my brother.

'But you said Hollister attacked him earlier today.'

'Only because Jeffrey thought I was in danger.'

'Then if Hollister thought you might be in danger again—'

'There was no reason for it!' It wasn't until my own sharp words ricocheted back at me from the high ceiling that I realized I must bridle my temper. I wrapped my hands around my glass and drew in a breath. 'I was in my office all day except to pay our oddities, and when I gave him his wages, Jeffrey was calm. He asked after my welfare.'

'And you told him?'

'The truth. That I was fine. That Mr Emerson had never meant me any harm. That he was, in fact, a friend who I have known these many years. And yes, before you ask, I did remind Jeffrey that he must never resort to violence inside the walls of the museum because that would be bad for the reputation of the place and, while I was at it, I mentioned that such behavior reflects badly on your reputation, too. You know how much he admires you, Phin. I don't think he would dare do anything to arouse your anger or make you look bad in the eyes of the world. To kill a man in so public a place? No.' I shook my head. 'I cannot believe Jeffrey Hollister had it in his heart, and I cannot believe he would be so careless with the welfare of our family.'

'Then who?' Phin sank into the chair recently vacated by Charity and, just as I had in mine, squirmed against the seat. 'And why there? Why in my museum?'

I was sure he wouldn't be satisfied with a lift of my shoulders so I sighed and tried to reason my way through the morass. 'He was not robbed,' I said and knew the moment I did – and the second Phin's eyebrows rose a fraction of an inch – that I should not have mentioned it. 'His watch,' I said because it seemed a far more acceptable explanation than admitting I had gone through Andrew's pockets. 'When I saw the body, I could easily see that his watch was not taken.'

'Perhaps his money was. As deplorable as it is, greed at least is a reason a man might take another man's life. I will speak to Slater about it in the morning.'

A tiny noise of derision escaped me before I could stop it. 'Slater cares only if you might allow him free admission into the museum.'

'Bah! Why not!' Phin waved away my concerns with one thick-fingered hand. 'It will cost me but fifty cents to allow him and his good wife into the place.'

'No doubt they will bring a gaggle of children,' I told my brother.

His eyes sparkled with amusement. 'No doubt you are right. I wonder how many of them will actually be related to the constable!' He wagged a finger in my direction. 'You see, Evie, you are finally learning to trust your instincts and to read people much the way I do. Soon, you'll truly be working at my side, not just studying the books and keeping them tidy and making sure the staff is working to the best of their abilities, though you know I appreciate it all and how well you discharge your duties. But soon, you'll be dreaming of new exhibits the way I do. You'll be looking for new ways to entice the public into entering our magical fairyland.'

'Oh, no!' It was such an impossibility to think my mind might ever work as my brother's, it made me laugh and I realized how grateful I was to feel such lightness after hours of grief and worry. No doubt Phin had known exactly how I would respond. No doubt it was exactly why he'd brought up the subject. 'I have no showman's blood in me. Not like you do, Phin.'

'I come by it honestly from our Grandpa Taylor.' Phin's eyes lit up the way they always did when he talked of our maternal grandfather, Phineas Taylor. 'He liked nothing better than a jest, and he wasn't shy about poking fun, was he? When I was born . . .' He threw back his head and laughed and, though I'd heard the story more times than I could count, I couldn't help but join in. Phin's laughter was infectious. 'When I was born he deeded me a parcel of land and he reminded me of it often in my growing-up years. The land, the land. How I had hopes for that land! Until I was ten, of course, and finally saw it. Worthless and barren, and not given in spite or to offend or wound me. Put in my name simply because Grandpa Taylor found it endlessly funny to talk about it and get me to believe in what was no more than a preposterous yarn!' He wiped tears from his eyes. 'You have his blood, too, Evie. You'll see. Someday when your life is settled down and you allow yourself some joy in it again—'

I did not mean to interrupt him. At least not with a sigh. 'For now I will concentrate on the museum's books,' I told him and pushed my chair back from the table. 'Don't get up,' I said because I knew he would the moment I stood. 'You have had a difficult evening, too, and you needn't bother with formalities, not with me.'

'You're going up to bed?' he asked.

I pressed a hand to my stomach. 'As impossible as it seems, I'm hungry. I thought I might go to the kitchen.'

Phin stood and walked me to the door. 'We had lamb tonight, and I know Cook saved a plate of it for you.'

I was actually thinking of something more soothing, a wedge of bread spread with butter, perhaps, or a bowl of Cook's delicious apple soup, but since lamb was Phin's favorite I did not mention it. Instead, I wished him a good night and headed to the back of the house and into the kitchen where I knew Cook would be waiting for me despite the late hour.

I found her at the table, a cup of tea in front of her and another already made and waiting for me.

'How did you know?' I asked her even before I sat down.

Ellen O'Donnell was a woman of forty with broad hands, a wide face and shoulders firm and steady enough to carry the weight of her household duties. She had come to this country from Ireland but four years before my brother happened upon her cooking at the home of a friend, Bernard Rathbone. Phin – as he does – decided instantly that the good Mrs O'Donnell was the most talented and wonderful cook in the world, offered to double her salary and stole her away, and it says something about both Phin and his friend that Rathbone never held it against him. After all, Ellen was a widow and had three children to support;

she needed the money and Phin was certain to invite Rathbone for dinner at least once every month so that he might still partake of her wonderful meals.

'It's a night you've had, to be sure.' Without asking yet somehow knowing, Cook got up and went to the sideboard for the piece of bread with butter she had there waiting for me. 'You'll need to settle your stomach.'

'Yes. Thank you.' I bit through the crunchy crust and the heavenly brown bread and chewed, then smiled gratefully before the sadness settled again and I said, 'He was a friend. From back home.'

When she nodded, Cook's golden hair glimmered in the light. Her cheeks were always ruddy so it was hard to tell if my talk of home caused her embarrassment, yet I thought not. If there was one thing I'd learned from her it was that life is not always easy and that there are challenges we all must face.

'I'm sorry to hear it,' she said and sipped her tea. 'As sorry as I am to hear that you were the one to find him.' Her look was innocence itself. 'That is, if the gossip I've been hearing is true.'

'True. Yes. It was . . .' My throat closed with emotion and I set down the slab of bread so that I might try and wash away the sensation with a sip of hot tea.

'There, there, now.'

I had a feeling Cook would have reached across the table and patted my hand if she didn't think it unseemly.

'You've had a shock and no doubt.'

'Yes, so everyone keeps reminding me.'

Cook's eyes were as green as she claimed the fields were back home, and I met her level gaze.

'It was truly a horrible sight, and I am saddened to think so promising a life has been cut so short. Yet now that the reality has taken hold, I do not find myself as shocked as I do . . . Heaven help me, Mrs O'Donnell, I do believe that, more than anything, I am curious.'

As if this was no surprise, she nodded. 'You're a bright one, to be sure. It's only natural you'd wonder what happened.'

'And why,' I admitted.

She finished her tea. 'You'll get to the heart of it.'

'It isn't my place,' I reminded her.

'Just as it isn't your place there in that grand museum, riding herd on Mr Barnum and making certain things are done right.' Her eyes gleamed. 'You will get to the heart of it.'

I finished my bread and pushed away the plate at the same time I scraped back my chair. 'I hope you are right. For now . . .'

'You're tired, to be sure. You need to rest. No need to rouse yourself too early in the morning. I'll have one of the girls bring up a tray.'

My feet were leaden and my legs were heavy, but I was already at the door when her voice stopped me.

'Had he a family?'

'Family?' As if it might help me find an excuse for what had surely been an unforgivable oversight, I pressed a finger to my lips. 'I hadn't thought of it. My goodness! How could I have been so—'

'You've been preoccupied. It's no wonder you didn't have time to think about it. Not to worry. You'll make it right.'

'Andrew . . . Mr Emerson . . . his mother and his father have passed. But yes, he has a sister. Madeline. Andrew and I are . . . we were . . . we were of the same age, and Madeline is but a year younger. We were fast friends back in Bethel. I must . . .' My heart bumped and suddenly I wasn't nearly as exhausted as I had been when I entered the kitchen. 'I must write to her immediately, and tomorrow I'll find a way to send the message.'

'No need to wait.' Cook had followed me to the door and I turned to see her give me a wink. 'My Patrick, he's been asleep behind the stables most of the day. You go on up and write that letter and I'll have him saddle a horse. It's a far enough ride and bad enough news. It shouldn't be delayed. He can start out for Bethel tonight.'

I thanked her and hurried to my room.

Though I had not asked for it, Charity had insisted I take the bedchamber at the back of the house, and though I was always grateful for the quiet, this night I was most thankful, indeed. My windows overlooked the garden behind the house, not Fifth Avenue, and though if I bent my head and listened hard enough I could still sometimes hear the gentle clop of horses' hooves and the whirr of carriage wheels out on the street, here with the quiet surrounding me and the deep shadows shielding me from the outside world, I was always better able to collect my thoughts and compose my emotions. I prayed on this night, when it was more important than ever, that I might also be able to find the words to deliver what would surely be a stunning blow to Madeline.

I lit a lamp and sat down at the desk that had been Phin's back in Bethel. Here in the great house the great showman had built, Charity had insisted his private rooms be furnished with the newest and the finest. But a country desk was good enough for me and I gratefully accepted it when Phin offered. Now I ran a finger over the pitted surface, drawing strength from the memories and the history, and drew out a sheet of the thick, expensive writing paper Phin bought for household use. I dipped my pen and began my task.

Fifteen minutes later, I reread the letter and wiped a tear from my eye.

'Poor Madeline.' I waved the paper in the air, the better to dry the ink, then folded the missive and prepared to take it out to Patrick O'Donnell waiting in the stable. I would have left with it immediately if another thought hadn't struck.

'Paper.' I looked at the letter, and the single word from my lips fell dull against the blackness outside the circle of my lamp. 'I took papers from Andrew.'

The thought, now hot and fresh, had lain dormant beneath the sorrow that had weighed down on my spirit all night, yet now that it was again real, it touched me like fire. I hurried to the other side of the room to retrieve my reticule and sat down with it so that I might go through it by the light of the lamp.

Though I knew the memory was blunted by the horror I had felt at the time, I clearly recollected retrieving two papers from Andrew's pocket, and I found the first and looked it over. It did not surprise me in the least. On it, in his fine, strong hand, Andrew had written the words 'Franklin House Hotel' along with the address of that establishment. It was a place with a good reputation and it appealed to professional men such as Andrew. I had no doubt he'd spent his nights in New York there.

Satisfied, I set aside that paper and turned my attention to the second. This paper was thicker, creamy-colored and I recognized it as the one Andrew had tried to press into my hands – the one he had begged me to read – but, looking over it, I thought its purpose far from clear.

Hoping that better light might help me interpret the words, I slid my chair closer to the lamp and tipped the paper toward its luminous halo. The writing here was not Andrew's, surely, for the letters were smaller, finer and far more feminine.

'And drat it all, it is just a draft of some sort,' I mumbled to myself, seeing the fragments of sentences and places where words had been crossed out and replaced with others. My eyesight had always been good, but it was late and it had been a long and trying day. I squinted and forced myself to focus on what few words I could read.

My dearest darling . . . Thinking, I tipped my head. 'A love letter then.'

I count the days until we can . . . Here the words were scratched across with stuttering, anxious lines.

I count the minutes, the very moments . . .

Had some woman sent Andrew these loving lines?

I turned the paper over but there was no indication of where the letter might have originated or who might have sent it. Failing in that task, I once again concentrated on those few words I could read.

Until we meet again . . .

I long for the touch of your hands, the fire against my bare skin.

'Oh, my.' I waved a hand in front of my face, feeling suddenly as if I were a party to information I should not possess. Fortunately for me and for the heat that rose in my cheeks, the anonymous writer did not finish these words, though I was left imagining where they might have led.

Rather than think about it, I squinted and read further.

I love you with all my heart. I love you, my dearest James.

Those were the final words on the page and, reading them, my blood ran cold and my heart pounded out a beat that filled my ears and deafened me.

My dearest James.

I sat frozen for some moments, staring at the paper in my hand, before I shook myself to reality.

'There are many men named James in this world,' I told myself, my voice razor sharp. 'And many a female, too, eager to fall in love.'

I told myself not to forget it when I tucked the papers back in my reticule and went downstairs to hand Patrick O'Donnell my letter to Madeline so that he might start on his journey.

And I reminded myself of it all again once I was back in my room and changed into my nightdress, tucked under the blankets but with sleep refusing to come.

'There are many men named James in the world.'

But that did not keep me from shedding a tear. For myself, for the past, for Andrew and for the poor, lovesick female who had been so foolish to give her heart to her dearest James.

FOUR

As wise as I knew it was, I did not follow Cook's advice and keep to my bed the next morning. It was Saturday and the museum would open at eight as it did every day but Sunday. I had work to do and no desire to shirk it and thus allow my mind to wander and my imagination – and the memories of all I had seen the night before and thoughts of how dear Madeline would grieve so in response to the news – to upend my hard-won composure.

Before I left the house, long before Charity even thought to be up and about, I stole into the nursery and wished the children a good morning, being sure to give each of them a pat and a cuddle as any doting aunt would, then I was on my way. Once inside the museum and in the Portrait Gallery, I firmly ignored the tremors of foreboding that cascaded over my shoulders when I walked by our Feejee lovely and the newly washed and polished floorboards directly in front of her and went straight to my office. By the time the long line of people who'd been waiting out on Broadway began to snake its way into the museum, I had the lamp lit on my desk, the door closed and my plans for the day firmly in mind.

I had devoted myself so steadfastly to working the day before in the hopes of avoiding any further confrontation with Andrew Emerson that there was little for me to do that day, and for that I was grateful. I quickly looked over some correspondence, checked the receipts from the day before (colossal, indeed, which only served to again confirm my brother's genius) and waited – not very patiently – for the clock to strike ten. It was then our human oddities were set to go on display and, once I knew they were away from their rooms, I left my office and climbed the back stairs to the fifth floor of the building.

I had heard it said (sometimes mumbled from person to person as if it were some great embarrassment to discuss and other times screamed out with righteous indignation) that it was cruel of P.T. Barnum to put on display people who were odd and freakish in nature, that he took advantage of them and profited from their woes.

Though I could see how this was in some ways true, it was not an equitable telling of the story.

Yes, the people Phin advertised as the human oddities – or as he sometimes called them, human curiosities – were presented to the public and yes, their strange appearance elicited gasps and finger pointing and, sometimes, ill-mannered comments. But here is the thing . . . Phin discovered these poor souls living in the streets or touring with circuses. Because of their physical appearance, they were often maligned from birth, rejected by their families and living as outcasts in a society that would pay to see them on the other side of a railing or the bars of a cage but would never think to greet them or talk to them or even acknowledge their existence had they chanced upon them in public.

Working at the museum gave our curiosities a purpose and provided them with protection. It kept them safe from the cruel impresarios who, before the oddities arrived at our door, often beat them and starved them and imprisoned them as a way to encourage them to work. Phin gave them a home inside the museum and he treated them well. He paid them royally so that each of their rooms was decorated to their taste and adorned with plush carpeting, fine furnishings and other comforts, the likes of which they had never dared dream of when they were on the streets.

As kind as Phin had always been to them and as much as I both accepted them and cherished their friendships and their talents and the personalities that made me see beyond their physical peculiarities to the essence of their beings, it was natural that only another curiosity could completely understand the challenges of the others. Theirs was a close-knit secret society of sorts, and those of us who were lucky enough to get to know them and who were welcomed into their inner circle had always to be aware that we were strangers there, curiosities in our own way.

It is no wonder when I opened the door and stepped onto the fifth floor, I felt a trespasser in their inner sanctum.

At the end of the hallway where the women were housed, I paused. I knew I had little to worry about, that I would not be interrupted, and yet my heart beat like a horse's hooves inside my chest and my breaths came in quick, short gasps that sounded to my ears like thunder in the thick silence.

The next time I took a breath, I forced myself to hold it deep in my lungs and raised my chin. So steadying my nerves, I moved into the men's wing.

I had been to Bess Buttle's room any number of times and been welcomed there with her usual good humor. I had talked to our Nova Scotia giantess in her quarters, too, and always marveled at how Phin had somehow been able to provide her with a bed and chairs that accommodated her more than seven feet of height.

I had never, of course, been in any of the men's rooms.

'And won't have a chance to do it now either if you don't get a move on,' I advised myself in no uncertain terms and, thus encouraged, I found the door with the small brass plaque on it that said *Jeffrey Hollister*.

Though I knew he wasn't there, I knocked and, when there was no answer, I opened the door and stepped inside.

Like the other rooms that belonged to his fellow curiosities, Jeffrey's was neat and tidy, kept so by a staff firmly admonished to treat our performers no differently than they treated me or my brother. Jeffrey's room was clean but sparse. There was a spool bed against the far wall, so called because its headboard and footboard were made up of multiple spindles that looked like sewing spools, and they gleamed with the beeswax polish the staff applied. To my right was a desk near the window and, to my left and in front of the fireplace, a table and chairs where Jeffrey might sit and entertain guests or partake of a meal.

The attendant Phin had sent up in search of Jeffrey the night before had been right in his assessment: there were no books anywhere, and Jeffrey cherished his books. There were no clothes in the wardrobe either, and no shoes tucked under the bed.

Jeffrey Hollister was truly gone.

The thought weighed on my mind and sat on my shoulders like a stone, and I sighed and sank down in the chair before the desk. Through the sparkling bits of dust that danced in a sunbeam from the window, I caught a glimpse of St Paul's, the church where George Washington had prayed after his inauguration as president some fifty-three years before and, seeing the church, I silently thanked my brother for his compassion. Jeffrey Hollister was an angry and fragile man, and Phin knew it, just as surely as he knew that giving Jeffrey a room here at the front of the building with a fine view might help reinforce his worth.

It did not, however, help me think my way to what might have happened to Andrew or what might have caused Jeffrey to flee.

Had Jeffrey seen something? Did he know something? Had he done something?

Now, like all the other times the thought crossed my mind, I dismissed this last question instantly.

'I need your help, Jeffrey,' I mumbled into the still air. 'I need a clue or some sign of where you might have gone and why.'

But of course, that was not to come. After a few moments of considering the situation and getting nowhere, I did another turn around the room. Jeffrey's bed had not been slept in the night before and the blankets were smooth and neat. One pillow, though, sat crooked upon the bed, and even though Jeffrey was not there to see it in disarray, I picked it up and fluffed it. I was ready to put it back down when something caught my eye.

Something written on the wall behind Jeffrey's bed.

I could see but little of whatever was there, the looping tops and bottoms of letters written on the wall in pencil.

I cannot say why so innocent a thing caused so peculiar a sensation to tingle inside me. I only knew I had to see more. I put my shoulder to the headboard and pushed it away from the wall so that I might read the words.

In fact, though, it was not *words*.

It was *one* word.

Just one.

Written there on the wall over and over again, sometimes soldier straight with heavy, precise letters and other times scrawled as if by the delicate touch of a fairy's wings, the letters curled and fluttering. One instance of it was written on its side, as if Jeffrey had done the writing while lying down in bed.

One word.

One name.

Evangeline.

* * *

I cannot say how long I stood there and stared at my own name written over and over again on the wall. I do know that in those minutes when time was suspended, my insides turned to ice, my breath caught against a ball of emotion in my throat and my head thumped as if it had been squeezed between the plates of a letterpress.

When the door popped open and Bess Buttle called out, 'And there you are!' I spun around and put a hand to my heart. It was impossible to contain the shriek of surprise that escaped my lips.

As if that was exactly the reaction she'd been expecting, Bess grinned, then darted a look into the hallway before she closed the door. 'When I didn't find you in your office, I knew where you would be.'

'Am I that transparent?' I collected what I could of my dignity and hoped I didn't look the complete fool. 'I thought that if I might—'

'Look about, yes.' Bess did just that, her beard jutting out when she lifted her chin and sent a gaze around the room. 'There's nothing much here to see, is there?'

'True.' The single word did not convey my disappointment so much as did the sigh that went along with it.

'And the paper in his pocket?' she asked. 'The one you snatched last night from the poor, dead gentleman?'

Ah, the paper.

What Bess didn't know was that there were two papers, the one with a hotel name and address on it and the other . . .

Rather than betray the sensations that cascaded through me when I thought of the fragment of love letter I'd found, I turned my back on Bess, the better to collect my thoughts and wayward emotions.

'It was simply the address of the place where Andrew Emerson was staying here in New York,' I told her, and continued through the lie. 'My thought is that Mr Emerson hoped to talk to my brother and wanted me to relay the location to him so that they might arrange a meeting.'

'You said he was most especially anxious for you to see that there paper.'

'Yes.' I whirled again to face her. 'Mr Emerson must have had urgent business he wished to discuss with Mr Barnum. It is a shame we will never know what that business was.'

Because Bess is herself an honest woman, she did not think to question me and, for that, I was grateful. Until I knew who had written the letter to 'dearest James,' until I knew what it meant and how Andrew thought I might somehow help him in the matter, I thought it best to keep the information to myself. For now, the surest way to do that was to concentrate on the matter at hand.

'If we knew where Mr Hollister might have gone . . .' I lifted my arms and let them flap back down again to my sides.

'We've been thinking about it, don't think we haven't.' Bess went back to the door, opened it, motioned out to the hallway and, with a start, I realized how long I must have stood frozen, staring at the wall where my name was scrawled. The morning's display of our oddities had ended and now some of them paraded into the room.

Jimmy O'Connell, our tattooed man, led the way, still dressed as he was for the morning's show in sit-upons but without a shirt, the better to display the birds and flowers and swirling designs he told our patrons had been inked onto his chest and arms and back by voluptuous virgins when he was stranded on a South Seas island. He was followed by George and Harry, our one-legged gymnasts, still in the costumes that made them look like jesters at a medieval court, then by Clara Foyle, our fat lady, and finally by Prince Mongo, who, three times a day, six days a week, regaled the crowd with stories of his life as a Zulu chief in the wilds of Africa. Had our patrons known his real name was Charles Hemple and that he was a free colored man from Vermont, it is my opinion they might not have hung so upon his every word.

'So . . .' It was clear from the start that Bess had been elected the spokesperson of the group, but she looked from one to the other of the curiosities in any case, just to be sure she had their permission to speak. When no one objected, she clutched her hands together at her waist. 'We couldn't talk of nothing else last night, nothing but Jeffrey and that poor young man what lost his life here.'

'And do any of you think Mr Hollister responsible for what happened in the Portrait Gallery?' I asked them.

When Clara Foyle made to sweep around the table and stroll to the other side of the room, both George and Harry had no choice but to move; Clara was as wide as she was tall and, in her rose-colored gown, she reminded me of a plump cloud bedecked with sunset hues.

'You know he had a temper. I reminded you all of as much last night.' Clara raised all three of her chins. 'Jeffrey had a temper.'

'But he had no reason to take it out on Andrew Emerson,' I reminded her. 'He didn't know Andrew.'

'He knew you.' Our Zulu chief gave the wall behind the bed a knowing look and I felt heat rush into my cheeks. I could not say if anyone else noticed Jeffrey's scribbles – Charles didn't give them a chance. As if it were the most natural thing in the world, he moved forward and pushed the bed back to its original position, the better to hide the telltale writing on the wall. 'He always held you in high esteem,' Charles told me. 'Perhaps you didn't know.'

I feared my cheeks were the color of Clara's gown and struggled to find the words that would explain away the whole thing as impossible. 'I . . . I don't think . . .'

'It ain't like it's your fault,' Bess said. 'And so it's nothing to be ashamed of. He's a gentle sort of soul is Jeffrey.'

To which Clara snorted her opinion.

'Well, he is,' Bess insisted, and just in case Clara thought to again dispute this, Bess gave her a narrow-eyed glare. 'He feels things. Down deep inside. Sometimes so much that he can't control what he says or what he does.' When she turned her gaze to me, Bess's expression softened. 'He wouldn't never have said anything to you about how he felt, of course, knowing how unseemly it was. But we all knew . . .' Again she glanced around at her fellow performers so as to elicit their support. 'We all saw the way he looked at you. We know he admired you and felt a sort of . . . well, I suppose you could call it affection. Not that he meant it as inappropriate!'

'Yes, I know that.' I wasn't sure I did, not right then, not when this news of a fondness offered me by Jeffrey Hollister was so fresh and so unexpected. 'But still . . .'

'You don't think he done it,' Bess said.

'We don't, either,' George put in, hopping closer on his one leg. Harry, his partner in the act, was missing a left leg, George a right. Nevertheless, they managed to tumble and juggle and twirl for the audience, uncannily graceful and as agile as if they were full-bodied. 'We saw him come up here to his room last night.'

This was the first real news I'd heard all morning and, encouraged, I looked from George to Harry. 'How did he act?'

Harry had an unfortunate stutter, the result, no doubt, of years of being taunted and belittled for his unusual appearance. 'H . . . he was agitated. H . . . h . . . Jeffrey fairly run up them steps and here into his room.'

'And then?' I asked them.

George and Harry exchanged looks and, just like they did in every precisely timed acrobatic feat in their act, they moved in unison when they shrugged.

'S-slammed the door and that was that,' Harry said.

'Didn't see him again,' George added.

'Did anyone see him leave?'

None of them had an answer, and I was forced to try and find another avenue of investigation. 'Then tell me this,' I said. 'Do any of you know where he came from? Before he joined us here at the museum, where did Jeffrey live?'

Like Cook back home, Jimmy O'Connell had been born and bred in Ireland and his words had the musical lilt of his homeland. 'On the streets, or so I hear tell.'

'Here in New York?' I asked.

O'Connell nodded. 'Five Points, he once told me. Over near Reade Street.'

'Well, you won't be going there!' Bess – and her beard – bristled with indignation. 'That's no place for a woman, and to be sure.'

'Not a place for anyone.' A shiver snaked over Clara's wide shoulders. 'Sin and villainy, that's all you'll find in Five Points. Sin and villainy.'

'And perhaps answers?'

'No!' Charles and Bess both spoke at once and, when I looked from one of them to the other, I was just in time to see Charles shake his head. He was a handsome man with a thick mane of hair which, for the purposes of his appearance as Prince Mongo, was frizzled around his head with the help of a daily washing in beer. He had a wide, noble nose, strong hands and dark eyes. 'Your brother can send someone to inquire,' he said in no uncertain terms.

As much as I was loath to admit it, I knew he was right. I had never myself ventured into Five Points, of course, but I knew about the area well enough from the stories I'd heard. As Clara had been so quick to point out, it was a place where whorehouses and gambling dens shared space with taverns and the small, squalid houses called rookeries that are built one atop the other in tumbledown disarray. Truth to tell, I feared neither the poverty of the area nor its residents, but there were even more sinister scoundrels about in Five Points, or so I'd heard, including pinch-purses, thieves and those shanghaiers who were said to waylay the unwary, drug them and drag them off to sea, where they were made to work out their lives on ships in servitude.

'I am not going to Five Points,' I told the oddities and reminded myself.

'W-w-we would come with you,' George volunteered.

I gave him a smile. 'I thank you for your kindness, and I know you are earnest, but I don't think it's wise for any of us to venture there. As a group, we might attract far too much attention.'

'And alone, you'll dice with death if you go there, and that's for certain,' Bess added.

'Then what are we to do?' I asked no one in particular. 'There must be some way of finding Mr Hollister.'

'Well, there is Carey's, of course,' Jimmy O'Connell said, and when I looked at him in wonder because he would keep such an important morsel of information so much to himself for so long, he grinned and tugged at one tattooed earlobe. 'Just thought of it. And it might not mean a thing. But Carey's, you see, is—'

'No place for a lady!' Bess snapped.

I did my best to shush her with the waving of one hand. 'Carey's is . . .' I asked O'Connell.

'The freak house.' Clara's opinion was clear from the way she clicked her tongue. 'Devils, every one of them there. Sinners and godless men who take cruel advantage of those such as us.'

'And Mr Hollister . . .' Again I looked O'Connell's way. 'He knows of this place?'

'Worked there, he did. Some five years or more. Before he left for the circus where Mr Barnum found him.'

'And this Carey's . . .' My excitement at hearing what actually might be helpful information nearly got the best of me, and I reined it in with a deep breath. 'Carey's is not in Five Points, is it?'

'Nah!' Bess ran a hand through her beard. 'Which don't mean it's a place a woman should go alone.'

'And I'm certainly not saying I'm going to.' This was not a lie, for I had not come right out and said that no matter where Carey's was I was planning a trip there. 'But it would be helpful to know where Carey's is located.'

'That's an easy one!' O'Connell grinned. 'To find Carey's place, you must head for the Bowery.'

FIVE

I t is a well-known fact to those of us who live on the island of Manhattan that the Bowery is a step up from Five Points.

It was no wonder then that though I was not nearly courageous enough to attempt a trip to the latter, I had few qualms about a visit to the former – at least once the oddities had returned to work for their two o'clock performance and thus would not notice my absence and report it to my brother.

It is not that Phin is like so many others and assumes that a woman should have neither a healthy amount of curiosity about life nor interesting work to occupy her. The fact that he employs me at his museum proves as much. No; in fact, Phin believes women are equal to men in every way and have every bit as much intellect as men.

Still, I was convinced he would not take to me traveling to the Bowery on my own. Especially if he knew I planned a stop at Carey's while I was there.

Assured that I would not be followed or interfered with, I set out in search of the aforementioned establishment in the hopes that Jeffrey Hollister might be there. I knew it would not be hard to find Carey's, for it was often advertised in the newspapers, as was our own museum, and I committed the address to memory and headed for the avenue known as Bowery.

It was the island's oldest thoroughfare, or so Phin had told me soon after I'd arrived in New York. Having begun life as an Indian path, the Bowery was first settled by ten families of freed slaves nearly two hundred years earlier. In later days, it was lined with the farms and estates of prosperous Dutchmen and then the row houses of Federalists. These days, those houses, with their steeply pitched roofs and the fan-shaped windows above their doors, served as taverns and brothels, and the Bowery had metamorphosed from a street of stately homes to—

The moment I turned from Delancey and my boots hit the pavement of the Bowery, all thoughts of the history and significance of the place flew out of my head. The music of a brass band thrummed through the air, the weighty rhythm of its song in counterpoint to the cheerful tune of a piano being played in a nearby tavern. Across the street, a man in brown held one end of a leash with a bear on the other end of it, and the people who gathered around threw pennies and applauded when the bear stood on its hind legs and caught an apple in its mouth.

'Well, hello there, miss!' The sound of a voice so near startled me back to awareness, and I turned just in time to see a young man with long sideburns tip his stovepipe hat to me. He was dressed as was typical of the jaunty and rambunctious fellows from the neighborhood who were known as b'hoys, in a black frock coat and with his sit-down-upons tucked into heavy boots. He smelled of a great deal of rum.

He stared at me intently, no doubt to try and bring me into focus. 'What's a beauty like you doin' here all by your lonesome?'

Yes, I was alone, but I had no fear of the man. It was daylight, after all, and at the museum we saw a large number of Bowery b'hoys and g'hals. They were hard workers, most of them. Butchers and bakers and other laborers like those who manned the German-owned breweries that proliferated nearby, and they were, for the most part, a jolly crowd, more interested in amusement than harassment.

I offered this b'hoy a smile. 'Carey's,' I said quite simply. 'If you could point me in the right direction.'

He bowed at the waist and made a sweeping gesture to his left, and when he stood again I did not wait for him to steady himself on his feet and offer to show me the way but headed off.

I saw other such men on my way past cheap dancehalls and dime museums I wished I might have stopped in so I could see how they compared to our own establishment. Where Broome Street crossed Bowery, three b'hoys, arm in arm, sang (badly, I must say) along to the music of an organ grinder who played while a lively little monkey squawked from his shoulder. Nearby, a lemon and orange seller plied his trade and a woman sold apples from the steps of a theater. There was another woman nearby and, though it was a cool afternoon, she wore no cloak, the better to show off the dress of flimsy fabric that she wore low over her shoulders. I might have been away from Bethel for

only two years but I knew full well what it was she was selling.
It was not apples.

I quickened my pace. Across the street beyond a stately brick
Federal home that had been turned into a place called the Three
Horse Tavern, I saw the sign for Carey's swinging in the breeze
and walked faster. I suppose, in some ways, it was a pity I did.
Had I been moving slower and paying more attention to my
surroundings, I might have been able to dart out of the way when
the doors of the boxing emporium I was just passing bumped
open. In that one second, I was overwhelmed with the smell of
tobacco, the odor of sweat and the sound of a rough voice
screaming, 'And don't you ever dare come back!'

It was but a second after that when a man, cursing to beat all,
came hurtling out of the door and slammed into me.

For one moment, I was too astounded to do anything other
than let out a surprised, 'Ooph,' but that moment did not last
long. The next thing I knew, the full weight of the man took me
down and I found myself flat against the pavement, the man –
still swearing – atop me.

'Darnation!' he growled.

I had landed on my back, the man on his stomach, and when
he raised himself up I saw that the stump of the cigar clenched
between his teeth was smashed at the end. He was a rough-looking
fellow with a beard and dark hair that spilled over his shoulders,
and he was dressed as I'd seen many of the boatmen who worked
along the Erie Canal, in fawn-colored buckskin sit-down-upons
and a jacket made of the same material that was fringed at the
sleeves, the hem and across the chest.

'It's a mercy I'm out here and not in there to beat the Dutch
out of you, Kimbal!' he called over his shoulder, but though
there were men with their noses pressed to the windows of the
building this man had so recently and so quickly exited, Mr
Kimbal did not appear.

'Blast the cussed old imp,' the man growled.

To which I decided I had no choice but to respond. 'Excuse me.'

He plucked the cigar butt out of his mouth and glowered at it
before he cast it away.

I tried again. 'Excuse me.'

'Eh?' As strange as it seemed – at least to me, considering

the fact that he was sprawled on top of me – the man looked at me as if he had no idea where I'd come from. 'What in tarnation are you doing there?' he asked.

'It seems I am the one who prevented you from having your nose smashed against the pavement.' I made to sit up and, when I did, he finally came to his senses and rolled off me. He sat on the pavement, his knees bent, and I took the opportunity to collect what I could of my dignity and untwist my cloak and my skirts from around my ankles. When I made to pull myself off the ground, he sprang to his feet.

'Are you telling me you weren't there the whole time?' he asked. 'When I walked out of Kimbal's? Are you telling me . . .?'

'Really!' I gathered my skirts and got to my knees and, when he offered a hand to help me to my feet, I accepted it. His hands were rough and his fingers strong. They wrapped around mine and, with a tug, he lifted me as if I weighed no more than a feather.

My knees shook but my chin was high and my head was steady when I reminded him, 'You hardly walked out of Kimbal's. You were thrown out. And of course I wasn't just lying there on the pavement. You exited the boxing emporium—'

'And knocked you down.'

It was difficult to say because of his whiskers, but I thought his cheeks darkened to the same deep red of the primitive beads he wore around his neck. He cleared his throat with a cough. 'I do beg your pardon.' He made a bow that wasn't nearly as showy as the one I'd been given so recently by the b'hoy. 'Are you injured?'

Was I?

I tried out my limbs and found them to be working sufficiently. 'It doesn't appear so.'

'Then are you thirsty?' His dark eyes lit up. 'I am nothing if not a gentleman,' he insisted. 'After I've been on top of a woman, I always offer to buy her a drink.'

I am hardly prudish. But, unlike my brother, I am not glib-tongued. I opened my mouth to say something – anything – and, when nothing came out, I snapped it shut again.

'Sorry.' As if the very word was painful, he squeezed his eyes shut. 'I've been away from polite company for quite some time. It seems I've forgotten there are certain women . . .' He looked

me over quickly, head to toe. 'Certain women one talks to in
such a way and certain women who are of better quality. You
are not a sister to those who ply their wares up and down the
street, I can see that. Though what a lady such as you is doing
here alone . . .'

I clutched my reticule at my waist. 'What makes you think
I'm alone?'

'If you weren't, whatever man you were with should have
come to your aid instantly when I knocked into you and taught
me what for while he was at it for putting you in danger. Hence,
you are either alone or the man you are with is a total and utter
fool to take the chance of offering such an insult to so pretty a
woman.'

'I am here looking for a man.' This seemed a better course in
which to steer the conversation than the one in which it was so
obviously headed. 'I thought I might find him at Carey's and I
was just on my way there.'

The gleam in his eyes disappeared and his smile faded. 'I am
truly sorry I delayed your search. Burke, ma'am.' He dispensed
with another bow and gave me a nod. 'At your service.'

'Well, Mr Burke—'

'Not mister. Just Burke.' A smile lit up his dark eyes.

'Well, Burke, as I was saying, I am looking to find a man who
may be at Carey's. That's where I was headed—'

'When I upended you.' His smile twisted with regret. 'If it
wasn't for that dadblasted Kimbal—'

'We would not have met.' I stepped back and away from him.
'Good day to you, Mister . . . er . . . good day to you, Burke.'

He wasn't wearing a hat but he made to tip one. 'Good day
to you, miss.'

I turned and left his company as quickly as I could, grateful
that, on the Bowery, there was so much activity and so much of
interest that no one seemed to have noticed our clumsy encounter.
I kept my gaze focused on Carey's, waited for a carriage with a
lively, strutting team of horses to pass and crossed to the other
side of the avenue. At the front of Carey's, a man in a red-and-
white-striped sit-down-upons (or unmentionables as they were
sometimes called) and wearing a white jacket stood on a wooden
crate in front of a blue-curtained doorway, outside of which hung

a larger-than-life drawing of a woman whose head was topped with the mane of a lion and whose teeth were man-eating fangs.

'Half-lion! Half-woman! All ferocious!' The man tapped the picture with the tip of a cane. 'Come inside and see Lionette, the strangest wonder in the world!'

'Strange, indeed,' I mumbled to myself, for I knew from first-hand experience that though Lionette looked lion-like enough in the drawing, my brother had come to see her for himself and had come away chuckling.

'Poor makeup,' Phin had told me at the time. 'Terrible false teeth.'

And still people paid their pennies to see her.

I was about to do the same – not so much that I might gape at Lionette but so that I could get inside Carey's and thus search for Jeffrey Hollister – when Burke stepped in front of me, blocking my way.

'You don't really want to go in there, do you?' he asked.

I was sure I did, so why my voice wavered when I looked past his buckskin and beads, I cannot say. 'I . . . I'm sure I need to go inside. I'm looking for—'

'A man.' The corners of Burke's mouth tugged into a look of disgust. 'Are you sure you wish to find such a man? Someone who comes to a place like this so he might make sport of the unfortunate freaks Carey puts on display is not the type of man who is worthy of your concern.'

Had he been talking about Phin, I would have disputed his observations. But when it came to Carey's, I knew better. I had heard stories of Nathaniel Carey's cruelty from our own oddities. I knew he baited his performers with food and beat them when they could not or would not obey. My stomach clutched.

I was no fool; I knew the patrons of our American Museum were sometimes known to taunt our performers, but I knew, too, that when my brother was about none of them dared. Yet here at Carey's I'd been told the more boisterous the crowd, the more Carey poked his performers, so as to whip the audience into a frenzy.

'I have no desire to look for anyone who might patronize this establishment,' I told Burke.

'Then you're looking for someone who works here? One of the freaks?'

It was not a word that sat well with me. I swallowed down my distaste. 'I am looking for a man named Jeffrey Hollister. He worked here once and might again.'

'We could ask.'

'And be lied to.'

He conceded the correctness of my observation with a tip of his head. 'But we'll ask anyway, why don't we?' And with that and a shiver of the fringe at the seams of his clothing, Burke whirled around and strode up to the barker at the door.

I had no illusions that this was the path to the truth. While Burke engaged the barker in conversation, I scooted past them, parted the blue curtain and ventured into Carey's.

I had heard about the jeering crowds, the prods, the performers who were treated as less than human and left to sleep in filth inside cages.

But I had never before seen such depravity, and I suppose in my heart I had hoped the reports of such were nothing more than tales told to frighten and titillate. Behind the blue curtain, I am sorry to report, I saw the stories were true.

There were four cages lined up one against the other just inside the door as a tease of things to come, an oddity in each, and the stench of the place and the inhumanity of the patrons who lined the entryway and pelted the cages with rotten fruit and called the oddities cruel names took my breath away. I stood frozen with loathing and disgust, bile rising in my throat, and I thought to race out the way I'd come in.

Until I remembered Jeffrey.

Beyond the entryway was a large open room and a stage, now empty. The seats in front of the stage were filling quickly with b'hoys and g'hals in high and ugly spirits and a smattering of patrons who looked to be of a better class but were no less excited to see the show begin. I did not take my seat on the benches with them but walked to the side and, since there was no one there to stop me, I slipped behind the stage.

Here there were no tallow candles flickering from the ceiling as there were in the outer theater, no odor of burning fat and curling trails of smoke. The darkness behind the stage was heavy with the smell of sweat and desperation. I stepped carefully over the rope that would be used to pull up the curtain when it was time for the show and ignored the man whose job it was, no doubt, to do the pulling. He hardly cared, being so engrossed in a mug of beer he paid me no mind.

Further into the bowels of Carey's, I found Lionette sitting on a low bench in front of a cracked mirror, adjusting her wig.

She did not spare me a look. 'Ain't nobody supposed to be back here.'

'I'm well aware of that, but I thought you might be able to help me.' I introduced myself and held out my hand.

Just as I expected, the Barnum name worked its magic.

Lionette turned in her seat, the better to shake my hand. 'You're looking for performers, are you?'

'We might be.' I consoled myself with the fact that this wasn't exactly a lie. My brother always had an eye out for the new and the unusual. 'I am actually looking for Jeffrey Hollister.'

She wrinkled her nose and reached for the wooden teeth, painted white, she would fit into her mouth before she made her appearance on stage. 'Who?'

I swallowed down my disappointment. 'It was some time ago. He worked here. He's a young man and his skin . . .' I was unsure how to describe Jeffrey. 'He works for us now at the American Museum. As the Lizard Man.'

'Lizard, eh? Well, ain't no lizards around here.' For reasons I cannot explain, Lionette found this particularly funny; she threw back her head and laughed, exposing gaping holes where her teeth used to be, now just gums that were swollen and bleeding from hours of wearing the lion fangs. 'I've only been here a year or so. You might ask . . .' She waved one hand in an indeterminate direction, somewhere back in the darkness. 'Samuelson's been here since he was a lad, or so I've been told. Per'aps he can help you. And if someday I should have a chance to come around there to Mr Barnum's museum . . .'

She didn't dare to come right out and ask but dangled the question.

'Ask for me. Or for my brother, Mr Barnum. I'm sure he'd be most happy to talk to you.'

Before she could get any further commitment out of me, I headed in the direction she'd pointed.

There were more draperies here, separating the backstage area from the place the performers lived. I parted them and choked on a stench like the worst muckheap. I clapped a hand over my nose and mouth.

'Mr Samuelson!' My voice was small but I could hardly blame myself. There was no breath in my lungs. 'Mr Samuelson, are you here?'

'Out back,' a voice answered, and what I'd thought was a pile of rags in a nearby cage shifted to reveal a man with no arms, his eyes devoid of hope. 'You'll find Sam out back.'

I thanked him and hurried away.

I found a door and stepped into a stone enclosure no bigger than my room a world away on Fifth Avenue. There were buildings on all sides of the little courtyard and their walls kept out the sunlight but, blessedly, not the hint of fresher air. Just as I gulped down a mouthful of it, a knife whizzed by not a foot in front of my nose. The blade slammed into a bare and twisted tree over on my right with enough force to bury itself to the hilt.

'So what do you think of that, eh? Mighty fine aim. Mighty fine throwing.'

My heartbeat, suspended for that one moment of surprise, started again with a thump and I looked to my left and the man who must have been Samuelson. His ears stuck out from either side of his head like enormous, misshapen sails. Proud of his accomplishment, he rubbed his hands together and I saw that his fingers, all ten of them, were nothing more than stumps.

'You don't see precision like that, do you? You don't see anyone who can throw a knife like ol' Sam can.'

'It is quite impressive.'

'Should have yelled to let me know you were coming out,' he told me on his way past so that he could wedge his palms on either side of the knife and pull it from the tree. 'You might have gotten hurt. Make no mistake about that. When Sam throws, his aim is strong and true. Surely, you might have gotten hurt.'

'I was depending on your accuracy,' I told him and offered him a smile. 'And your memory, too, Mr Samuelson. Lionette says you might know a man named Jeffrey Hollister.'

'Jeffrey? Got himself a cracking position over at Barnum's place. Lucky devil.'

'He does, indeed, work for Mr Barnum. But he's currently missing and I thought you might—'

'Missing?' Samuelson examined the tip of his knife, testing its sharpness against the tip of his tongue. 'Where's he gone to?'

'I thought you might be able to tell me that. Is he here?'

'Jeff?' As if he actually had to think about it, Samuelson tipped his head and the bit of light that seeped into the yard showed through his right ear, turning it pink and highlighting a network of purple veins. 'Nah. Not here. Never here. Ol' Carey just about went all to pieces when Jeff left and went away with the circus. Jeff was just a young man then and he'd lived here with Carey two, three years.'

'In a cage.' The words tasted bitter in my mouth.

'Don't take no offense there, miss. Sometimes it's for our own good.' Samuelson shrugged as if there might actually be a kernel of truth in the statement. 'At least we don't have to worry. You know, at night, when the b'hoys might come back looking for a little excitement.'

It was not something I could stomach thinking about. 'So Jeffrey left with the circus.'

Samuelson nodded and his ears flapped. 'And then went to Barnum's from there, or so I'm told. Haven't seen him since.'

My shoulders drooped. 'I hoped you might know where he is.'

Samuelson plodded across the yard and planted his feet, rolling the hilt of the knife between his palms, ready to throw it again. 'Can't say. Wouldn't know.' He squinted, aimed and, though I was not in the path of the blade, I stepped back instinctively just as he let the knife fly. Again it slammed into the tree, and Samuelson threw back his shoulders and crowed, 'Now there's some pretty throwing!'

I acknowledged it with a smile but refused to digress. 'Do you happen to know where Jeffrey came from? Before he came to Carey's, who were his people? Where did he live?'

'People!' He didn't so much spit out the word as he laughed around its syllables, as if they were foreign to him. 'We ain't got no people. Not the likes of me and Jeffrey and the others in there. But I heard him say once that when he was a boy,

after he was tossed out of the house on account of how odd
looking he was and how his father didn't want to spend a penny
to feed him, he used to sleep behind St Patrick's Cathedral at
night.'

St Patrick's.

I did not need to commit the name to memory, for I knew
well enough where it was and where I had to go.

Five Points.

The last of the afternoon sunlight touched the facade of St
Patrick's there at Mott and Prince Streets with gold, softening
the look of the sturdy stone building and the brick wall that
surrounded the churchyard beside it. Like all churches, this one
should have been a haven of peace in the bustling city but, like
so many other New Yorkers, I knew the truth – Five Points was
disease-ridden and crime-infested, and much of the violence that
tore through the area was between Protestants who had long
made the neighborhood their home and the Irish Catholics who
increasingly came to this country from their homeland and settled
in the tumbledown tenements and bedraggled shanties that were
packed one on top of the other on every street in Five Points.
The wall around the church and the burial ground was not for
aesthetic purposes. For the Irish Catholics, it was a rampart
meant for self-defense.

About to enter the burial grounds through the doorway in the
red brick wall, I looked both left and right. For now, there was
no one about but me and three pigs that rooted in the refuse that
littered the street, and for this I was grateful. None other than
Charles Dickens had visited Five Points earlier that year and had
declared it as wretched a place as any he'd ever been; my insides
would be tied into far fewer knots if I could find Jeffrey quickly
and leave before anyone took note of me.

My heart in my mouth, I stepped into the burial ground, its
standing monuments gray and ghostly in the long shadow of the
wall. Not far away a man sat on the ground, his back to me, and
my fears instantly vanished in a surge of hope.

'Jeffrey!' I hurried around to stand in front of the man and
my excitement plummeted. This was not Jeffrey but a thin, elderly
fellow with ashen skin and sunken eyes who looked neither

surprised to see me nor even the slightest bit interested in why I might be there.

'Jeffrey Hollister?' I asked him. 'Have you seen him? He is a man with . . .' I twiddled my fingers up and down my arms by way of indicating Jeffrey's peculiar skin condition. 'You would certainly remember him. He is green.'

But the man did not answer.

There were others huddled in the shadows of the gravestones not far away, dressed like the first man, in rags and with all their earthly belongings tied in sacks beside them. But when I asked after Jeffrey they either ignored me or shook their heads. I think they weren't so much telling me they did not know Jeffrey as they were simply dismissing me altogether, insignificant to their misery.

Disheartened, I left the burial ground and looked briefly into the church with the thought of asking God why so many lived in wretchedness. There was no answer forthcoming, and I decided to be on my way.

It was only then that something caught my eye from across the way, its passing so fleeting as to make me wonder if perhaps I was imagining it – the flash of fawn-colored buckskin and the vague impression of an amused, and bemused, smile.

SIX

The next day being Sunday, I did not have the opportunity to continue in my search for Jeffrey. As a family, we attended Universalist services in the South Reformed Dutch Church on Murray Street, and it wasn't until we were in our carriage and traveling toward home that Charity bothered to address me.

'We are calling on Sebastian Richter this afternoon.'

I confess I was paying little attention as the carriage that contained the children was behind ours and I'd turned to see how it was progressing.

I shook away my momentary confusion. 'A call on . . .'

Charity's sigh filled the carriage. 'Sebastian Richter. The man who lives across the way.'

'From?'

My brother sought to save me embarrassment by erupting into laughter. 'Across the way from us, of course,' he said, and he reached across the space that separated the two facing seats of the carriage so that he might pat my hand. 'You know our Evie,' he added, leaning closer to his wife who sat on the bench next to him. 'She does nothing but work all day and isn't one for poking around the neighborhood. Her head is filled with the details of the museum. She hardly pays attention to what's happening out in the world.'

'Well, perhaps she should.' Charity smoothed one hand through the fringe on one end of the fine wool shawl thrown over her shoulders. 'Richter is an influential man. He owns a good many breweries and I've been told he's quite wealthy.'

'But not as wealthy as we are, is he?' Again my brother laughed. 'Why is it you said we're going to visit the man?'

Charity had thin lips that pulled into a line when she shot her husband a look. 'Because he invited us.' She turned the same look on me. 'All of us.'

In an attempt to make her relent, I offered a smile. 'I

thought perhaps I would take the children to the park. There are ponies at—'

'The girls have no need to see ponies,' Charity said.

'But I thought perhaps Walter might like riding them and—'

'My son is too young to ride.' Her word was the final say, or so the mettle in her voice told me. 'Nurse will keep them at home where they belong. We, on the other hand, are going to Sebastian Richter's.'

We went to Sebastian Richter's.

Lest it be said that I am not sociable, I must defend the fact that I was less than enthusiastic about the prospect. It was a beautiful September day, warmer than it had been when I had ventured to the Bowery and Five Points, and I would have liked nothing better than to be out of the house, preferably with the children. Barring that, I would have enjoyed a walk on my own and taken a book along so that I might find a place to read and, while I was at it, to contemplate the mystery that was Andrew Emerson's death and the place Jeffrey Hollister had in it.

Calling on the neighbors seemed far less enticing.

Especially when it was finally time and we stepped out of the house and I looked at the grand, turreted home across the way and at an angle from Phin's and realized just how many guests there would be. The path to Richter's front door was crammed with carriages and, even as we watched, another couple – well-dressed and in a carriage that made even Phin's seem small and plain by comparison – arrived.

I touched a hand to my dress, a wool challis gown in a shade of blue much like my eyes, the fabric printed with sprigs of white flowers and greenery.

'You look fine.' As if he were reading my thoughts, my brother wound an arm through mine and whispered in my ear, 'You always look fine. And even if you didn't, I hardly think you'd care.'

'I wouldn't. I don't. But . . .' It was difficult to explain how such groups of people made me feel. In the museum, whether I was talking to one or one hundred, I was at ease. Yet in such social situations, when I was expected to talk of nothing more interesting than the weather or the latest fashions from Paris, I often felt awkward and tongue-tied. Then again, I reminded myself, I was with my brother and I had nothing to worry about. When he was in a room, it wasn't often that anyone else had a chance to speak!

Thus encouraged, we crossed the road and entered Richter's property through two iron gates thrown open in welcome. The front garden was a riot of color thanks to a proliferation of dahlias, and I stopped to admire them and was noticed by a man in brown tweed who sauntered up beside me. It was Sunday and he was certainly not working, but still, there was a permanent layer of dirt under the man's fingernails and a smile so wide and so proprietary on his face I had no doubt he was Richter's gardener.

'What do you think, miss?' He waved an arm to encompass the flowers in every shade of pink, red, purple and yellow. 'They are a thing of beauty to behold!'

'They are, indeed. I have never seen dahlias except in drawings, and I hear they are difficult to cultivate.'

'Not if you've got the gift as I do.' The wink he gave me was exaggerated and, thus, good-natured. 'Just you wait, miss. Just you wait until spring. Got my hands on some of them tulips you might have heard about. From across the ocean, all the way from Holland. Planted them just yesterday. Hundreds of them. Oh, yes, next spring Mr Richter's will be a showplace. I do hope you'll have a chance to see it.'

As I lived just across the way, I had no doubt of it and told the gardener I looked forward to seeing his flowers.

By this time, Phin and Charity, who had not stopped to discuss flora, were nearing the door and I hurried to catch up. We were greeted and our shawls and bonnets taken by a butler who handed them off and then showed us into a grand parlor painted in a shade of green that matched the sprigs in my gown, decorated as only a man with money could, with plush carpets, fine, heavy mahogany tables and chairs upholstered in fabric darker and even more soothing than the green on the walls. Nearby, our fellow guests – a whole boodle of them – were served egg sandwiches, thin slices of ham and smoked fish from one table, and there was an array of pastries, fruit and bits of candied ginger on another.

'Champagne?'

I was so absorbed by the scene and the elegant people who

surrounded us, as tightly packed and as colorful as the dahlias in the garden, I was hardly paying attention, at least not until I turned and found a tall man dressed all in black except for the brilliantly white shirt beneath his waistcoat and the small ribbon of red and yellow pinned to his jacket. He held a crystal flute in my direction.

'Sebastian Richter,' he said, and when I accepted the drink he lifted his own glass by way of salute. We sipped. He smiled. 'I must be sure you don't get the wrong idea and think that I usually serve the drinks in my own home. I saw you standing here alone and thought to introduce myself.'

He was a handsome man with strong, even features, broad shoulders, hair the color of ripe corn with a just few threads of silver in it and just the slightest trace of a Germanic accent.

I introduced myself.

'Oh, I am well aware of who you are.' His smile was dazzling. 'It was one of the reasons I appropriated a glass of champagne and brought it over here, so that I might meet you.'

I wasn't quite sure what to say, so it was just as well I didn't have to say anything at all. From across the room, my brother spied us talking and made his way over, the crowd parting in front of him like the Red Sea before Moses.

'Nice of you to ask us to stop by!' Phin pumped Richter's hand. 'We are neighbors but hardly neighborly, eh? Never seems to be time for that sort of thing for the working man.'

'Which is why we must make the time to get to know each other.' Richter was talking to Phin but he was looking at me. 'I hope you'll excuse the early hour. I know it is not usual to have a social gathering before candle-lighting. I've heard this sort of thing is something new they're doing in England – they call it a tea party.'

'Darned civilized.' Phin grinned from ear to ear. 'Though I have to say, the champagne helps.'

'And your good wife looks to be talking to my cousin, Sonya.' Richter glanced over Phin's shoulder to where the two ladies had their heads together. 'I must go and introduce myself and save Mrs Barnum. Sonya has been known to talk the ears off a rabbit! You'll excuse me.' He nodded to Phin and bowed ever so slightly to me.

Watching him go, Phin leaned nearer. 'I swan, there's a fine figure of a man. Seems the congenial sort.'

'Indeed.' I sipped my champagne.

'Handsome, too.'

'That much is undeniable.'

'And charming.'

My brother is anything but subtle. Knowing he was right about our host, I laughed, but my amusement stilled when I realized I felt exactly the same. Our host was handsome. He was charming. The tiny bit of warmth that curled inside me felt unfamiliar, like a friend I hadn't seen in too long a time and, uncomfortable, I sloughed it off.

By this time, Phin had caught the eye of someone he knew and he called a greeting and raced away to chat with the man. Left on my own, I accepted an egg sandwich from a girl offering them from a tray and drifted to the fringes of the crowd to eat it, far more content watching than interacting. From my spot near the doorway, I could see into the dining room, and the painting above the sideboard caught my eye. I closed in on it, the better to take in the broad brush strokes and colors that were so vivid and true, and it seemed as if the scene was happening right before my eyes. The painting showed a horse fair, and every sinew of every animal vibrated with life, as did the bulging muscles in the arms of the horse traders, the tilted heads of the buyers and the amazing, animated looks on the faces of the men who watched the goings-on.

'So what do you think?'

I didn't need to glance to my side to know that Richter had again joined me.

My words escaped on the end of an awestruck sigh. 'I can nearly taste the grit of the dirt from the horses' hooves between my teeth.'

His laughter was low and smooth. 'Ah, an art lover! I knew the moment I saw you that I had found a kindred spirit. The painting, it is not too vulgar for you?'

'You mean because it shows real people doing real things rather than the cavorting gods and goddesses that are so common in so many paintings?' I bent nearer for a closer look at the flashing hooves of a coal-black stallion. 'I have never felt drawn to such classical works but this is different. This is—'

'Intriguing?'

I stepped back and looked his way. 'It is astonishing.'

His smile never wavered. 'The artist is William Kobieta Walker. Perhaps you have heard of him, for he is all the talk of the town. He is a relative newcomer to New York, or so I'm told, but is fast gaining a reputation and a following. I'll have you know I am quite the rebel to hang a painting so modern and so unusual.'

'Then here's to being rebellious.' It was my turn to raise my glass to him. 'You have excellent taste, Mr Richter, and I—'

'Papa! Papa!'

Before I could finish complimenting Richter, the front door flew open and two children raced into the house and hurtled in our direction. Their red-faced nurse followed behind, breathing hard, one hand pressed to her bosom, but Richter waved her off and handed me his champagne glass so that he might get to his knees, the better to be prepared when the children slammed into him. He put an arm around each of them.

'Did you have a pleasant day at the park?' he asked a little girl of five or so with the face of a cherub. 'And did you float the new boat Papa made for you in the pond?' he asked a boy of perhaps seven who had the same golden hair as Richter's, the same eyes, as blue as sapphires, and the same patrician nose.

The children assured him they'd had a wonderful day. He instructed them to go upstairs with Nurse and change so that they might come down and greet his guests and they were gone in a swirl of cloaks and laughter.

'You must forgive Frida and Otto,' he said. He smiled when he got to his feet and took his glass. 'They are full of energy. Full of life. I know I should better discipline them but I don't have the heart.'

I couldn't help but smile, too, when I found myself staring after the children. 'You and your wife must be very proud.'

'My wife . . .'

The moment Richter spoke the words, the way he said them and imbued them with so much reverence, I knew I'd made a mistake. I whirled again to face him and felt my heart thump against my ribs.

He saw the mortification in my eyes and didn't hold my blunder against me but offered a soft smile. 'Marta has been gone these few years now. She went home to our Lord when our Frida was born. So you see . . .' He sloughed off his sadness. 'You see why I indulge them so. My children, they are my world.'

'And they are beautiful.' I finished my champagne, and when a young man with a tray came along he took my glass. 'They look so much like you.'

'They may have my looks but let us hope they have their mother's good sense! It will serve them well in the world. Let us hope they have her good heart, too. She was a sweet, benevolent woman.'

'Ah, you must be talking about Marta!' The woman who joined us and wrapped an arm through Richter's was the same woman I'd seen talking to Charity earlier – his cousin, Sonya. She was a small woman with dark hair and eyes that were a shade of gray that reminded me of marble. She wore a ribbon just like Richter's pinned to her crimson gown. 'Has he started lecturing you about Marta's charities yet?'

Sonya was offering a tease and Richter knew it. Still, he did not look sorry when Phin approached.

'Speaking of charities . . .' Richter didn't apologize for seizing the opportunity when he saw it and I thought it refreshing. In the time I'd been in New York and Phin's financial star had risen, I'd witnessed so many who wanted his assistance pretend it didn't matter to them at the same time they nearly drooled for his attention. 'Mr Barnum, I thought perhaps I might mention that the new St Paul's Evangelical Lutheran Church is readying to lay the cornerstone for a church and school. I thought perhaps you might—'

With one hand out, Phin stopped him. 'It is Sunday, sir, and I never talk money on Sunday.' He allowed Richter to have exactly three seconds of disappointment before Phin broke into a grin. 'But send someone around to the museum tomorrow, why don't you.' Still smiling, Phin backed away when another acquaintance approached. 'I'll be sure he doesn't come back to you empty-handed!'

Richter's eyes lit up. 'It is just as I have always heard. Your brother is an amazing man.'

'And this new church, is this one of your late wife's good causes?' I asked him.

'The church. The school.'

'And don't forget Succor,' Sonya added, touching a hand to the red and yellow ribbon. 'The Society for the Relief and Succor of Needy Women. You may have noticed Sebastian and I wear its symbol as a reminder of all we have accomplished in Marta's name and all that still needs to be done. Succor was the one thing dear Marta loved nearly as much as she did her husband and her children, a place where women who are in trouble . . .' She endowed the word with an odd little accent that twisted through my stomach and clutched further when she added, 'Well, I am sure a woman such as you knows exactly what I'm talking about, Miss Barnum. From what we have heard, you are out in the world, working! My goodness, I can hardly comprehend such a thing, but I can understand that, under the circumstances, you surely have heard of such women and perhaps even seen them, too, as you travel to and from your brother's museum. Women who are alone. And desperate. Women who have no hope in this world.'

I had more experience with such than she could imagine.

I swallowed the sudden ball of emotion in my throat and hid my discomfort beneath an interest I hardly needed to feign. 'Your late wife,' I asked Richter, 'she was involved in a charity that benefitted such women?'

'She was, indeed,' he said. 'Though she was not just involved. I hope you do not think me too boastful when I tell you that Marta was the force behind Succor and the rest of us were caught up in her fervor and her mission.'

'Which is exactly why I've just been discussing Succor with Mrs Barnum,' Sonya said, glancing over her shoulder to where my sister-in-law was chatting with a white-haired woman dressed ever-so-fashionably in a gray dress of *peau de soie* with tight-fitting sleeves and a bell-shaped skirt who, like others in the room, wore the Succor ribbon. 'She most specifically asked me to mention Succor to you and to point out the plight of such poor, unfortunate women, so many of them left alone and with no family to turn to. Mrs Barnum insisted that, as she is, you would be interested in joining in our cause.

'We are meeting tomorrow,' Sonya continued. 'At the office of Succor that my cousin Sebastian' – she gave Richter's arm a warm squeeze – 'has been so generous as to lend us. He allows us to use offices in a building he owns. We are always in need of women of character who are willing to lend a hand to those less fortunate. Will you join us?'

'Has my sister-in-law agreed to attend?' I asked.

'Oh, yes.' Sonya's exhilaration was palpable. 'She told me you would surely come with her, and we are most grateful.'

'I will,' I said.

'Then may I . . .' Sonya produced another of the little ribbons, pinned it to my dress and stepped back to beam me a smile. 'If you will be so kind to wear the ribbon when you are out, it will remind people of our good works.'

'Yes, of course.' By that time Sonya had already seen a woman she knew across the room and excused herself.

'You really don't have to go,' Sebastian Richter told me. 'Sonya can be—'

'It's fine. Really. I am not sure what I can do to help but I can surely try.'

'A woman of your intelligence . . .' Richter did not finish the statement and, for that, I was grateful. The gleam in his eye wasn't off-putting but rather entrancing.

And I am not a woman who is comfortable being entranced.

With that in mind, I excused myself and would have walked away if Richter hadn't stopped me.

'I thought perhaps . . .' For a man of such reputation and such stature, he suddenly looked ill at ease. 'That is, if Mrs Barnum would allow it, I noticed how much you seemed to enjoy the company of my children. I know your brother and his wife have children of their own, and I thought that we might take them – all of them – to the park some afternoon. That is, if you think you might enjoy the outing.'

I couldn't help but think of what his cousin had mentioned earlier. 'And it wouldn't bother you to be seen in public with a woman who is employed at the American Museum?'

Richter's unease was gone in an instant.

'Your work at the museum, Miss Barnum . . .' His smile warmed me through to the bone. 'I hope you won't think it too forward of me, but the fact that you are intelligent and capable enough to work is one of the things I find so fascinating about you.'

I had in the past been told I was fair enough of face and figure, and though some men I had met did not think it an asset in a woman, I had been also told that I talked like a book and was as smart as a steel trap.

As far as I could remember, I do not think that anyone – man, woman or child, able-bodied or oddity – had ever called me fascinating.

I do confess, the thought bolstered my spirits and made it difficult for me to sleep that night. I stayed up to the small hours and, most naturally, thinking about being deemed fascinating made me think of Sebastian Richter.

It is no wonder that when the sun rose the next morning I was hardly at my best, and it was just as well that when I arrived in the breakfast room there was no one about. When I was seated, Cook brought me a cup of coffee and offered boiled eggs, sausages and fried potatoes, but I had no time to decide if I wanted more than the bread and butter that had been left on the table when Phin bumped through the door.

His face was a thundercloud.

'You'll excuse us, Mrs O'Donnell,' was all he said.

She left the coffee pot on the table and exited the room and I sat up, a sudden dread filling my veins with ice.

'What is it?' I was out of my chair in an instant. 'The children? They aren't—'

'They are fine. Every single one of them.' Phin plunked into a chair and poured coffee for himself, and I sat back down. 'That is not what I need to talk to you about. It is . . . it is Madeline Emerson.'

'Andrew's sister?' Thinking of poor Madeline receiving the news of Andrew's untimely end made my heart squeeze, and when I made to take a drink of my own coffee, my hands shook. I set cup on saucer with a clink. 'I've written to her,' I told my brother. 'The night . . .' He knew exactly which night I was talking about – I did not need to elaborate. 'I sent the letter to Bethel with—'

'Yes, yes. The O'Donnell boy. Not the most industrious of lads, I think you'll agree. Knowing that, I sent a letter, too, and a rider who was faster and more experienced and with better horses. I have already received a reply.'

He pulled a folded piece of paper from his pocket and smoothed it open in front of him on the table.

From where I was sitting, I could not read what was written there, but I saw the letters were small and cramped.

'It is from Sarah Hanks,' Phin told me. 'Andrew and Madeline's aunt.'

I remembered the woman well, for she had an orchard and, when we were children, she often let us pick the apples. 'She must be distressed by news of Andrew's death.'

'Yes, of course.' Phin tapped a finger against the paper. 'But that is not all she's worried about. You see, Evie, it seems Madeline is no longer in Bethel.'

'Not in Bethel? Then where—'

Phin cleared his throat. 'No one has seen Madeline Emerson in weeks,' he said. 'No one has heard from her. The last time she was seen . . .' Even my brother, who was so audacious in so much else, could not look me in the eye when he spoke the words. He stared at the chandelier above our heads. 'The last time she was seen she was getting on the coach that was traveling from Bethel here to New York City. She was with James Crockett.'

SEVEN

I could not help myself. I tried, and oh, how I prayed that I might succeed!

But as it was, I simply could not help myself.

I spent that morning in my office at the museum, the ledger books open in front of me, my lamp lit and the door closed. Yet I could not work. I could not think.

Not of anything but what Phin had told me.

Madeline had been seen leaving Bethel for New York City.

With James Crockett.

Even now, hours after first hearing the news, the enormity of it brought tears to my eyes.

She needs your help.

Dear God, if Madeline was truly with James Crockett, she did need my help.

And I had turned away from him when Andrew came to seek it.

My heart squeezed, and I again reread the fragment of writing Andrew had tried to press into my hands as we stood together in front of the Feejee Mermaid.

I love you with all my heart. I love you, my dearest James.

As things so often do after it is too late to change them, it all made sense now – Madeline had written a love letter to James Crockett and her brother had found evidence of it. It was, no doubt, why Andrew had followed his sister to New York and why he thought I might help, for, like everyone else in Bethel, Andrew knew that James and I had once been friends.

No.

Even to myself, even when I so desperately wanted to, I could not lie.

James and I had been more than friends.

Back in Bethel, when I stopped walking out with James, when people no longer saw him calling at our door, word went around – as it always does in towns both large and small – that there had been a falling out between us, that perhaps the whispered rumors of James's true character had finally worked to change my mind and my heart. No doubt Andrew thought I might speak to Madeline and deliver her from the unhappy destiny that was the fate of any young woman who had the misfortune of falling in love with James Crockett.

If only he knew the enormity of the truth!

My gaze on the fragment of Madeline's letter and my hands clasped together on my desktop, I realized that thinking about it no longer clutched at my heart and did not keep me up at night as it had for so many months. It was simple fact. Andrew could not have known – no one except my own family would know that if James's good looks and his fortune, his charm and his honeyed tongue had seduced Madeline as they had me, she was in far more danger than he might have imagined.

For James Crockett was the father of my child.

I cannot say how long I sat lost in my thoughts. I knew only that I'd just put away the scrap of the letter when my door flew open and Phin stuck his head in my office.

'Come on, Evie! It's Monday.'

For what I feared was far too long, I gawped at him, my mind in such a whirl I could not think what he meant.

With a click of his tongue, Phin dashed into the office and grabbed my hand, the better to tug me to my feet. 'Monday, Evie, and we have sellers we need to receive. You must come down to my office, it's nearly eleven.'

As if they were buried in tabby, my feet kept their place and Phin relented, at least for a moment, gentling his hold on my hand. His smile melted and his eyes brimmed with the kind of sympathy only a man who so keenly gauges the moods of others can offer. 'The sellers who are downstairs will take your mind off the bad news I gave you earlier, and besides, if you leave the buying to me . . .' As suddenly as the laughter in them had stilled, his eyes gleamed again. 'If you are not there to keep me in check I'm bound to spend far more money than I ought. You are the only one who can stop me!'

By the time we made our way to Phin's office, there was already a line outside it, young and old, men and women, all eager to show their wares to my brother in the hopes he might purchase what they offered and display it in the museum.

He was right in the observation that this, our usual Monday routine, helped keep my mind focused on things other than Madeline's plight.

But then, boredom is sure to do that to a person.

Over the course of the next hours, I watched a man from Maine spill a box of rocks on Phin's desk and do his best to convince us that they were the product of the eruption of Vesuvius and, thus, of interest to one and all. Another man, this one surely from the Bowery for he had both the long sideburns called soaplocks and the swagger that were the sure signs of that neighborhood, swore he had a three-legged chicken he would be most delighted to present to us – if only we would give him the sum of ten dollars so that he might have the creature shipped from Pennsylvania. A third man, so old he teetered as he stood before us, was convinced the discarded black glass bottles he'd collected from the nearby breweries were as valuable as the gemstones we displayed in the gallery.

Phin gave the man a dollar coin for his bottles and sent him on his way.

'One woman left and then that's the last of them,' Mr Dewey told us. 'She's got a bag with her, and the bag . . .'

The woman, the bag in question under her arm, strode into the office. The bag wiggled and a mournful meow emanated from its depths.

'Got a cat here,' the woman said, plunking the bag and the mewling animal inside it on Phin's desk. 'He's the color of a cherry.'

After a morning that had been decidedly disappointing even by Phin's somewhat loose standards, this piqued his interest.

'A cherry, you say?' He sat up straight and looked my way. 'That surely sounds like something our patrons would enjoy. A cat the color of a cherry! Madame, I would be most interested in your cat,' he told the woman.

She had not taken her hand off the bag and now she clutched it a little tighter. 'I'd like nothing better than to give him over to you, Mr Barnum. But it will cost you. Twenty-five dollars.'

It was a large sum, indeed, but that hardly dampened Phin's

interest. More intrigued than ever, he went into his desk drawer, drew out the sum of money and handed it over.

The woman tucked away the money and overturned the bag on the desk.

A black cat tumbled out.

'But—'

The single word was barely out of my mouth when Phin cut me off. 'I've been duped!' he yelled. 'Madam, you told me—'

'That he was the color of a cherry, Mr Barnum!' Her eyes sparkling, the woman turned on her heels and headed for the door. 'And as you well know, sir, some cherries are black!'

Phin froze in amazement for a second, long enough for the woman to leave and, once she was gone, he burst into laughter. 'Black cherries! The color of black cherries!' The cat had already made himself at home atop of pile of papers and Phin ruffled a hand over its head. 'We shall surely cause a sensation with this, Evie. We'll advertise him as a cat the color of cherries and when people come to see him, they will surely enjoy the jest, just as I have. What do you say?'

I would have said that the cat looked comfortable and I did not have the heart to turn him out, but I never had the time because Mr Dewey stepped into the office again.

'Sorry, Mr Barnum. Another gentleman has just arrived. I told him to come back next Monday, but he told me that by next Monday he will have already set sail for Zanzibar.'

'Zanzibar, you say? Now that sounds like an interesting fellow! What do you say, Evie?'

There was no use in my saying anything because, from the gleam in his eyes, I knew Phin had already made up his mind. I was not surprised when he told Mr Dewey to show the fellow in.

But I was surprised when the man walked into the office.

His beard had been shaved to reveal a face that was far more appealing than I remembered it: a strong chin, a well-shaped nose, lips that were full. His hair was cut and combed to the side. He was cleanly and fashionably dressed, much as Phin was that day, in light-colored unmentionables and a dark frock coat. His waistcoat was a brilliant red.

Just like the string of primitive beads that peeked from below the edge of his black cravat.

At the same time he caught sight of me and closed in, a sly smile on his face, I blinked away my astonishment.

'It is good to see you again, Miss . . .'

'Barnum.' My brother supplied the name. 'Evangeline Barnum, though I wonder that I need to inform you of as much, sir. Something tells me you have already made the acquaintance of my sister.'

'We have . . .' his smile intensified, '. . . bumped into each other.'

My own smile in return was tight. Then again, I couldn't help but remember I had last seen him outside St Patrick's Church. He had followed me to Five Points and, because I didn't know why, the thought sat uneasy with me. I gave him a nod. 'Mr Burke.'

'Just Burke.'

'Well, Burke, I am especially delighted to meet you since you are a friend of Evie's.' Phin rubbed his hands together. 'What do you have to show me?'

'Nothing at all, sir. But there are crates outside on the rig I hired. Ten of them all told. Rather than go through the trouble of unloading them, I assumed you'd be intrigued enough to—'

'So intrigued that we would simply hand over our receipts in exchange for merchandise we haven't seen?' I didn't dare look at the cat when I said this since, in buying him, it was exactly what we'd just done. I rose to my feet and made my way across the office. 'Really, this beats the Dutch! Phin, you cannot possibly think—'

His palms flat and his hands out, my brother backed away from the argument. 'If this fellow is a friend of yours, Evie, I leave the decision solely to you.'

'Then that decision is easy enough.' At the door, I turned to face Burke. 'We are not interested. Good day, sir.'

I was scarcely out into the lobby when Burke caught up with me.

'The least you can do is pay me something for saving your hide on Saturday.'

I had no intention of any further interaction but, astonished, I turned to face him. 'You? Saved me? The way I remember it, sir, you are the one who nearly broke my every bone.'

'And I apologized for it.' A smile skimmed his lips. 'And nicely, too, the way I remember it.'

I would give him that much but didn't dare let him know it. I stiffened my shoulders. 'Still—'

'Still, I've been around the world and back and have a grand collection of artifacts you might find interesting.'

'Is that what you do?' I had not meant to ask the question and thus prolong our encounter, yet I could not help myself. My curiosity got the better of me. 'Are you an adventurer?'

Without the beard, his smile was even more disturbing than it had been in the Bowery. It was too broad, too knowing, and it made me anxious in ways I did not want to consider. 'A traveler, an explorer, a finder of treasures, a trader, a dealer. I dig in the dirt. I haggle with the natives. I've even risked my life a time or two, though I try to avoid that sort of thing as much as possible. I leave on my next voyage tomorrow and would like nothing better than to take good memories along with me.'

'You mean the good memories of us paying you money for wares we haven't seen.'

'I was thinking more of the good memories of the two of us having dinner together this evening. Then I could set sail tomorrow a happy man.'

Fortunately, I remembered the gathering at Succor and my promise to attend along with Charity. Otherwise, I'm not at all sure I wouldn't have succumbed to the magic of his smile. 'I have an engagement,' I told him.

'Then luncheon. Right now. Surely you must eat.'

'Not when I have other business to attend to.' I backed away.

His grin faded, his dark brows dropped low over his eyes and he laid a hand over his heart. 'Then perhaps I'll see you when I return, Miss Barnum. If I return. The world is full of dangers. Tell me you'll regret not sharing a meal with me if I never come back.'

'I hardly know you. Certainly not well enough to know if I might regret it.'

'Then tell me you'll regret not getting to know me better.'

In spite of myself, I couldn't help but smile.

'Ah, see!' He wagged a finger at me. 'You do appreciate the fact that I watched over you on Saturday.'

'You mean the way you followed me to Five Points?'

'Saw me, did you?' One corner of his mouth pulled tight. 'Actually, I was thinking more of Carey's. Nasty place, and had I not kept the fellow at the door engaged he certainly would have seen you slip inside without paying. The least you can do in return for my services is buy those crates that wait outside.'

He was maddening. And I knew that one more minute in Burke's company and I might forget all about Succor.

Looking to be done with Burke, his infuriating manner and his disquieting smile, I reached into my reticule and came out with a stack of coins. I dropped them into his hand. 'There. I have no interest in your merchandise, sir, but there is my payment for your services on Saturday. Goodbye.'

I am not sure how I expected him to react; I know only that when Burke was done studying the coins, he clapped his hat upon his head and, when he turned for the door, he was whistling a jaunty tune.

The Society for the Relief and Succor of Needy Women was housed on the second floor of a tidy and unpretentious building not far from the museum. By the time I arrived, Charity was already there, teacup in hand, as were a dozen other well-heeled ladies, all of them wearing the red-and-yellow Succor ribbon just as I was on my cloak.

'There you are, Miss Barnum. It's good to see you again!' Sebastian Richter's cousin, Sonya, greeted me warmly and handed off my bonnet and cloak to a woman with a pinched face who was dressed all in black. Sonya showed me to a seat near the windows that looked over the street. 'We were just about to get started.' She glanced toward the woman in black who'd left to deposit my cloak in another room and was back. 'Matron, why don't you tell the ladies a bit about Succor.'

'Of course.' The woman known as Matron stood before us in front of a sturdy desk, her hands clutched at her waist. She was tall and thin, with hair that was neither blonde nor brown and was streaked through with gray, and she had a pair of spectacles pinched to the bridge of a long, slender nose. 'There are many women in this city who are alone,' she said simply, her voice high-pitched and so brittle I had the impression that her spectacles were cutting off her air supply. 'They arrive here in New York thinking they will somehow provide for themselves and discover soon enough that it is nearly impossible without either the benefit of a husband or the assistance of family.'

It was not my imagination; Charity glanced my way. I pretended not to notice but I could feel her eyes on me.

'Many of these women are immigrants,' Matron continued, imbuing the word with a twist that made me think it must have tasted bad in her mouth. 'They have few skills when they land on our shores and fewer prospects once they are ensconced in the dreadful tenements where so many of them gather.'

'They should know better.' The comment came from a woman in a gown of dark plum and was met with nods of assent from the women seated all around. 'To come across the ocean, all by themselves.'

'But isn't it true that many don't come by themselves?' I thought it nothing more than a question worthy of discussion, yet the scowls on the faces of the women who turned my way when I spoke made me feel as if I'd offered an insult.

'They do come with their families,' I was quick to explain. 'But so many die on the voyage. It's only natural the women who are young and strong survive when others don't, and so once they make port of course they are alone. It is not how they intended to begin a new life here.'

'Yes, of course.' Matron's words crackled. 'Then there are others, of course. American girls who find themselves in . . .' She coughed politely behind one hand. 'Difficulties.'

Had I been a kinder person, I would have thought it nothing more than coincidence that Charity chose that particular moment to clink teacup on saucer. The small, crisp sound reverberated through my bones like a rifle shot.

'These women deserve no pity for their poor and immoral choices,' Matron said, and again, a number of the women nodded. 'Yet it is our Christian duty not to turn them away. We at Succor, inspired by the work of the late Mrs Sebastian Richter, provide them with training so that they may eventually learn correct behavior and serve in large houses. We offer them assistance and hope and a place to stay if they have no other. When all the world has turned its back on them, we give them succor.'

I don't know if Matron was finished but the woman in purple applauded and the other women joined in. I waited until they were done to ask, 'And who may come here for help?'

'Our doors are open to any woman who finds herself alone in the city,' Matron told me with a sniff that said she apparently shouldn't have had to. 'Our first duty is to find out if they have family who might take them in and care for them and, if that is the case, we reunite them. If not, then the ladies are trained and employed. They stay here on premise.' Matron glanced at the ceiling, which told me there was an apartment somewhere above where the women being aided by Succor slept. 'But, of course, it takes a great deal of money to keep such important work going, which is why we are confident that all of you—'

When the door flew open and Sebastian Richter breezed in, Matron's words dissolved like an icicle in sunlight. He tipped his tall top hat to her, then turned to those of us who were seated and listening.

'Good evening, ladies.' When he saw me, Richter's eyes lit up. 'Miss Barnum, I'm so glad you could be here tonight.' He looked to Matron. 'You are done, are you not?'

'Yes, of course.' Her lips pinched, she marched around to the far side of the desk and stood as stiff and as firm as a soldier awaiting orders.

'Matron has done a marvelous job of explaining everything.' Sonya got up to greet her cousin with a kiss on the check. 'She has let everyone know about the important mission Succor carries out.'

'That's very good.' When Richter looked my way and smiled, I found myself smiling back.

Our silent communication lasted no more than a second or two before the woman in purple asked a question about the daily operations of Succor and Richter shook himself back to reality and began a conversation with her. The rest of the ladies chatted among themselves.

'Well, it is certainly heartening to see such good works being done.' In a rustle of skirts, Charity moved by me to deposit her teacup on a nearby table and, when she was done, she met my gaze. 'Where would such women be without such as Succor?'

I refused to be lured by her bait. 'It does seem a worthy cause. Will you tell Phin to give his financial assistance?'

She tossed her head. 'No doubt you will influence him in his thinking far more than I ever could. I know, dear Evie, that you have it in your heart to feel sorry for women such as those that Succor aids.' She swept by me and toward Sonya.

As I had been doing since the day I had arrived in New York and told my brother I was with child and cast off by its father, I shook off the sting of her words, pretending to be interested in the scene outside the window until my anger waned. Yet I could not still the sudden whirring in my mind. If Madeline had come to New York with James . . . I knew James's character. He was cold and cruel, and I doubted he'd changed much in the time since I'd known him and loved him. Madeline may very well have been forsaken as I had been.

I went to where Matron stood alone, quietly watching the interaction as Richter went from woman to woman, thanking each of them for attending.

'You locate people.'

As if she wasn't used to being addressed, Matron flinched and turned my way. 'We locate—'

'People. That is correct, isn't it?' I made sure to keep my voice down. For all I knew, Phin and I were the only ones who knew the fate that had befallen Madeline. There was no use letting the rumor go abroad. 'You talked about reuniting women with their families. I wondered how you locate them.'

Her lips were thin and nearly the same color as her sallow skin. She pressed them together and reached for a book propped on a shelf behind the desk. 'We have the woman sign,' she said and she flipped open the book so that I could see the pages. Each line was filled, some with a signature, others with only an X and the woman's name printed beside it in cramped lettering. 'When they arrive upon our doorstep, we have them sign and ask them questions and, yes, we are often able to find their families. We do our best to reunite them.'

'Might I . . .' I didn't wait to finish the question or for Matron to answer it. I reached for the book and turned the pages to the most recent and scanned the names and dates there.

Of course, I didn't really expect to see Madeline Emerson's name. Still, I could not help but feel the hot sting of disappointment.

'Satisfied?' Matron asked.

'Just . . .' Carefully, I closed the book. 'Just curious,' I told her with a smile she did not return. 'I wondered how many women—'

'Too many,' she told me. 'But we do not shirk our Christian duty. Not to any of them.'

'It is admirable,' I told her.

'Admirable, indeed.' Behind me, Sebastian Richter's voice was warm with appreciation. 'And admirable of you to join us, Miss Barnum. Especially when you are so busy with your own work. I hear Sonya is going to ask you if you would like to join the ladies in serving soup to the newly arriving immigrant women when they disembark.'

I took his comment as a signal that I could politely turn away from Matron, and I was glad. There was something about the woman's eyes – too small and set too close together – that made me feel as if I were one of the butterflies pinned under glass at the museum.

I smiled Richter's way. 'I'm grateful I can help.'

'And I am glad we can continue Marta's good works.' He twitched his broad shoulders. 'I must apologize for sounding like a sentimental fool. What's past is past, and I am a man who knows he must move on to the future.'

'Speaking of moving on . . .' The other ladies had already headed for the exit and I moved that way, too, waiting only long enough for my cloak and bonnet. At the door I turned again to Richter. 'Your work here at Succor is important as well as benevolent, and my brother will be glad to hear of it.'

'For that, I thank you.' He took my hand and brushed it with a kiss. 'Have a pleasant evening, Miss Barnum.'

The warmth of that kiss still shivered over my skin once I was out in my carriage and my head was filled with the image of Richter's smile. It was a good thing I had that to lighten my mood for it was obvious from the start that I would not be getting home anytime soon. A cart had overturned just up the way and horses and carriages were snarled up in a jumble that took more than a few minutes to sort itself out. By the time it had, and I'd settled back in my seat, it was nearly dark. I suppose that is why I saw no more than a gray shape when a person darted out from two buildings just as we passed. I hardly paid it any mind. That is, until the person raised a dueling pistol and shot it too close to my horse's ear.

My coachman was Mercer, one of Phin's most skilled drivers, but even he could not contain the animal's terror.

The horse reared, bucked and bolted.

EIGHT

For a few breathless minutes, it was all I could do to keep myself upon my seat. The carriage lurched this way and that, and the horse, usually one of the most docile in Phin's stable, flashed its hooves and raced past pedestrians whose terrified faces – mouths open and eyes wide – I could see out of the window as they leapt to safety.

I braced a hand against the diamond-pleated burgundy satin upholstery.

'Miss Barnum? Miss Barnum? Are you all right?'

From his perch, Mercer called out, and through the window at the front of the carriage I saw him shoot a look at me over his shoulder, but I knew he had more important things to worry about and yelled to tell him so just as we rounded a corner on but two wheels. I slammed against one side of the carriage, then was immediately thrown the other way and my bonnet drooped over my eyes, blinding me. I plucked it off with desperate fingers and skidded across the seat yet again, and this time my shoulder met the door with a smack I knew would mean a bruise by morning.

All the while, Mercer yelled commands, using all his strength and skill to rein in the frightened animal.

When he finally did, we stopped with bone-rattling abruptness.

Mercer was down off his perch in an instant and had the door open.

'Miss Barnum, are you—'

'I am fine. Really,' I assured the man, because except for the fact that my heart clattered and my blood raced, my teeth chattered and my hair hung in my eyes, I knew I was.

What I didn't know, and what kept me up half the night once we finally made our way home and I had sung the praises of Mercer's bravery to Phin, was why anyone would shoot a pistol so near a carriage.

My carriage.

And if the actions of that shrouded figure had anything to do with the fact that I was asking questions about Jeffrey Hollister, Madeline Emerson and Andrew's murder.

The thought sat uneasy with me, and it could not be so easily soothed with witch hazel as was the bruise on my shoulder. I suppose it should have frightened me to think someone wanted me to keep to my own business and stop asking questions, or at least it should have made me more cautious.

Instead, all it did was ignite my anger and inspire me to continue my inquiries at full chisel.

The next day, I arrived at the museum at my usual hour, prepared to tell Mr Dewey that I would be out for a portion of the day, and I would have done so immediately if I hadn't turned into the passageway that led to my office and found it nearly completely blocked.

'Mr Dewey!' I had seen him only moments before on the stairs so I knew he was still nearby. 'Mr Dewey, there are . . .' I did my best to count, but when Mr Dewey appeared I lost my thought so instead merely pointed. 'There are crates of merchandise here. Many of them. What are they doing outside my office? And where on earth did they come from?'

Mr Dewey was a small, slim man, efficient and orderly by nature. He pulled at his earlobe. 'He said you were expecting them, Miss Barnum. He assured me you told him they were to be delivered to your door and nowhere else the very first thing this morning.'

Hearing this, I had a sudden suspicion, and it was confirmed when I sidled down the slim pathway between the crates and found a note pinned to the door where I couldn't fail to see it.

The handwriting was far more elegant than I expected, the paper heavier and it carried the unmistakable scent of bay rum.

I cannot accept money from a lady without giving her something in return, the note said. *Until next time, Miss Barnum, I remain your ever faithful—*

'Burke.' I did not so much mumble the name as I did grumble it.

'That's right, Miss Barnum.' Mr Dewey had followed me into the maze and nodded and smiled. 'He said you'd know exactly what to do with these things and, yes, he did say his name was Mr Burke.'

'Just Burke. As for what to do with these things . . .' I looked around at the array of crates large and small and surrendered with a sigh. 'Oh, just leave them for now. I will look through them later and then . . .'

Because I had not the slightest idea of what I might do then, I sailed into my office and closed the door behind me. I will not report the thoughts that tumbled through my head for the next few minutes. Since Burke wasn't there to hear me give voice to exactly what I thought of him, it hardly seemed to matter.

I allowed myself time for my blood to stop pumping like Mr Fulton's steam engine through my veins, took care of a few of my normal morning duties and, once I was feeling more in command of both my anger and my thoughts, I went downstairs and told the man at the door I had an appointment and was going out. Just a short while after, I found myself in front of the Franklin House Hotel.

The why is no mystery. The name of the establishment was written on one of the pieces of paper I had found in Andrew's pocket, and the hotel was well-located, nicely furnished and known for the sort of clientele that would appeal to a man like Andrew. I intended to find out if, as I suspected, he had stayed there during his time in New York.

The man I found behind the front desk was short and round and smelled of peppermint.

Hoping to gauge his reaction, I gave nothing away. 'I'm looking for Mr Andrew Emerson.'

Whatever response I had expected, it wasn't a low whistle or the slow slide of the man's brows up his long, sloping forehead. 'Now there's a popular young man,' he said.

'Popular? Is he?' I pretended nothing more than the slightest interest. 'Why?'

'Well, that young lady there . . .' The man behind the desk looked across the lobby and I turned that way, too, just in time to see a woman in a most remarkable – and brassy – sunflower-yellow coat walk toward the door. 'Not two minutes ago, that young lady asked after Mr Emerson, too.'

'Did she?' I did not wait for him to answer. When the woman stepped outside I was right behind her.

'Excuse me.'

Surprised, she turned. Her face was round and her lips were full. She had dark eyes and hair the same color as her coat that peeped out from beneath a large red bonnet festooned with green veils, a blue flower and a sweep of peacock feathers.

'Do I know you?' she asked.

'You know Andrew Emerson.'

Her polite smile froze. 'Why do you say that?'

'You came here looking for him, just as I did.'

'Did you?' She looked me up and down the way a woman does when she is assessing the cut of another woman's gown, the style of her hat, the worth of her boots. 'Why?'

'I believe that's exactly what I asked you.'

Her dark eyes sparkled. 'Actually, you claimed I know Andrew Emerson. You did not ask why I was here looking for him.'

'Why are you here looking for him?'

She carried a reticule embroidered with an abundance of red poppies and held it up by way of demonstration. 'I owe him money.'

I glanced toward the door of the hotel. 'And what did the man behind the desk tell you when you inquired about Andrew?'

'Andrew.' She savored the syllables. 'You know him well.'

'Perhaps not as well as you do.'

The woman threw back her head and laughed, revealing straight, pearly teeth. 'He said he had a sister. Are you Madeline?'

'I'm not,' I admitted. 'But if you know Andrew has a sister—'

'Then I must know Andrew well.' The woman wound an arm through mine. 'It seems we have a great deal to talk about. If you're a romantic rival—'

I loosened myself from her grasp. What I had to tell her was best said face-to-face. 'You don't know, do you?'

Her smile sobered. 'Know? About Andrew? Oh, tell me he hasn't gone and done something foolish like get married. He always threatened it, and in truth I have no objection. As long as it isn't me he's marrying!'

I ran a tongue over my lips. 'Andrew is dead,' I told her.

In an instant, the high color drained from her face and she grasped my arm. 'When?'

'Friday last.'

'It can't be.'

'I'm sorry. Yes. It's true.'

Her gaze flickered to the Franklin House. 'Then it's no wonder he hasn't been here when I've stopped in. I am dreadful sorry to hear the news. Especially if you and Andrew were—'

'No more than friends,' I assured her. 'How could we be anything but if you were the one he wanted to marry?'

Her smile was bittersweet. 'I am not sorry I refused him. You understand that, don't you? There is no earthly reason why a woman should come under any man's command, and such is the relationship between husband and wife. Why legally give yourself over to such tyranny when you may have all the benefits of marriage without ring and preacher?'

I was not so much scandalized as I was surprised she had the mettle to speak her mind so openly to a stranger. When my mouth dropped open, the woman laughed. 'It is a new age, Miss . . .'

'Barnum,' I told her. 'Evangeline Barnum.'

'Clarice Carrington,' she introduced herself. 'I'm sorry if I shocked you, but I am not known for keeping silent on subjects I feel strongly about.'

'Then we have something in common, Miss Carrington.'

'You mean, other than poor Andrew.'

Andrew.

My heart sank.

Traveling to the Franklin House, I'd had such high hopes of learning more about what Andrew was doing there and how his visit to the city might shine a light on his search for Madeline and his murder.

I backed away from Miss Carrington. 'I must speak with the man behind the desk.'

'About Andrew?'

'I have questions that must be answered.'

'His death was mysterious?'

'He was searching for his sister,' I said, because I could not bring myself to tell her Andrew had been murdered.

Miss Carrington's mouth puckered. 'Here in New York? He never told me she was here.'

'Her arrival was recent. I thought Madeline might help provide the answers as to what Andrew was doing in the city, who he saw and where he went. I need to find the thread that might lead me to Andrew's killer.'

In spite of her every attempt at insouciance, Miss Carrington's bottom lip trembled. 'Murdered?' Again, she wound an arm through mine. 'Then we must find out what happened.'

Together, we went again into the Franklin House and I explained to the man behind the desk that I was a friend of Andrew's and knew he wouldn't be coming back to his room. If I could go upstairs and collect his things . . .

Of course, the man refused. At least until I scrawled out a note which would allow him and any number of guests he chose to visit the American Museum without charge.

'Only you can't go up to his room,' the man said when Miss Carrington and I made for the stairway. 'He's been gone these few days and we didn't know if Mr Emerson was coming back. We're a busy establishment.' He shrugged by way of telling us it wasn't his decision. 'His things have been moved to the cellar.'

To the cellar we went, and to a room with windows high up on the walls that allowed small streaks of light to stain the floor. There was a pile of traveling bags there, and I located one with Andrew's name attached to it and dragged it into the middle of the floor where the light was better.

In spite of her progressive beliefs about marriage, it seemed Miss Carrington had qualms about rooting around in the valise of a dead man. I had no such misgivings.

While she stood a distance back and watched, I opened the bag and proceeded to take everything out of it so that I might look carefully through it all.

There wasn't much of interest. Clothing, combs, shaving supplies. Setting those aside, I looked across the bag at Miss Carrington.

'You knew where Andrew stayed when he was in New York.'

'Of course.' Her hands clutched behind her back, she bent forward to better watch me work. 'I often stayed here with him though, of course, we could not be so public about it that anyone here recognizes me. Philistines!' She laughed, but the laughter stilled soon enough. 'He was not here just to see me. Each time Andrew visited New York he wrote articles about his adventures here for his newspaper back home,' she explained, then coughed away her discomfort. 'Do they know who—'

'The constable is looking for a man named Jeffrey Hollister in connection with the murder and I am searching for Jeffrey, too.' I ran my hand around the inside of Andrew's bag. 'I am sure he had nothing to do with Andrew's death. If only I could talk to Jeffrey, perhaps I might find—'

When my fingers came in contact with a piece of paper, I drew it out of the bag and held it to the light.

'It is a receipt,' I explained. 'For rooms at the Astor House.'

Miss Carrington's mouth twisted. 'Andrew never stayed there.'

'Are you sure?'

'I am sure I never stayed there with Andrew. If there was someone else—'

'I think not. Andrew was not such a man.' Thinking, I cocked my head. 'But that is exactly why this note acknowledging payment is so interesting.' I tucked the paper into my reticule. 'Why would a man staying at the Franklin House have a receipt for rooms at the Astor?'

She thought through my question and twitched her shoulders when she had no answer, then watched as I looked through the rest of the contents of the bag. 'So who is this Hollister fellow?'

'Well, he's green, for one thing,' I said and laughed at the look on her face. 'He's the Lizard Man from Borneo. At least when he's within the walls of the American Museum.'

I finished looking through the bag, replaced its contents carefully and stood.

'Nothing helpful?' she asked.

'Perhaps the receipt from the Astor House.'

'Perhaps . . .' Thinking, Miss Carrington pressed her lips together. 'We dined often at Delmonico's. There is a chance someone there might know something about Andrew.'

'There is,' I agreed. 'And it's nearly time for luncheon.'

We shared broiled bluefish, new potatoes and string beans. Miss Carrington told me she had lived in New York all her life and that her father was a prominent physician who, on his death, had left her so financially well-off she did not need to depend on a man to support her. She was an artist, and she invited me to join the salon she held at her home in Chelsea each month.

By the time we had finished our chestnut pudding we were on a first-name basis and, because the man who waited at our table could not help us when it came to telling us anything about Andrew, I continued my questioning of Clarice.

'How long did you know Andrew?'

'Two years,' she told me. 'No, three. We met when he was here in town looking into information for an article his late father was writing for his newspaper. I believe it involved some scandal. A banker by the name of—'

'Withnower, yes.' Every person in Bethel knew the story, for Maynard Withnower had been found to be taking large sums of money from his own bank. Or at least that's what everyone thought. It was only later, after Maynard Withnower hanged himself from an oak tree, that the evidence against him was found to be false.

'We had a mutual acquaintance,' Clarice told me. 'A man by the name of Forsythe. He introduced us and, from that time on, Andrew and I saw each other each time he was in New York.'

'And when was the last time you saw him?' I asked her.

She considered the question for a moment. 'At least a week ago,' she told me. 'He sent me a message to tell me he'd arrived in New York and he wanted to see me.'

'And did you see him?'

'Yes. Here.' She gave her pudding spoon one final lick. 'I thought it best if we met in public.'

'Because . . .'

'Because as I told you, Andrew wanted to marry me. I wasn't interested. That doesn't mean I didn't admire him. Andrew was a wonderful person.'

I could not have agreed more.

'That is precisely why I ended our relationship,' Clarice went on. 'It wasn't fair for Andrew to hold out hope that I might someday change my mind. He needed to find a woman who would appreciate him, someone who could be the helpmate he so wanted.'

The tall clock that stood nearby rang the hour and Clarice rose to leave. 'I have a model coming soon for the sketches for a new painting. You'll excuse me, Evie?'

'Of course.'

'And you will come to my salon?' She grinned. 'There are a number of handsome poets who attend. You might find the gathering very interesting.'

I had no doubt of it.

I paid for my luncheon and stopped at the front of the restaurant while Jonathan – a man I knew since I dined there often – retrieved my cloak. He helped me into it and glanced out the window. 'Happier today than she was last time she was here,' he said.

I looked over my shoulder to the window where I could see a flash of yellow as Clarice crossed the road. 'You mean Miss Carrington?'

Jonathan pursed his lips. 'I'm hardly one to tell tales, but then, anyone who was here that night knew there was something afoot between the two of them. Oh, what a dust-up they had!'

'Miss Carrington and—'

'And Mr Emerson, of course. One of the boys clearing the table heard the whole thing.'

'You mean about how Mr Emerson wanted to marry Miss Carrington and she wasn't interested?'

'Is that what she told you?' Jonathan rolled his eyes. 'The way I heard the story, he was the one who told her it was over between them.'

I contained my astonishment. 'And what was her response?'

He leaned nearer, sharing the secret. 'She kept her voice down, I'll give her that. Otherwise, I swear she wouldn't have the nerve to show her face here again. But there was no mistaking her anger. The boy cleaning the tables, he says she just about popped a cork.'

'Really?' I looked again toward the window but Clarice was already gone. 'Did you say when this was?' I asked Jonathan.

'Early for dinner. Maybe five or six o'clock. Last Friday.'

Friday.

How odd that Clarice had said she hadn't seen Andrew in at least a week. Nearly as odd as the fact that she'd forgotten to mention that she and Andrew had had an argument on the very night he had been murdered.

NINE

I t is a long journey from New York City to Bethel so I started out very early Wednesday so that I was sure to be there on time. I did not tell Charity where I was going, nor did I mention it to Phin. She would not give me a second thought, and in fact, would probably be relieved to think I was busy at the museum, leaving early and coming late, and that our paths simply had not crossed for several days. He was more perceptive, of course. On thinking it through, Phin would know exactly where I'd gone and why. Andrew was a dear friend; I could not miss his funeral.

Of course, I also could not let anyone in Bethel know I was there. They would ask too many questions: where had I been these last years? And why had I left? I could not risk exposing my shameful secret and hurting my family's reputation. It was exactly why I had agreed to give over my child to adoption, exactly why each time I thought of my sweet babe my heart broke just a little more.

I also had no desire to have contact with my mother while in Bethel. It was nearly as painful to remember the day I had told her I was to have James's child and she had sent me out of the house and told me she never wanted to see me again as it was to think of when I had told James the news and he had turned his back and walked away.

That next day, Thursday, the memories swirled around me, each more painful than the last, and I sat at the back of St Thomas's Episcopal Church, away from the knot of mourners in the pews at the front, swathed in a black dress and cloak and with a heavy black veil across my face. It was not so easy to disguise the waves of emotion that engulfed me when, outcast, I watched old friends and neighbors together there and then my mother and sisters, who walked in and joined the mourners.

I shouldn't have come.

The thought slammed into me and left me breathless and I

nearly fled. That is, until I took another look at Andrew's casket there near the altar.

And I wondered again what had happened to him in those last moments in front of the Feejee Mermaid.

I was able to occupy myself with these thoughts throughout the service and keep the sadness at bay and, before I knew it, the assembly processed out of the church and to the Center Street Cemetery.

Following at a distance, I again kept to myself at the burial ground, hiding behind a tall standing stone, far enough from the grave so as not to be noticed.

I am not an Episcopalian but I hardly think it mattered. I prayed along with the assembled congregation, my head bowed and my heart heavy. When the short service was over, the crowd scattered and I waited in the gathering silence so the laborers might be done with their work and I might approach the grave and say my final goodbyes.

There was a copse of trees directly across from where I stood and as soon as the last shovelful of dirt was piled on the grave and the workers left the grounds, a man stepped out of the shadows and walked toward it. I recognized him at once.

Frederick Withnower, son of Maynard, the banker whose reputation had been ruined when Andrew's father had published an article about him in *The Intelligencer*, a man shamed who had taken his own life and had only been proven innocent later.

I was certainly surprised to see Frederick there and outraged when he stopped only long enough at the mound of freshly turned earth to spit on Andrew's grave.

I could understand the anger. Though the incident had happened three years earlier, before Andrew's father died and Andrew took over operation of the newspaper, the Withnower family had been ruined by the accusations.

That didn't make it any easier to watch the desecration, and when Frederick left and I stepped to the grave, I apologized to Andrew on his behalf.

It did not make it any easier to forget.

I was still thinking about the disturbing event the next morning when I left the inn where I'd stayed the night under a false name and boarded the coach that would take me back to New York, still swathed head to toe in veils and cloaks so as to keep the secrecy of my visit.

I could not have been more surprised when Frederick Withnower climbed into the coach after me.

As we were the only two in it, we exchanged polite greetings but no more, and I was just as glad. I had no wish to make conversation. He settled back in the uncomfortable seat, sullen and silent, and the veil I kept over my face gave me the opportunity to observe him without his knowledge.

He was a man nearing forty, dusky-skinned with strong features and dark hair shot through with gray. His boots, I noticed, were worn at the toes, and the cuffs of his jacket were frayed, as were the hems of his unmentionables.

At each stop we made over the sixteen-hour journey, I expected Frederick to leave the coach, but though we were joined by other passengers along the way and stopped now and again to spend time walking and to partake of meals, each time he got back into the coach along with me. Together, we made the journey all the way to New York City.

Once we arrived, he allowed me to leave the coach first but, when I did, I took my bag and walked only as far as the nearest building. It was already dark, and I waited there in the shadows for Frederick to pass then fell into step behind him, grateful that he must have been as weary as I was from the long journey and did not walk too quickly.

I was not familiar with the area of the city where we traveled and knew neither the streets nor the landmarks we passed. I only know that, a short while later, he stopped in front of a church and I watched from the shadows across the road. He did not enter the building but went around to the side. I waited as long as I dared, then slipped from shadow to shadow to see where he might have gone.

Not far, it seemed, for the passage that Frederick had entered ended in a wall with a doorway in it and no way out except the way I had come. Even as I stood there, two men walked by unshaven, ragged and so corned they smelled to the high heavens of whiskey and were so busy holding each other upright they paid no attention at all to me. They, too, went inside the building and, more curious than ever, I neared the door and saw a small brass plaque on the wall beside it.

St John's House of Hospitality, it said. *Enter here and find hope and comfort.*

Hope and comfort were two blessings I imagined had been hard for Frederick Withnower to enjoy since his father's untimely death. It was clear he had lost everything and been forced to seek refuge far from where people knew his history and his family's disgrace.

It may have been commendable for me to have these thoughts if I intended to use my brother's wealth and influence to help allay the misery beyond St John's door, but I will admit that helping those far less fortunate than I was the last thing on my mind at present.

I started for home, and I could not help but think that, because of Andrew's family, Frederick Withnower had lost everything.

And a man who had lost everything might well seek revenge.

We had left Bethel long before sun up and, by the time I arrived home, it was late and I was bone weary. I had already cast my black veils away from me as I walked home, and now I handed my cloak and bonnet to Portman and asked if Cook was still awake so I might get something to eat.

Before he ever had a chance to answer, the front bell rang.

All too aware that news brought to the door at night is often unwelcome, Portman and I exchanged looks, but he is nothing if not conscientious. He wiped away the friendly smile he'd offered when I arrived, pulled back his shoulders and went to the door. From where I stood near the stairs I could see little more than Portman's back. That is, until he stepped aside to allow a visitor in.

'I am terribly sorry to bother you so late.' Sebastian Richter didn't look the least bit sorry and, had I been less tired, I might have pointed that out. His eyes were bright, his smile was warm and he was dressed in evening attire – dark jacket and unmentionables, white vest and shirt and a white cravat tied loosely and secured with a diamond-studded stickpin. The little red and yellow Succor ribbon pinned to his jacket provided a splash of color and he smelled slightly of brandy and beeswax candles.

'I just arrived home,' he said, his tall hat in both hands, 'when I saw you walk up to your door. I thought if I came over quickly you would not yet have had a chance to retire. It is ill-mannered of me to stop over unannounced, I know, but as I said, I hated to waste the opportunity.'

'Would you like a glass of sherry?' I asked him. I was hardly being sociable, simply thirsty and feeling in need of something stronger than tea after the day I'd had. I led the way into the parlor.

'Your brother won't mind?' Richter asked.

I filled two glasses and handed one to Richter. 'As you said yourself, I've been out. I haven't seen Phin all day. For all I know, he may still be at the museum.'

'Even at this late hour?' He sipped and smiled his approval of the sherry. 'It seems you Barnums take too much upon yourselves.'

He was talking about the museum and knew nothing about how I'd been tracking a man who might be a murderer.

Too tired to keep to my feet, I took a seat at the table and sipped my sherry. 'I doubt you've come across the street to tell us we work too hard, Mr Richter. No doubt you work hard yourself. You have your breweries. And Succor, of course.'

'Yes. Succor.' He touched a hand to the ribbon and took the seat across from mine. 'It is one of the things I came to speak to you about, to thank you for your support. It is heartening to know that women of your character can show such empathy to those who are less fortunate.'

What would Richter say if he knew that, without my brother, I might very well have been one of those women?

Had I not been so tired, so sorry for Andrew's fate and so immersed in thoughts of Frederick Withnower, his animosity toward the Emerson family and the fact that it looked as if he might have been in New York at the time of Andrew's death—

'It is not the only reason, of course, that I've come to bother you at this late hour.'

Richter's voice snapped me out of my thoughts and, startled, I winced.

He pushed back his chair. 'Of course, if it is inconvenient . . .'

'No. Really.' With the motion of one hand, I bid him to remain at the same time shaking my head to clear it of the thoughts that had pounded through it since I had seen Frederick in the grave-yard. 'Now I am the one being rude,' I told him. 'I'm sorry. I'm a bit tired. It has been a long day.'

'Yes. Which means if I was any sort of gentleman, I would get to my business and be done with it so that you might get some rest.' He set down his glass, picked it up again and took a sip of sherry. 'You are far more lively and intelligent than most of the women I meet,' he said, and before I could deny it – for I was feeling less lively by the moment – he stopped me with a smile. 'I hope I do not overstep my bounds by mentioning it but, Miss Barnum, I cannot stop thinking about you! I saw the way you watched my children the other day and you must know they are the most important thing in my life. They need a mama who can tend to them and mind their education and their manners. And I need a woman . . .' He was a handsome and sophisticated man so there was something especially endearing about the fact that the tips of his ears turned red. 'I need a woman who is my intellectual equal. One with whom I can discuss art and politics and religion. Though I hardly know you well, I would like to find out if you are that woman. Miss Barnum . . .' He sat up very straight and pulled back his shoulders. 'Evangeline, I wondered if perhaps you might give me permission to call upon you.'

It was not what I expected. Not at this hour. Not from this man. Not so soon after we'd met.

For a few moments, while the tall-case clock ticked away the seconds in the corner, I wondered how to respond.

As it turned out, I didn't have a chance.

Charity stepped into the parlor.

'Perhaps,' she said, her words like gunshot in the heavy silence, 'that is a question better left to Mr Barnum rather than Evie.'

Richter stood and offered her a bow. 'Yes, of course. I thought only to gauge Miss Barnum's reaction to my proposal before I—'

'Yes, of course.' It was clear that, when the bell rang, Charity had been roused from her bed. She was enveloped in her night-gown and a white satin night jacket and had a shawl thrown around her shoulders that was a match to the lace cap tied under her chin. Her sheepskin slippers were as silent against the parlor carpet as they must have been upon the stairs. It was no wonder I'd had no warning of her approach.

She swept farther into the room, the better to intimidate Sebastian Richter. To his credit, he pretended she did.

He gave her another bow. 'I do believe I shall be going,' he said, as if it had been his idea all along. 'I will call another time and speak to your husband, Mrs Barnum.'

She did not wish him a good night.

A minute later, when the front door closed behind Richter, Charity was still looking that way.

'He's very pleasant,' she said and turned to me, a sly smile lighting her expression. 'And very wealthy.'

'And I am very tired,' I said and finished my sherry. I had just stood to leave the room when another thought occurred to me. 'Did you know the Withnower family back in Bethel?' I asked Charity. 'The children of the family were all older than me and we had no mutual acquaintances. Did you know them?'

She sniffed. 'We would hardly socialize with their like.'

Tired or not, I could not help but laugh. 'When we lived in Bethel, Phin sold newspapers and worked at our father's inn. The Barnums were hardly anyone's social superiors!'

She ran one finger along the surface of the table. 'That may be true, but that doesn't mean we were foolish. We wouldn't have been friendly with the Withnowers. Maynard was a thief.'

'He was thought to be a thief,' I reminded her. 'The accusation proved false.'

Her lips folded in on themselves. 'Why do you care? What do you know of the Withnowers?'

'I just thought perhaps you might have heard from someone back home. One of my sisters, perhaps. Have you heard that Frederick, Maynard's son, has left Bethel and is living now in New York?'

'Is he?' The way she twitched her shoulders told me how little she cared, yet I could not help but notice she refused to meet my eyes.

'You did know.' Since she would not look my way, I moved to stand in front of Charity so she could not avoid me. 'You knew Frederick was here in New York.'

'What difference does it make? Or do you have your eye on him, too?'

She should have known better than to bait a tired woman who had an entire glass of sherry in her.

I propped my fists on my hips. 'I do not have my eye on Sebastian Richter or Frederick Withnower or anyone else. Besides, I thought you approved of Richter.'

'Oh, I do. The right sort of marriage would go a long way toward cementing our place in New York society.'

'No one is talking marriage,' I reminded her.

'But you are talking about Frederick Withnower. Why? Why do you care?'

'Why do you?'

When she studied the chandelier, I moved a step closer. 'Come now, Charity, you look as if you've bitten a lemon, and I doubt you would have such strong feelings about a family you claim you barely know.'

She pressed her lips together. 'I wouldn't care. Not at all. Not if your brother . . .' She had a way of saying the word that made it seem as if Phin were a creature from some other world, alien and thus impossible to fathom. 'He can be foolish, and sometimes I need to remind him of such.' She made to step toward the door, but as I stood between her and it and refused to move, she had no choice but to stay put.

'What do you mean?' I asked her. 'About Phin being foolish?'

She made a tiny clicking sound with her tongue. 'If he is seen in the company of such as Frederick Withnower, a man whose father took his own life . . .' Charity sucked in a breath of horror. 'How might it affect what people think of us?'

'So Phin has met with Frederick?'

She gave in with a sigh that ruffled the lace on her night jacket. 'I told him not to. I told Phin it was the wrong thing to do. But he agreed to a meeting, and Frederick came around to see Phin and ask about employment at the museum. Imagine! It's not as if they were old friends. Yet there was Frederick, hat in hand.'

'And has Phin offered him employment?'

'He has not,' Charity said. 'Not as far as I know.' She dismissed the topic with the wave of one hand. 'It was months ago.'

Months ago.

I do not know what I expected, but hearing that Frederick had been at the museum long before Andrew met his end there left me feeling more exhausted than ever.

Eager for my bed, I went to the door and stopped there only when Charity spoke again.

'But then he came back,' she said, and I turned to see her with her head tilted, thinking. 'Frederick came back to the museum last week. If I'm not mistaken, it was the very night Andrew Emerson died.'

My exhaustion forgotten, I closed in on her. 'Do you know the time?'

'Really, Evie!' Charity swept past me and out of the parlor. 'You set your mind on the strangest things. What difference does it make what time Withnower was at the museum? After all his family has been through, I'm surprised he hasn't just disappeared into the wilderness so as not to cause anyone any embarrassment. And speaking of that . . .'

It wasn't what she said, it was the way she said it that made me stop just as I was about to walk out of the parlor. I studied my sister-in-law as carefully as she examined me.

'I won't ask where you've been,' she said. 'I do not need to. I will ask you to keep in mind that your own past is every bit as shameful as the Withnowers'. You mustn't risk your future and the future of my family with visits to places where you are no longer welcome. My goodness!' Without excusing herself, she brushed around me and to the stairs and didn't look at me again until she was on the steps, one hand on the mahogany bannister.

'What on earth would happen if word got out about your past?' she asked. 'You don't think a man like Sebastian Richter would come to call upon you again if he knew the truth about you, do you?'

TEN

I kept to my bed too long the next morning and was not ready to leave for the museum at my usual hour. As it happened, this was not so terrible a thing because, by the time I was up and dressed, Charity had gone out on a social call. That left me free to visit the nursery and share breakfast with the children. I cradled Walter in my lap while we ate buttery toast and drank warm milk, but nine-year-old Caroline and Helen, just two, did not seem to mind and the youngest, Frances sat with Nurse.

Walter, like the girls, had the high cheekbones of a Barnum and the same honey-toned hair and smile as Phin. His eyes, though, were a bright, fresh green and there were times, like that morning there in the sun-spilled nursery, when I could not look into them without thinking what my life might have been if I had not been forced to give up my own child.

Certainly Sebastian Richter would never have abandoned his dear Marta as James had forsaken me.

The thought crept up on me, and I must have winced for Caroline, who was just singing 'Yankee Doodle' for me in her high, sweet soprano, stopped.

'Are you feeling ill, Aunt Evie?' she asked.

'I am fine,' I assured her. 'But I must get to the museum.'

'Will you see my father there?' she wanted to know.

'I will.' After I kissed him on the cheek, I set Walter on his bed. 'Shall I tell him to come up and see you when he arrives home this evening?'

Caroline pouted. 'He's always home too late. Just as you are. You work in the museum all day and have little time for us.'

The criticism clutched at my heart and, as much as I knew it was but the product of a child's peevishness, I could not help but think about it all that day as I worked in my office.

If they'd been mine, I would have been more than happy to spend my days with the children and not be shut up in the confines of the museum and, if it were my decision, I would never have

Nurse there for more than just those times when it was necessary to go out. We would play in the park, the children and I. We would ride ponies and pick flowers in the garden and read books like the animal tales of Edward Augustus Kendall or the fantastical stories of Hans Christian Anderson.

If I were to marry Sebastian Richter, I would have the time and his permission for such things. I would have Frida and Otto to love and perhaps be blessed with more children of my own, and I would live just across the way, where I could watch Walter and the girls grow up and they would be friends to my children.

Coming at me out of nowhere the way it did, the thoughts upended me and I sucked in a breath.

'I do not love Sebastian Richter,' I told myself, then laughed. I hardly knew the man well enough to know if I even liked him!

Because I was uncomfortable with my own musings, I rose and did a turn around my small office and went to the window. It was a fine afternoon and the sun shone down on the crowds out on Broadway, so many of them heading here to the museum.

But even the heartening realization that they would relinquish their twenty-five cents to us could not still the murky thoughts that overtook me – if Sebastian Richter knew my real character, if he knew about James, he would never wish to call on me.

Could I ever hope to make a life with a man if I could not find it in myself to tell him the whole truth of my past?

'It is early days for such as that,' I reminded myself. For all I knew, Richter had had too much brandy the night before and had not meant a word of what he had said.

I brushed the thought off. The best way to keep it gone was to occupy my hands and my mind, and I knew exactly how to do it.

My passageway was still crammed with the crates and boxes left there on Burke's instructions, and I opened the door and dragged the nearest box inside. I might as well see what I had spent my hard-earned money to buy.

By the time another hour had passed, I'd been through not just the first crate but three of the other smallest ones besides, and they were piled there in my office, one on top of the other, their contents displayed across my floor. I would give Burke this much, he had eclectic tastes.

The worst of the hodgepodge I set aside and would let our

staff look through and take with them if they so desired. There were a number of decks of playing cards, none of them unusual or interesting, and books that, as far as I could tell, were of little value. There were any number of trinkets, too, such as seashells and pen nibs and even a string of blue beads crudely made and similar to those I'd seen Burke wear.

These I picked up and thought of keeping for myself but, just considering the possibility, I could see Burke's brazen smile and practically hear him purr, 'Ah, I knew you'd finally have to admit I have good taste!'

'Indeed!' I set the beads aside and concentrated instead on the other, more interesting things I'd found in the packing crates. There was a handsome spice chest that would look good displayed in our Oriental gallery and a number of baskets artistically woven from palm leaves. They were certainly not valuable but they were exotic looking, and there was little Phin liked more than the exotic. I set these things on my desk and pulled another small crate into the office.

'Last one for today,' I promised myself, and I began my search.

More seashells. A wooden mask carved as a grotesque face with a wide mouth and bulging eyes. Surely Phin would love it, as he would the small replica of a South Seas islands war canoe.

The last thing in the crate was heavy and I hefted it with both hands. It was a little more than a foot long and shaped like a paddle with large areas of geometric incising all around its cylindrical handle. I could not help but smile when I wondered how many other young ladies in the city of New York would recognize a Tongan *pakipaki* when she saw it, and I supposed I had Phin to thank for that; the museum had a collection of South Seas islands battle clubs.

'It seems you have very good taste when it comes to some things.' It was easy to compliment Burke when he wasn't there. Perhaps when he returned – if he returned as he had so ominously put it – he would see this war club on display with our others.

No sooner had I set the club down on my desk than a thought hit and knocked me into a cocked hat.

'A South Seas island war club,' I murmured to myself, and I took off into the museum.

It was not so easy to get to our display as I'd hoped. In the days since, word had gone around about Andrew's death, and there is nothing that draws a crowd as much as tales of a mysterious murder. Our establishment was even more busy than usual, and I had to excuse myself through crowds of visitors. If any of them thought it odd when I opened the glass case and took out an armful of war clubs, they never said a thing. But then, this was the American Museum and they expected spectacle the moment they were through the doors.

The clubs were heavy and awkward, and when I came upon Bess Buttle in the back passageway that led to my office, I enlisted her help. Together, we went inside and set them down. I closed the office door behind us.

'You're fixin' to start a fight of some sort?' she asked, her beard twitching.

'Hardly.' I lifted the first club, a short instrument that I knew could be thrown at an opponent. If it hit, it was heavy enough to cause serious harm. 'But I was thinking.'

'About these here odd things.'

'War clubs.' I tried the next. 'You see, this one has a blunt tip. It's used for smashing small bones.' I swung it at Bess but stopped short of hitting her. This did not keep her from pressing a hand to her heart and backing up against the door.

'I could break your arm with this,' I told her, putting the club safely on the desk so she no longer needed to feel in peril. 'But if I hit you on the head with it, it would crush your skull, not make a nice, neat hole.'

Her eyes grew wide. 'Like the head of the poor unfortunate young man what was killed here.'

'Exactly.' I tried the next weapon, but it, too, had the wrong shape, as did all the others arrayed upon my desk. I stood back, fists on my hips. 'It isn't here,' I said.

Bess stepped up beside me. 'It . . . isn't . . .'

'I am not intimately familiar with every item we display,' I told her. 'But I am willing to wager that we had a war club that is called . . .' I thought about it for a moment. 'A *totokia*, yes, that's it. It has a handle, you see, like this one.' I lifted one of the clubs for Bess to see. 'But instead of a flat head, it has what looks to be a large acorn on the end of it. Round at the base.' With one hand, I outlined the shape of the weapon as I did my best to describe it. 'But with a sharp, pointed end. It's designed to drive a neat hole through an enemy's skull.'

Bess sucked in a breath. 'And you think . . .'

'That the *totokia* we had on display is now missing. I do believe it was used to murder Mr Emerson.'

'And no wonder the constable never noticed,' Bess said. 'I mean, aside from the fact that the man was a pudden-head. Who would think of an instrument such as that!'

'I never did, not until now,' I admitted, though I did not point out I never would have if not for Burke.

'What does it tell us?' Bess wanted to know.

This, I couldn't say. Not for certain. My arms crossed over my chest, I leaned back against the desk to think.

'That the assailant did not come prepared. That is one possibility,' I said. 'He used a weapon close to hand.'

'And took it along with him.'

This, too, seemed a fact since the *totokia* was not in the display with the other weapons.

'But why?' I wondered.

'Knew it was valuable? Wanted it as a sort of memento?' Though she was the one who suggested it, the thought did not sit easy with Bess and she twitched it away. 'If he was some ruffian off the streets he may have thought he could use it again.'

'We will never know,' I admitted. 'But at least I can tell Phin about the *totokia* and he can tell the constable. If they could find the weapon—'

'They would find the murderer what caused that young man to make a die of it.'

'I will talk to Phin right now.' I stood and crossed the office. 'He can send a message around to the constable.' I paused, my hand on the doorknob. 'That way we can—'

When I pushed the door, it didn't budge. I gave off talking and tried it again.

The door didn't move.

'It's as if . . .' I put my shoulder to the door and pushed but it did not yield. 'It's as if there's something right up against it,' I told Bess. I had just stepped back to consider my options when the first curls of smoke snaked under the door.

*   *   *

I simply stared at the thick, gray smoke, too stunned to speak.

Bess had no such problem.

'Fire!' Her voice itself was like an alarm, high and shrill. She grasped my arm in both hands and gave me a fierce shake. 'It's a fire! And we are trapped!'

She was afraid enough for the both of us. I suppose that is why my voice was calm and my steps sure when I rounded the desk. 'We will call out for help,' I told her and opened my window. On the street below there were people coming and going and one woman was nearest. I could see the top of her bonnet, the sweep of her cloak and a flash of green from her gown when she stepped to the street.

'Madam! Madam!' I shouted as loudly as I could, carefully choosing my words so as not to cause a panic. 'You must get the attendants at the museum. There is a problem here on the second floor. We need help immediately!'

The woman did not hear me. Without looking up, she rounded the corner to the side of the building and disappeared.

When I spun back to Bess, I saw the smoke had grown heavier. It curled around my desk like a wraith's fingers and rose into the air, sticking in my throat.

When Bess coughed, I hauled her to the window. 'Here,' I told her. 'Breathe deep and, while you're at it, yell for help!'

She did and I went back to the door, putting my shoulder to it, kicking and pounding it with my fists. When nothing worked, I had only one choice.

I snatched up the closest war club and used it as an axe.

It was an old building and sturdily built; the club bit into the wood but not through it, and I was forced to swing again and again.

By now, the commotion of Bess's piercing screams and the thud of the club had attracted attention. On the other side of the door, I heard one of the museum attendants call out. Help was on the way!

I wasn't about to wait for it.

By the time I heard footsteps pounding down the passageway outside, I had smashed a hole through the door, but I could see nothing except the crate that had been pushed against it.

'Coming, Miss Barnum!' someone called out. 'We have sand

to douse the flames and we've called for the fire brigade. We are coming!'

The smoke bellowed, thicker than ever, and flames licked the crate. They caught the corner of a piece of fabric that peeked from the lid and erupted, and I fell back. Ash speckled my cheeks and smoke caught my lungs. Behind me, Bess cried, but I didn't spare her a look. The club still in my hands, I swung at the door again. The hole got bigger and, just as it did, someone on the other side hauled the crate away from the door.

'Don't move, not yet!' a voice cried out, and I saw four figures through the smoke, buckets of sand in their hands. They doused the flames and the next second the door burst open and Phin strode in, his face smeared with soot. He didn't say a word, just folded me into his arms, his breaths as rough as mine. He gave me a pat on the back then went to see if Bess was all right, and I was left to stare out into the passageway at the crates that had been wedged in front of the door and at the dark, oily stain on the carpet where someone had put a flame to a puddle of whale oil.

Phin insisted I go home for the remainder of the day.

I did not argue with him, for while he was left to ponder how such a terrible accident might have happened, I could not help but remember the figure that had come out of the darkness and shot a pistol so near my carriage horse.

And now this.

Any right-thinking person would have known better than to think the two incidents could possibly be related.

But no one had ever said the Barnums were rational.

More than ever, I needed answers.

I stopped home only long enough to race to my room, wash my face and get the piece of paper I needed, then I was back in my carriage. Andrew Emerson had stayed at the Franklin House Hotel on his visits to New York. But among the things Clarice and I had found when we went through his possessions was a receipt for rooms at the Astor House.

'And why would a man who was staying at one hotel need rooms at another?' I asked myself.

Rather than have Mercer question where I might be going and

why, I had him return me to the museum. I waited until he had
taken the carriage around to the stables and then I walked the
short distance to the Astor House.

John Jacob Astor was as much celebrated in New York as my
brother. He was a man who'd made his wealth in the fur trade,
and just eight years before he had opened the five-story hotel
that bore his name. It was considered the finest hostelry in the
country.

I kept the thought in mind when I walked into the lobby and
up to the main desk. Like so many establishments in the city, I
knew the Astor House would not allow me – a woman alone – to
eat in the dining room. I hoped there were no such rules against
simply talking to the employees.

At the sight of me, the man behind the desk raised one silvery
eyebrow. When he sniffed every so delicately, I cursed myself
for not taking the time to change out of my smoky clothes.

'Yes?'

I gave him the smile that had been called sweet back in
Bethel. Before I met James Crockett. Though I never traded on
the fame of my brother's name, I introduced myself.

The man's eyebrow rose another fraction of an inch.

'I am hoping you can help me,' I told him, and smoothed the
paper from Andrew's valise onto the desk. 'Mr Andrew Emerson
was here not long ago. He paid for a week's lodging.'

His lips pursed, the man studied the paper. 'It's my writing.
And the man—'

'Young, polite. Coppery haired.'

'Ah, yes.' As if it would somehow help him clear the fog
from his brain, he lifted the paper for a better look. 'I remember
him now.'

'Did he stay here?'

The man glanced at me over the paper. 'I am hardly in a
position to tell tales, miss.'

'And I do appreciate that as would . . . as does Andrew Emerson.
But you see, he has gone on a journey and, in his absence, I am
to take care of his financial obligations. Before I can enter this
expense into his ledger, I would like to know what it is for.'

He leaned over the desk and lowered his voice. 'You mean to
say, who it is for.'

I caught the suggestion. 'It was not for rooms Mr Emerson himself stayed in.'

He shook his head. 'Mr Emerson was here asking after a couple, a young man and a woman who registered here as' – he coughed politely – 'husband and wife, Mr and Mrs Smith.'

'The woman, Mrs Smith – she had hair like Mr Emerson's?'

'Only more fiery, if you know what I mean.'

I did. I had heard the color of Madeline's hair compared to that of carrots.

'And the man?' I could hardly make the words form around the sudden knot in my throat. 'You said he was young, and—'

'Young, fit, handsome of face, or so I imagine the ladies might say. Golden-haired, like one of the gods you see in paintings.'

A golden-haired god.

Then the rumor Phin had heard out of Bethel was true: Madeline and James had come to New York together.

'So you are telling me the room Mr Emerson paid for—'

'Was the Smiths',' the man said. 'The young man, this Mr Emerson, he insisted on settling the debt.'

'Because the Smiths had not settled it themselves.' It was not a question.

'I saw Mr Smith go out one morning,' the man said. 'It was very early and he had a bag with him but I thought nothing of it. Not an hour later, Mrs Smith came down asking for him.'

'And you told her . . .?'

'That I was sure he would be back, though truth be told, I wasn't. I am sorry to say we see things at a hotel, even at a place as grand as this. Mr Smith, he had that look in his eye. Begging your pardon for bringing it up, Miss Barnum, but as you are in charge of Mr Emerson's finances I believe you have the right to know. Mr Smith looked as if he was searching for . . . for new horizons.'

It was a look I knew all too well, but rather than dwell on it, I asked, 'And Mrs Smith, what did she do?'

The man thought it over. 'Stayed another day. No, two,' he said. 'Then one evening I saw her go out and I didn't greet her because, my gracious, it would have been embarrassing. Her nose was red and her eyes were swollen as if she'd been crying them out. I didn't see her come back in and I heard the next day that the room hadn't been slept in and her bag was just left there.'

'And Mr Emerson?'

'Showed up days later, asking after the woman. Said he had been up and down New York searching and was finally led here. When I told him what I just told you, he said he was sure neither Mr nor Mrs Smith would be back.'

'And paid the bill.' Andrew had always been an honorable man.

I thanked the clerk and, while I was at it, I scrawled a note upon a piece of paper that said he and his family were most welcome at the museum as my guests. It was a small price to pay for the information he'd given; I only wished that it had been more hopeful.

For though the man's story supported what Phin had heard and confirmed my fears for Madeline, it also told me something else.

Madeline was alone, abandoned on the streets of New York.

ELEVEN

I returned to the museum to find the staff working outside my office to clean up the debris left from the fire. With no place else to go and no answers as to who set the fire – or why – I wandered to the first floor and Phin's office. It was a lucky thing I was there because a message arrived.

'For you, Miss Barnum.' The man who usually sat at a desk near the front door handed me an envelope heavily scented with roses and lavender. The paper was thick and expensive and the handwriting was decorated with any number of swirls and curlicues. I was not at all surprised to see that the note had come from Clarice Carrington.

You absolutely must meet Damien LaCrosse, it said, though Clarice did not bother to mention why this was so important. *He is a poet,* she continued, which made me think that perhaps I did not want to meet him. *He has just written a new work. You cannot wait until my next salon to hear it. You must come, dear Miss Barnum. It is of the utmost importance.*

I was not convinced, but I was also not busy. I called for my carriage and gave Mercer the address Clarice noted in her letter. A short while later I stood in an area of the city known as Chelsea in front of a charming row of red-brick townhouses. I did not need to consult the note from Clarice to know her home was the one to my right. It had a recessed front door gaily painted in robin's-egg blue. The home of an artist, I decided at once, and went to the door, where I found a note attached to it with a butter knife.

If I am not here, go right in! it said.

The note smelled of roses and lavender.

I knocked and, when there was no answer, I did as instructed and found myself in a long hallway, a stairway to my right and to my left, an expanse of wall covered not with paintings but with images painted right onto the wall. There were flowers, artfully done, and animals (not nearly as skillfully painted). There

were everyday objects like fruits and vases and carriages, some
painted with great skill and others that looked as if I'd given
paints and brushes to Caroline and Walter and told them to go
at it. Still, the whole thing was a marvel and I followed the
flowing images to where they ended. There was a basket of
brushes along with paints in the tin tubes I'd heard had recently
been devised by a clever fellow and were all the talk of the art
world because they provided a far better way to store paints than
the pig bladders that were usually used. There was another note
there in the same hand as the missive on the front door that
instructed the reader to *Paint!*

I did not. Aside from having little talent in that arena, I was
now at the back of the house and far more interested in my
surroundings than I was in dabbing color to the walls. The room
I found myself in had windows that rose floor to ceiling and
allowed a flow of marvelous light that spilled over the wooden
floor like melted butter. Over on the fireplace mantel, joss sticks
like the ones we burned at the museum sent up their scented
smoke, and all around me, on tables and the floor itself, cigarette
ends overflowed from china plates.

Around the room there were any number of easels with
canvases upon them and I strolled past some that had been simply
sketched upon in rough, quick strokes and others that were in
the process of being painted. One, larger than the others, showed
a silver-haired man in formal clothing, his expression so lifelike
it was as if he was sitting right there in front of me. Others were
less accomplished but no less interesting. A still life with flowers
and crockery. A study of the couch against the far wall and the
paisley shawl in shades of brown and orange thrown across
the back of it. A woman reposing on a bed with tussled blankets,
her bare thighs and breasts exposed.

None of these was nearly as spectacular as the painting
propped against the far wall and, captivated, I closed in on it.
It had yet to be framed but the canvas was taller than me and
wide enough to fill an entire wall even in a home as large and
spectacular as Phin's. The scene before me was that of a farmyard. There was a stone building in the background, its windows
dark and its door shut, and in front of building two ferocious
bulls (or as they were known in more polite company, cow

brutes) faced off against each other. Both animals were black and massive with eyes dark and fierce and hooves that looked deadly and kicked up eddies of dust. The muscles beneath the animals' skin rippled with strength and, though I knew I was being fanciful, I could have sworn I could feel their hot breath and hear each labored snort. The animal on the left had haunches larger than dinner plates. The one on the right had a plume of steam coming from its mouth.

I cannot say I was surprised when I saw the artist's signature in the corner.

'William Kobieta Walker.' I read the name aloud – the same artist who had painted the horse fair picture I'd seen at Sebastian Richter's.

And his painting, unframed, was here at Clarice's.

Before I had a chance to work through how that might be possible – if Clarice had perhaps bought the painting, or if Walker was an associate, a friend or more – the front door banged open and the sounds of footsteps, laughter and singing echoed through the house.

'So take your time, Miss Lucy, Miss Lucy, Lucy, oh!'

One voice, a man's, loud and completely out of tune, sang the popular ditty with far more enthusiasm than the others and hung onto that final 'oh!' as if he were drowning and needed it for his last breath.

His mouth still rounded by the word, he tumbled into the room, took one look at me and fell to his knees.

'There is a goddess among us!' he announced, though truth be told, the half-dozen others who piled into the room behind him did not look completely convinced.

The man himself had a riot of chestnut curls, a cleft chin and a straight, slim nose. He wore black unmentionables and a shirt that was undone at the front to reveal a good deal of bare flesh. When he came nearer, still on his knees and his eyes wide with wonder, I smelled the strong odor of liquor about him. 'She has come down to grace the mortals of this world with her beauty!' he announced.

'Don't be an ass, Michael. Miss Barnum has come because I invited her.' Clarice untangled herself from the knot at the doorway and came forward to greet me. Her cheeks were pink and she smelled of champagne and cigarettes. 'You must forgive Michael,' she said, her mouth thin with disgust when she tossed a look to where the man crawled away from me and propped himself against the couch. 'He fancies himself a French intellectual and feels he must say things like that.'

'Then I am not a goddess?' I asked her.

Clarice threw back her head and laughed. 'Each in her own way, we are all goddesses, my dear Evie,' she said, and she took me around and introduced me to her friends who had come tumbling into the room along with her.

A woman with blotchy skin and half-closed eyes was Abigail who, even before she could return my cordial greeting, collapsed upon the couch. A fleshy young fellow followed her there before I even learned his name. Another woman, golden-haired, plump and pretty, giggled and greeted me even as the man she was with – older and with bulging eyes – nibbled on her neck. No sooner had they finished saying hello than the couple took flight. Seconds later I heard their footsteps on the stairs.

'And this is Damien,' Clarice said.

Damien LaCrosse had hair as dark as ink and it flowed over his shoulders in glorious waves, framing a face with fiery eyes and full lips. He puffed on a cigarette and stepped back to study me in a way that reminded me of the looks the traders gave the horses in that painting I'd seen at Sebastian Richter's.

'Michael has low standards,' he announced.

His voice was deep and somehow intimate even in the presence of the others, and it sent prickles along my spine. Rather than stand there tongue-tied, I swallowed the sudden and inexplicable dryness that filled my mouth and managed a smile. 'Then it is just as I thought – I am not a goddess.'

'Hardly.' He gave me another look, from the tips of my boots to the top of my bonnet. 'Though it is difficult to say with woman who is as swaddled as you are.' He leaned closer, a little unsteady on his feet. 'Perhaps if you took off your clothes.'

'It is the absinthe talking,' Clarice said, and the fierce look in her eyes told me it was not the first time she'd used the excuse to apologize for Damien's behavior. She raised her chin, her shoulders rock steady. 'Damien is far too imaginative.'

He shot back, 'And far too drunk to listen to you moan.'

She hadn't moaned and she didn't comment, but that didn't keep Clarice from holding in her annoyance by sucking in her bottom lip.

'She's a terror,' Damien confided. As if we were longtime friends, he put a hand on my arm. His fingers were cool but his palm was hot and the warmth seeped through the sleeve of my gown and into every pore, surprising in its intensity. 'And I am but a gentle soul,' he crooned, 'looking for a sweet woman who will understand the workings of my heart. I do believe you are her.' He tightened his hold on my arm and fought for a moment to adjust the focus of his eyes. 'She.'

Another second under the gaze of those soulful eyes and I might have told him anything he wanted to hear. It was a good thing the man who had flopped onto the couch chose that particular moment to let out a burp that echoed through the room and brought me to my senses.

'There isn't a person in all of New York City who would say I am sweet,' I told Damien. 'I am sorry to tell you, I am not the woman you are looking for.'

'But we don't know that yet, do we?' He leaned nearer still, his lips far too near mine for propriety. 'We might find out some night when the moon rides high in the sky and spills its silvery light over our entwined limbs and bare flesh.'

'Spoken like a poet!' When she stepped between us, Clarice's voice was airy, but I did not fail to see her eyes shoot fire.

In spite of myself, I couldn't help but think of what I'd learned from Jonathan at Delmonico's. Andrew had been there with Clarice on the very night he'd been murdered, and when he'd told her he wanted to end their relationship her anger had been palpable.

When it came to the men in her life, was Clarice as jealous as all that?

At the same time a chill crawled up my spine, an idea formed in my mind.

'It is your poetry that interests Miss Barnum,' Clarice told Damien, winding her arm through mine. 'Not your sad attempts at romance.' She made a move to pilot me to the nearest chair.

I stood my ground, at least for the space of a heartbeat. The next moment, I removed my arm from hers and dared to step closer to Damien. Like Clarice's resentment, Damien's animal energy was easy to perceive and impossible to ignore. It wrapped around me like a living thing, the scent and the heat, the very essence of the man. I had never been a coquette. I had never needed to be with James Crockett whose affection, so I thought, was so immediate upon our introduction I did not need to try at being clever or pert. They were not behaviors that came easily, and I nerved myself and managed a smile I hoped was more mysterious than ridiculous.

Sure to keep my voice low so that Clarice could hear the murmur of it but not the words, I told Damien, 'Clarice does not know me all that well. Perhaps some night when the moon rides high—'

'Ah, when the moon rides high!' His sigh might have transported me if not for the heavy scent of spirits that came with it. 'I have a place nearby where I write. Small but private. We can meet at twilight, my dear Miss . . .' He dismissed the obvious fact that he did not remember my name. 'We'll watch the sun set the evening afire and then kindle a fire of our own. I can see you are the type. All cloaks and bonnets and petticoats. But once I get you out of them . . .'

I allowed my smile to inch up a notch. 'Once you get me out of them?'

'Really, Evie!' This time when Clarice tugged my arm, it was with enough force to yank me back a step. 'You mustn't get caught up in Damien's nonsense. He's a dreamer, after all. Or so he'd like the world to think. But we are not here to listen to him spin his fantasies. I asked you to stop by to listen to his poetry.'

It was so obvious a ploy, I had no choice but to obey. When Clarice waved me toward a chair, I took it and twined my fingers together on my lap, wondering what she'd think if she knew that, ruse or not, those few minutes in the pull of Damien's orbit had made my heart beat double time.

Once I was seated, Clarice whirled to face Damien. 'I told Miss Barnum about your newest poem.'

I cannot say I had ever met a poet before, yet something told me that, like all artists – painters and writers and makers of all the things of beauty that adorn our world – they can be caught up in their own vision of themselves. Damien obviously was. The simmering smile he'd turned my way when he'd talked of moonlight and naked limbs disappeared and was replaced with a look that was more self-important than sensual.

'My new poem.' His shoulders inched back. 'I've just completed it and it is a masterpiece. Finer than anything I've written before. More real. More carnal. Like that painting of your friend's over there, Clarice.' He slid a glance toward the barnyard scene and another at Clarice that made me wonder what silent secret passed between them. 'But then, there can be nothing more real than Walker's paintings, can there? We are but amateurs, artless in his presence.'

Clarice rolled her eyes. 'The poem, Damien.'

'The poem.' Damien cleared his throat. 'Miss . . .' A brief, pained expression crossed his face and he conceded to his forget-fulness with a shrug. 'She needs to know this poem is written not from a dream but from real experience,' he told Clarice.

'That is the point,' she shot back. 'But she will not know any of it, not until she hears the poem.'

'Yes, of course.' He pulled himself up to his full height and stood with his feet apart and his head high.

'Woe for the pain that banishes the brightness from the earth,' he said, and his words echoed through the room with its high ceilings and gilded walls. 'Woe for an Eden that has been lost. To sin. To shame. To those who remain unseen.'

I did my best to pretend understanding and reminded myself that, someday, such a skill might serve me well. Phin often talked of adding a sort of lecture room to the museum where he might present plays and speeches and public poetry readings. If his plans ever came to pass and I was forced to attend such events, I would have to know how to wear the mask of interest. Still, I could not help but slip Clarice a look of confusion.

With the small movement of one hand, she told me to be patient.

I did my best and focused again on Damien, who had lost his way through his stanzas and repeated himself quickly until he got to the place where he'd stopped. 'To sin. To shame. To those who remain unseen.' He coughed politely and slowed his speech again, endowing each syllable of his work with its own importance. 'And to the man whose visage peered through the darkness, his skin and face so green.'

Bad rhyme or not, I sat up like a shot. One look at Clarice's satisfied smile and I knew this was exactly what she'd wanted me to hear.

'A green man?' I could not keep to my seat. I closed in on Damien. 'You say you did not dream these images? That they are not flights of your imagination?'

'Exactly how Clarice tried to criminate me.' Damien's pouted. 'I reminded her that though I do have more imagination than the normal human, this was not one of those times. It is like Walker's work.' He turned to Clarice to say this. 'Realism. I saw him.'

'The green man?' I had to be sure. 'Tell me about him.'

Damien's top lip curled. 'My age, my height. I was trolling through the dark, looking for the grotesque so that I might give it immortality with my words.'

'And you saw him.' I forced myself to hide the excitement that made me feel as if I'd leap from my own skin. 'Where? When?'

'I wrote it all in one sitting. In one night.' Damien wanted me to be impressed, and I confess I was shameless enough to try and play the part, the better to have him continue with his story. 'The poem is very new and I have yet to let my stanzas marinate, yet I do think you will agree, they are quite brilliant.'

'Quite,' I agreed. 'And this green man, you saw him . . .'

He squeezed his eyes shut. 'Wednesday,' he said, then opened his eyes again. 'No, Thursday.'

Just two days earlier! I folded my fingers into my palms, the better to disguise my eagerness. 'And where? Where did you come upon such a unique specimen of a man?'

He stepped back and crossed his arms over his chest. 'Are you a poet?' Damien asked.

'Me? No, I'm—'

'A writer then? Looking for the macabre and the marvelous?'

'Not at all, sir. I'm simply—'

'Then another artist!' Damien threw his hands in the air and spun away. 'I am sick half to death of artists. If you're looking to find this hideous creature so that you might paint him, I have to warn you—'

'I have no intention of painting him or writing about him or immortalizing him in verse. The green man is . . . Jeffrey. Jeffrey is a friend.'

As quickly as he'd turned away, Damien spun around again and gave me the sort of look I'd seen men of wit and intelligence bestow on our Feejee beauty back at the museum. 'There is more to you, miss, than I imagined. You are friends with a green man?'

'Yes, and I must speak to him. I must find him. Where did you come upon him?'

'Not in a place where a woman should be alone.'

I nearly laughed. 'I've already scoured the Bowery. And Five Points.'

'And lived to tell the tale.' The gleam in Damien's eyes told me he was actually impressed. 'Will you quake in your boots, pretty miss, if I tell you to look for your friend along Water Street?'

'Near the docks?'

'You don't look the type of woman who would know of such places.'

I had no doubt he was right, just as I had no doubt he would be surprised to know I'd been to the Water Street docks any number of times to receive shipments for the museum.

'Has he taken a position on one of the ships?' I asked Damien.

His shrug was casual. 'I can only say that when I came across him, your green man was scurrying out from under an old tarp, like one of the rats that lives nearby. He clapped eyes on me and scuttled back the way he came.'

'Thank you.' I didn't wait for Damien to respond but made for the door. 'Thank you,' I told Clarice before I got there.

'It hardly helps,' she told me.

'Yet it is a place to start.'

'But, Evie.' She caught me by the sleeve before I could exit the house. 'You can't just go off to the docks on Water Street by yourself. Promise me you will be careful.'

'Of course I will.'

'And you must also promise me that you don't think less of me for introducing you to people like Damien.'

I couldn't help but smile, but it was an expression that did not last once I was outside. For I had learned two interesting things that day at Clarice's and neither cheered me. One was that I might find Jeffrey hiding somewhere near the East River.

And the other?

Before I entered my carriage, I glanced over my shoulder toward the house and found Clarice at the window watching me.

I could still feel her eyes on me as the carriage drove away, just as I could feel the weight of the thought that would not leave me alone.

Clarice was a jealous woman.

Was she jealous enough to kill?

TWELVE

A s I was expected at the dinner table that evening, I had no chance to go to Water Street to begin my search for Jeffrey. It did not matter, I told myself, for the next day was Sunday, the museum was closed and I would have all day to find him.

I did not count on Charity having other plans for me.

That Sunday morning, a list in her hand, she hurried into the breakfast room where Phin and I were already sharing a loaf of Cook's delicious, crusty bread, a plate of sausages and a pot of coffee. My brother and I exchanged wary looks.

When Charity makes a list, it usually costs Phin a great deal of money.

He managed a smile. 'More decorating ideas, my dear? I thought we were done.'

Charity's mind was clearly elsewhere. She waved away the question with one hand and waited while Delia, the girl who came in to help during the day, poured coffee.

'We'll need oranges,' Charity said.

'I thought there were to be artichokes,' Phin replied.

When Charity looked at him in wonder, he threw up his hands. 'On the wallpaper in the dining room, of course! I thought we were going to have—'

'I'm not talking about wall coverings.' Charity slapped her list on the table. 'I'm talking about luncheon. This afternoon at one.' She had ignored me completely since walking into the room but now she glanced my way, a tiny smile playing around her thin lips. 'Sebastian Richter is coming.'

This was not unpleasant news. Leastways, it would not have been on any other Sunday.

I set my cup on my saucer. 'I am sorry I will miss him.'

Charity had just picked up a piece of bread slathered with apricot jam and she froze with it at her lips, blinking rapidly like an owl surprised by a sudden light. She set down the bread and twined her fingers together on the table in front of her.

'He is hardly coming to call on me,' she said.

'If he is coming to call on me,' I replied, 'perhaps I should have been apprised of it.'

'I am telling you now.' Charity picked up the bread, snapped off a piece and chewed it, her gaze still on me. When she was finished, she swallowed down her coffee. 'I don't need to remind you—'

'No, you don't.' Phin was at the head of the table, and reached out and put a hand on hers. 'Evie knows.'

'Perhaps she doesn't.' With a look, Charity dismissed Delia, and once the girl was gone she leaned forward, her elbows on the table. 'You're fortunate he wants to call on you at all.'

'I cannot say if I am or I am not,' I told her. 'He seems pleasant enough but I hardly know the man.'

'That's not what I'm talking about and you know it,' she shot back. 'It is not Richter's character that's in question, it is yours, and yours being what it is—'

'Now, Charity, my sweet pigeon.'

It had taken me little time under Phin and Charity's roof to discover that when he called her *sweet pigeon* it was because he was doing his best to appease her. In that same, scant time, I had come to realize that when he tried to appease her, Charity only got more angry. Phin, it seemed, had never learned the same lesson.

He patted her hand. 'Evie needs no reminder—'

She swatted his hand away, at the same time pinning me with a look. 'Apparently she does. You are lucky, indeed, that he is interested. He wouldn't be. Not if he knew the truth about you.'

My shoulders shot back. 'If he is truly interested, he will know the truth about me. I could not spend my life with a man who doesn't know my history. All of it.'

'Then perhaps we should call the men from the newspapers in here right now!' Charity leapt out of her chair and her voice rose. 'Wouldn't they love to hear the story of Phineas T. Barnum's sister? Wouldn't that make for delicious gossip from one end of Manhattan to the other? Not to mention in Bethel. Oh, how delightful it would be for your mother to read the story in Bethel.'

'My mother knows the story,' I reminded her, my voice calm even while my insides twitched. 'She is the reason I am here with you today.'

'Oh, no!' Charity wagged a finger at me. 'Your good mother is not the reason. He . . .' She swung around to point that same finger at her husband. 'He is the reason you are here. If he wasn't so soft-hearted—'

'It was your decision, too.' Phin's voice was quieter than hers and, though I was sure it was designed to calm her, I knew all too well that it was also an attempt to make sure we weren't overheard; Delia may have been sent from the room but that did not mean she was very far away. 'You know it was the right thing to do,' he told his wife. 'The kindest way to deal with a situation that was difficult.'

Charity snorted. 'Difficult for us!'

'And not for me?' I had been complacent for too long, following my brother's advice to stay silent and depending on his wisdom to guide me, but now the pain of the last years clutched at my throat. 'I spend my every waking moment thinking of my child!'

'And so you dote on my son because of it,' Charity shot back. 'You must put your debased past behind you, Evie. I told you that from the day you came to us with the shame in your belly.'

I rose slowly and ever so carefully, and I think it was that more than anything that made Charity see the depth of my anger. No sooner was I on my feet than she plunked back into her chair, unable to keep her place beneath the rage that simmered through my words.

'That child is my flesh and my blood. He is my soul, and I will never be ashamed of him.'

My words hung in the air between us, punctuated only by Charity's sharp, rough breaths. I do not know how long I stood there, daring her to contradict me; I only know that when Phin jumped up and clapped his hands together, I flinched.

'It is good to get these things out in the open,' he said. 'It will make for smoother days down the road.'

I wasn't convinced, but when there was a gentle tap on the door I again took my seat and was relieved when Cook approached Charity with a question about the luncheon arrangements. When

I reached for my coffee cup, my sister-in-law didn't see my hands trembling.

They agreed on boiled salmon and mutton with caper sauce, followed by a custard, and then nuts and oranges for dessert. Before Cook retreated to the kitchen, Charity sent me the briefest of looks.

'For five,' she told Mrs O'Donnell. 'Mr Richter's cousin, Sonya, will be joining us.'

And so it was determined, and I might have argued if Phin hadn't implored me with a look.

At one o'clock, I was downstairs when Sebastian Richter and Sonya arrived.

They made a handsome couple. I never realized it until I walked into the parlor and saw them standing side by side, she – just a slip of a thing next to her tall, broad cousin – in a sweet gown of rose-colored silk brocade with the Succor ribbon pinned to her shoulder and Richter dressed all in black aside from his white shirt and twin ribbon. She greeted me as if we were old friends. His eyes lit up when I extended a hand to him.

'Your sister is too kind to ask us for a meal,' Richter said, and he gave my extended hand a quick squeeze.

'My sister-in-law' – Charity was on the other side of the room, supervising the pouring of lemonade and I shot her a look – 'is very happy that you could join us.'

'We look forward to you coming back to Succor to visit,' Sonya told me. 'We've been devising something of a plan to try and intercept young women before they are alone in the city.'

'Really, Sonya!' Richter's laugh was deep and rich. 'It is a beautiful Sunday afternoon, the sun is shining and the last of the flowers are in bloom. Do we really want to demoralize Miss Barnum's mood with such gloomy talk?'

'I don't mind. Really,' I told him. 'I am interested in Succor's work.'

'There. You see.' Sonya lifted her chin. 'Miss Barnum is not airy-headed as so many young women are. She is interested in our work.' She bent her head toward mine. 'We are thinking of organizing small groups of women to meet ships at the dock.' She apparently thought I might be abashed at such news (little could she have imagined my search for Jeffrey!) because she sent up a silvery laugh. 'I don't mean every ship, of course. That would be unseemly as well as impossible. I mean the immigrant ships. The ones that come from England and Ireland. If we could talk to the young ladies just as they disembark we would sooner find the ones who need our help before they are forced to take to the streets on their own. We will give them our ribbons as a sign of our commitment to them, and to remind them that if they are in need of friendship, they can find it with us.'

It was a clever plan, and I told her so. I also told her I would help when I was able.

'Would you?' Sonya's eyes sparkled, and when Delia came around with a tray and offered lemonade she took a glass, but before we had a chance to discuss the scheme further my brother came over and corralled her.

'I hear you play the piano and play it quite well,' he said. 'We've a new one in the next room and my dear daughter Caroline is the only one here with any talent for music. She is upstairs with Nurse. Would you do us the honor?'

Sonya smiled her agreement and stepped away with Phin and, a minute later, the strains of a lovely waltz floated to us from the room next door.

'Charming.' Richter sipped his lemonade. 'Sonya is a woman of many talents.'

'It must run in your family.'

He laughed. 'I'm afraid my family is more interested in business than in art. No, no, Sonya was Marta's cousin, not mine. But she is a good friend and she is an aunt of sorts to my children. She loves them dearly.'

'I saw them in the garden the other day,' I admitted. 'I watched them from the front window. They're happy children.'

He moved just a step closer. 'They could use a mother's love.'

My cheeks flushed with heat and Richter must have sensed my embarrassment. He stepped back immediately and just as quickly changed the subject. 'Speaking of Succor's work, your brother tells me you are searching for a missing friend.'

Phin couldn't have meant Jeffrey. He had no idea I was looking for Jeffrey. 'You mean Madeline.'

He nodded. 'Yes, that is the name he mentioned. A Miss

Madeline Emerson. After he inquired, I checked the books at Succor.'

'She's not listed.' The words were out of my mouth before I could stop them and I offered a smile by way of apology. 'I'm afraid I may have overstepped my bounds. When I was there to meet with your cousin and the other women who give so generously of their time, I asked Matron if I might have a look.'

'So you already knew this friend of yours . . . this Madeline . . . you knew even then that she was missing? That is not the impression I got from Mr Barnum.'

'I didn't know,' I said. 'Not really. I knew only that she was in the city and I thought . . .' I could hardly say what I thought because what I thought was that when the man at the Astor House told me James had walked out on Madeline, I hadn't been the least bit surprised. A man like James is forever heartless. When I visited Succor, it may not have been a wholly formed thought but, deep in my heart, I knew that Madeline might have been abandoned.

I twitched away the uncomfortable feeling. 'I thought it wouldn't hurt to ask. That is all. As long as I was there. I am sometimes too curious.'

'And altogether charming.' His smile was as gentle as the breeze that flowed through the room and brought with it the scent of autumn air. 'I'm not at all surprised you're industrious, that is for certain. But I am surprised . . .' He darted a look over his shoulder to where Charity and Phin stood listening to Sonya's music. 'Mrs Barnum seems the type who might not approve of a pretty woman spending so much time here on the other side of the room in intimate conversation with a man.'

'She's anxious to get me out of the house,' I confided, then realized I'd said too much.

When my eyes went wide, Richter didn't hold it against me. In fact, he laughed. 'Correct me if I am wrong, but I think there is wisdom in the old saying that two women under one roof means trouble. You have too strong a spirit for her. The very fact that you're looking for your missing friend tells me that.'

'I haven't exactly looked,' I admitted, and realizing it, my shoulders drooped. 'I've asked at Succor. I've gone around to the hotel where she once stayed here in the city.'

'And that is certainly looking! You are to be commended, Miss Barnum. If there's anything I can do to further your search, you will let me know? Or better still . . .' He thought for a moment. 'You are far too busy at the museum. You hardly need another worry. I will contact some of the people I've met through our efforts with Succor, people who work with the other charities that help women. Perhaps I may learn something and if, at the same time, it allows me to take some of the burden from your shoulders, I would consider it an honor.'

I was afraid that blurting out, 'Thank you!' my voice breathy and my cheeks hot, made me look like nothing more than a callow miss, yet I could hardly help myself. Fortunately, I was saved from further missteps when Phin announced it was time to eat.

The meal was delicious and the company pleasant. What had Richter once told me? That Sonya had been known to talk the ears off a rabbit? It was true, yet I was grateful for her constant chatter and the interesting stories she told about her recent travels in Europe. Listening to Sonya helped me forget that the hours were ticking away and Jeffrey was somewhere near Water Street while I sat eating custard on Fifth Avenue.

I had hoped to make a graceful exit after the meal but Phin suggested a game of Boston, and as there were four card players needed and Sonya offered to play the piano again, I had no choice but to remain. As I was partnered with Richter and he was a savvy player, I could hardly complain.

Boston was followed by a few quick rounds of charades – one of Phin's favorites for it gave him a chance to perform and to be the focus of attention – and then by coffee and cakes which Cook brought in on a silver tray.

By the time it was over, I realized I admired Sebastian Richter more than ever. He was clever and charming and he paid me far more attention than was allowed of an acquaintance. The realization that he was more than an acquaintance gladdened me, and when he and Sonya left I watched them walk across the street through the last of the evening light and found myself smiling.

I didn't realize Charity stood behind me at the window until she purred in my ear. 'If you're wise, you'll keep your mouth shut.'

I twitched away my surprise along with the suggestion. 'If I'm wise,' I told her, 'I won't assume he has more affection for me than he might.'

'Oh, I don't think you need to assume it. He's interested and will stay interested. If you keep your secrets to yourself.'

I turned from the window. 'And if I do tell?' I asked her.

She lifted one shoulder. 'He will surely reject you. And after that, word is bound to get out. You'll be an outcast and never find a decent man. But then, I suppose that before now decent men were never the kind that interested you.'

She was referring to James Crockett and I could hardly defend him. That didn't keep my shoulders from shooting back. 'It's been a long day.' I gathered the skirts of my blue dress and swept around her. 'I am going up to bed.'

If she noticed that I did not mention I was going to sleep, Charity didn't say. What she didn't know was that once I was in my room I changed out of my afternoon dress and house shoes and into a black gown and a pair of sturdy boots. I gathered the money I would need at the public stable where I hoped to hire a hack and a muffler to wrap around my face so I would not be recognized.

Ready, I waited for the house to grow quiet.

It should come as no surprise to learn that Phin often stayed awake until the small hours of the night. He was a man of great energy and possessed an intellect that was so quick-moving as to sometimes seem uncanny. He needed little sleep and often spent his nights at his desk. When I crept out of my own room, I saw a light from beneath the door of his study. Charity's bedroom, across the hall from Phin's, was dark but I was hardly willing to take a chance. As quickly and quietly as I could, I made my way to the servants' stairway at the back of the house and, from there, down to the kitchen.

When I walked in, Cook had a glass of beer on the table in front of her. 'It's late,' was all she said.

I glanced at the clock that ticked away the minutes on the shelf behind her. 'Just past eight,' I said. 'And I won't be long. If you would be so gracious as to not mention—'

She stood and went to the door that led into the kitchen garden. 'Whatever it is you're about, you best be careful and be home quick.'

I promised I would be.

I would make better time out on Fifth Avenue than I would if I kept to our neighbors' gardens, so I went around to the front of the house, pausing for a moment once there to make sure there was no one to take notice of me. A carriage whirred by and I waited until it was gone, then made my way down the street and around the corner to a stable where the man on duty pretended not to be too interested when a woman alone came to hire a rig after dark.

I gave the driver my destination, refused to react when his eyebrows shot up his forehead and settled in for the ride. A short while later, I disembarked and paid the man to wait.

I was no stranger to ships or the smell of salt air. Though his family originated in Bethel (as landlocked a place as any), James Crockett had considerable financial interests in shipping and owned a small fleet that regularly plied the waters along the eastern coast and down into the Caribbean, and from there to South America. In former days, we visited his ships and talked of his business interests, and remembering how he'd oftentimes told me that someday the two of us would board one of those ships and explore exotic ports together, my heart squeezed in spite of the advice from my head that told me to put his airy promises behind me.

In daylight, the slips on Water Street bustled with ships coming and going, the piers teemed with sailors and the warehouses that lined the street buzzed like beehives. But in the dark, the docks were a shadow of themselves. Warehouses loomed, dark and massive, to my right as I made my way along the street, and across the East River the lights of Brooklyn winked at me and danced a staccato rhythm against the inky water. Here on the Manhattan side, ships bobbed in the current, their sails furled and their masts like skeleton fingers against the night sky.

There would be fog that night and soon. I realized it when a tendril of moisture curled against my cheek and I found myself pulling my cloak tighter around me. Already the paving stones were slick and I slipped a bit when I stopped to let a rat scuttle across my pathway, followed by a large orange cat on the hunt. They disappeared into the shadows and I heard the rat shriek and told myself to pay it no mind. I had more important business to attend to.

I began my search near where Montgomery Street crosses Water and made my way west and south from there, stopping those few sailors I happened to pass to ask if they'd seen Jeffrey and trying my best not to be unnerved when they looked me up and down as if to judge if I was some crusader bent on doling out salvation to those along the docks or a woman looking to make the cost of an evening's lodging.

Fortunately for me, my plain dress and cloak and the muffler I wore wound around my neck made me look more like a reformist than a fallen woman, and they told me they couldn't help me and let me go on my way.

I continued thus for an hour or more, peering behind crates and barrels where they were stacked along the river, talking to those I came across and wondering what in the world I had been thinking when I had decided that a plan this ill-formed might actually have success.

And then I saw him.

Jeffrey Hollister stood in a fleeting pool of moonlight that was just as quickly extinguished when a cold breeze blew and the mist thickened. In the dark and with the fog swirling around us like the eddying currents on the river, he looked neither green nor an oddity but like any other man except for the way he stood, one foot out and his shoulders back, as if he was ready to bolt.

When he heard my footfalls, he tensed and would have run if I hadn't called out.

'Jeffrey!'

As if thinking he might be asleep and dreaming my presence, he shook his head. 'Miss? It cannot be you. Not here. Why are you—'

'I've come to find you, Jeffrey.' Careful of the slippery pavement, I closed the distance between us. Jeffrey had lost weight since last I saw him; his face was pinched and his eyes were wary. 'The constable thinks you killed Andrew Emerson.'

A wave of pain crossed his expression when he glanced left and right over his shoulder. 'I know they are looking for me as I've heard rumor now and again. They've been about, over on the Bowery—'

'At Carey's, yes. I searched for you there, as well.'

'They've been around here, too.' Jeffrey ran his tongue over his lips. 'They will surely be back. It's why I have to get out of here.'

'On a ship?' It made sense so I was not surprised when he nodded. 'When do you leave?'

'You are not . . .' He scraped his hands over his face. 'You won't tell them?'

'That I've seen you?' Against the sound of the water swishing around the docks, my laugh did not exactly sparkle. 'I am not here so the constable might find you, Jeffrey. I am here because I know you had nothing to do with Andrew Emerson's death. I've been trying to find you so that I might help you.'

He narrowed his eyes and stuck out his lower lip. 'I didn't like the way the gentleman touched Miss.'

'I know that, Jeffrey, but that does not mean you killed him.'

'I . . .' Jeffrey's shoulders sagged. 'I did not. I wish I might have, Miss, because he mistreated you. But to bash a man's head like that? I could never.'

'Yet you know Andrew's head was bashed, and you ran and you've been missing since. And now you tell me you're going to go to sea. What are you afraid of, Jeffrey?'

In the moonlight, his eyes looked like pieces of silver and his voice was no more substantial than the fog. 'Saw it, Miss,' he said.

My stomach clutched. 'You saw Andrew being killed? You saw who did it? Then you must come back with me, Jeffrey, and tell the constable.'

He backed away from my outstretched hand. 'No. No. They won't believe me. They'd never believe me. No one will believe a freak like me.'

'My brother will.' I closed the space between us. 'You know that, Jeffrey. You know if you tell Mr Barnum what happened he will listen, and he will believe you, and I will, too. We'll make sure the constable understands. Only you must tell me the truth, Jeffrey. What happened the night Andrew Emerson died?'

He passed a hand over his eyes. 'What happened? What happened is—'

I suppose I was so intent on listening to Jeffrey I never heard the footsteps behind me. Jeffrey didn't, either, not until it was too late. Then I saw his mouth fall open and his eyes go wide, and I would have responded to the alarm if only I'd realized what it meant.

'You must watch out, Miss!' He grabbed my hand, spun me around and did his best to push me out of the way, but by that time it was already too late. I saw a figure heavily cloaked, a deeper shadow in the darkness that surrounded us, and then the terrifying flash of pale moonlight against a silver blade.

'No, Miss, no!' Jeffrey called out, right before I felt the bite of steel in my side.

I gasped and grabbed at the spot that was already wet with my blood, then fell to my knees on the slick pavement.

The last thing I remember, it was as if the East River itself, deep and murky, had washed over me with its green water.

Then my world went black and the only thing I was aware of was the faintest scent of roses and lavender.

THIRTEEN

I woke to find my brother looking down at me, his usually jovial expression softened with worry.

It was not an unhappy thing to find him there, of course, but because of what felt like cotton wadding in my head it made little sense.

'Phin?' I did my best to focus my eyes, but that, too, proved something of a challenge because I was so distracted by my surroundings. There were no darkened warehouses, no ships, and I did not hear the rip and pull of the vicious East River current. Instead there was the glow of sunshine against the walls of what looked to be—

'My room?' My voice was rough and I ran my tongue over my lips. They were sticky and tasted sweet. Phin gently lifted my head from the pillows and put a glass of water to my lips. I drank like a desert nomad and, once he'd settled me, I felt better able to speak. 'How am I—'

'Not to worry.' He sat in a chair next to my bed and put a gentling hand on my shoulder.

'But how did I—'

'Evie!' There was steel in his eyes but his voice was honey. 'You needn't talk. You must rest.'

'Not until I know . . .' When I squirmed in an effort to sit up and a stab of pain hit my left side, a wave of frightening memory washed over me and I collapsed against the bed. 'What happened?'

'Precisely what I have been wanting to ask you since Sunday night when we found you.'

I was almost afraid to ask. 'And today . . .?'

'Monday. Late in the afternoon. The doctor gave you laudanum to ease your pain and help you sleep.'

'It cannot be that so much time has passed. Last I remember, it was Sunday night and I was—'

'Where?' Phin pinned me with a look.

Exhaustion washed over me and I closed my eyes and did my

best to make sense of the situation when I whispered, 'On Water Street.'

When I opened my eyes, it was to find him shaking his head, not so much in confusion as in wonder. 'What business would you have at the docks after dark?'

My head cleared and I was sorry for it. As the memories slowly seeped in to take the place of the confusion that had muddled my brain, I saw the scene again before my eyes – the swirl of fog, the flash of a knife and Jeffrey, fighting to keep me out of harm's way.

I tightened my hold on Phin's arm. 'Jeffrey?' I asked.

Phin is a cagey businessman. That does not mean he is not an open book to those of us who know him well. When the corners of his mouth thinned, I suspected the news wasn't good. 'He came to the door last night and told us you were in a hired carriage, wounded and bleeding. We were worried about you, Evie, and Jeffrey didn't tell us that he'd been injured as well.' His expression clouded. 'By the time we had you settled and came back to him . . . well, there was a great deal of blood and nothing we could do. It was too late.'

Hot tears stung my eyes and I did not brush them away. 'He saved me, Phin. He fought off my attacker and he somehow . . .' Again, as if it would help me fill in the missing pieces of all that had transpired, I glanced around the room. 'He brought me here. He must have located the carriage I had left waiting. I only wish . . .'

It did not matter what I wished and Phin knew it. He patted my hand, then, as if he was afraid I might take flight, he wound his fingers through mine. 'What is going on, Evie? You must tell me. First the fire at the museum and now this terrible assault—'

'And my carriage being shot at.' Phin did not know the story, so I relayed it and apologized. 'I know I should have told you but I didn't want you to worry. As to why . . .' I waited for another sip of water and, when I was done drinking, I pulled in as much of a breath as I was able to considering that I was swaddled around the middle with bandages.

'I think it is because of Andrew Emerson,' I told my brother. 'For I can think of no other reason, nothing that I've done that would cause someone to want to silence me. You see, I have been looking into the matter of Andrew's death.'

My brother, unshakable and composed in the face of everything from horridly deformed oddities to specimens of mummies and the bodies of dead animals, went ashen. 'That cannot be!' he announced. 'Evie, you cannot—'

'But I have been, because, you see, when Andrew came to see me that day at the museum, he asked for my help. From what I have learned since, I think it was because of Madeline, Madeline and . . . and James, but I never gave Andrew the chance to tell me. I was so worried that just by talking to him I might somehow reveal the reason I'm really here in New York. So concerned about my own reputation and my own secrets, I made excuses and sent him on his way. He came back that evening. No doubt to plead with me again. And it cost him his life. I owe him this at least, Phin, to find the truth behind his murder. So yes, I have been talking to people and asking questions, for, unlike the constable, I was not convinced that Jeffrey was the killer. Jeffrey can be . . .' I swallowed the lump in my throat. 'He could be quick to anger but Jeffrey did not hold onto his rage for long. He wouldn't have killed Andrew hours after assaulting him there before the Feejee Mermaid. When I found Jeffrey on Water Street, he told me as much and I believed him. He told me he didn't do it.'

'And now he is dead and cannot help us.' Phin hung his head. 'And the constable tells me that, with Jeffrey's death, he is considering the matter of Emerson's murder to be at an end.'

'No! We can't let that happen. Jeffrey told me why he ran from the museum and why he kept himself hidden all this time. He saw the murder happen, Phin. He knew who did it and he was afraid!'

'And now he cannot tell us. And you . . .' Phin gave me a sidelong glance. 'You cannot continue to look into the matter, Evie. It is too dangerous.'

'But I must.' Biting back a stab of pain, I propped myself against the pillows. 'Now more than ever, Phin, I must continue to try and find a solution to the mystery. If the constable has given up looking, it means there's a killer out there who will not be brought to justice. Not for Andrew's murder nor for Jeffrey's.'

*   *   *

Phin was not convinced, but he knew I was just as stubborn and just as determined as he was himself. He did not encourage me to continue my investigation but he did not forbid it, either, and it was just as well since I would not have listened if he had.

The next day I insisted on going to the museum and promised I would do nothing more strenuous than sit at my desk, but when I did venture out of my office to join Phin for luncheon and later to deliver an accounting of the previous days' receipts, I did not fail to notice a man – short and slim, with a thin face and beady eyes – who was so intent on studying our displays he spent the entire day there on the second floor. Bless Phin! He would have been embarrassed to accept my thanks for providing me protection, so I did not mention it. I did, though, breathe easier.

Now if only I could determine why anyone would want to kill me!

Back in my office, the thought pounded through my head to the same staccato tempo my fingers beat upon my desk. Whoever wanted to do me harm must think I was close to uncovering the murderer and yet . . .

Careful so as not to disturb the wound in my side, I shifted in my chair. Fortunately my cloak and gown, along with the layers of my chemise and corset, had prevented the injury from being too serious. Still, I had been cut just below the ribs, and the wound had a way of reminding me to move slowly. I was not about to ignore the advice.

I may have been comfortable enough in my chair but it was a shame I was not so at ease with the one thought that refused to leave me in peace. Try as I might, I could not forget that when I was attacked on Sunday I had caught the scent of roses and lavender.

Yes, it was true many women wore the scent. I had been known to do so myself.

But there was only one I could think of who wore it and was intimately connected with Andrew Emerson.

A shiver skittered up my spine, but even that wasn't enough to convince me to change my mind about what I knew I must do. Since I had promised Phin I would not stay late at the museum that day, no one questioned me when I called for my carriage a little before six. I did not check to see if I was followed by the beady-eyed man. If he trailed behind me – and I had no doubt he did – he would think nothing more than that I was off to visit a friend.

Was I?

Or was I in search of a foe who had followed me to Water Street and waylaid me?

Knowing I would not rest easy until I discovered the answer, I arrived in Chelsea a short while later and found the robin's-egg blue door that led into Clarice's home standing ajar. There was no one in the hallway and no young Bohemians in the studio at the back of the house, either. Clarice's friends weren't the only thing missing.

There was an empty space against the wall where, when last I'd visited, the William Kobieta Walker painting had stood. Without the farmyard picture and the vitality and power of the bulls in it, the room seemed chilled and empty.

'Ah, you've come back!'

A voice from the doorway brought me spinning around in time to see Damien LaCrosse prop himself against the doorjamb, the better to keep upright. His long, dark hair was a-tumble over his shoulders, his shirt was open at the neck and he was in his stocking feet. 'I knew you couldn't stay far away from me for long.'

'Actually, I am here to see Clarice,' I told him. 'I have much to discuss with her.'

He sauntered close enough for me to catch the scent of brandy and, with a tip of his head, indicated the blank space behind me. 'That painting, you mean? Don't tell me you're as besotted by Walker as everyone else in this town. It seems all of New York City thinks he is a genius.'

'You don't agree? The man has a great deal of talent.'

'The man' – he lifted his shoulders – 'has not one bit of talent at all, not real talent. Painting isn't nearly as demanding as wrestling with words. Yet I hear no one singing my praises as they do Walker's. Do they pay for my poems? Hardly, and if they did it would not be as heftily as they do for his paint daubs.'

'You're jealous.'

'Yes,' he admitted. 'Though for the life of me I cannot see why. I would hate to be a painter.' He gave an exaggerated shiver then shot me a grin that had all the heat of a winter night's fire in it. 'Except, of course, for the part about painting nymphs. You would pose as my nymph, would you not? I can picture you now in a sylvan setting, your hair loose and your legs bare.'

I looked beyond him. 'Did you say Clarice was in?'

'Clarice is . . .' As if he weren't quite sure, he turned to examine the expanse of empty room dotted here and there with easels and paintings, then turned to smile my way. 'She has flown the nest and left me here to tend the chicks.'

'Yet there seem to be no chicks about.'

'Well, there's you!' He inched closer. 'Would you like a glass of wine?'

'I would like to find Clarice.'

'Ah, Clarice!' Damien threw back his head and laughed. 'Oh, if you knew the truth, pretty miss.'

'You mean about Clarice and Walker? I thought they might be acquainted. Is that why his painting was here?'

'Acquainted.' As if they were delicious, he rolled the syllables over his tongue. 'They are far more than acquainted.'

'And I am hardly interested in gossip.'

'You would be if you knew the whole of it. You would be greedy for details, begging me to feed you every last morsel.'

'Or you might simply tell me where Clarice has gone.'

Anyone not as peculiar as a poet might have just answered and been done with it. But Damien was a poet, after all, and if there was one thing I'd learned on my last visit, it was that he had a flare for the dramatic and a love of listening to his own voice. Rather than say anything at all, he turned and strutted to the other side of the room, and I had no doubt he knew full well that, standing there, the evening light from the windows behind him melted over his shoulders and touched his hair with golden glimmers.

'I have a new poem,' he said. 'Would you like to hear it?'

I didn't, but I did need to know where Clarice was and it looked like LaCrosse was the only one who might be able to help.

I forced a smile. 'Of course.'

'Ah, wise as well as pretty.' He inched back his shoulders. 'You must listen carefully, for it's the best work I've done.'

'That's what you said about the last poem you recited to me,' I told him, but Damien was hardly listening. He was too busy settling himself like an actor on the stage, his elbows bent and his hands at his waist.

He tossed his head and his voice oozed through the room, each word precise and rounded.

'Wither do you wander, with your colors and your paints? Your hat upon your head, your scarf over your face. Wither do you travel, my fine and gorgeous dab? To farm and field, through mist. Wither do thou goest, Renaissance man and miss?'

'Stuff and nonsense,' I mumbled to myself before I remembered that Damien had information I needed and I could not afford to offend him. 'It is quite the ode,' I called across the room to him.

'Walker is quite the painter.'

'You said he had no talent.'

'He hasn't. None at all.'

More stuff and nonsense, and I was not in the humor for it.

'Did you say where I might find Clarice?' I asked him again.

'At an art salon, of course.' Damien strolled from one to the other of the paintings still displayed around the room. 'She wouldn't miss tonight's festivities. They will be unveiling the new Walker painting.'

'The bulls?'

'Such language!' He pretended to be outraged, but as he ended up laughing it carried no weight.

'Why aren't they exhibiting one of Clarice's paintings?' I asked.

'Clarice's paintings are . . .' He stopped in front of the easel closest to the windows and motioned to it with one hand. It was the painting I'd seen on my first visit there, the man with iron-gray hair, and it was so lifelike as to make me feel as if his blue eyes were watching me.

'This is one of hers?' I asked.

'Portraits.' The way he spoke the word told me he wasn't terribly impressed. 'Clarice does them well.'

'She does, indeed. Yet hers isn't the painting that's being featured at the salon tonight. Will Walker be there?'

Damien shot me a look. 'If Clarice is there, Walker will be there.'

'Yet he wasn't here when I stopped in last week.'

'Wasn't he?' Perhaps Damien really was surprised. Or perhaps he'd been too drunk to remember. 'They are usually inseparable.'

'Not so inseparable that Clarice didn't have the freedom to enjoy an acquaintance with Andrew Emerson.'

Damien's eyes lost their brandy sheen and he looked at me with new interest. 'The man who died?'

'She was angry at him.'

'Clarice is always angry at men for one thing or another. She's even been angry at me a time or two.' A grin split his face. 'Can you believe it?'

'I believe the two of them had a falling out the very night Mr Emerson was killed.'

'And you think Clarice did it?' Damien threw back his head and laughed. 'That is golden. Truly. Clarice with a knife in her hand, dripping blood from every finger. Oh, I do love the image it makes inside my head. I may have to write a poem about it.'

'She might be offended.'

'She will think it eminently amusing. Clarice is not the murdering type.'

'But the night Andrew died—'

'There was a salon. There are always salons! I find them endlessly boring, but then I am intellectually superior to most of those who attend and pretend to be wise and educated and oh-so erudite. But I do remember that one because Clarice came home from dinner that evening in a foul mood and insisted that nothing would cheer her up except me coming along to the salon.'

'And did you cheer her up?'

Damien's eyes lit up. 'The way I remember it, we were both cheered considerably before we even left the house.'

'You were with her all that evening?'

Damien strolled toward the door. 'Ask her yourself.'

'I will.' My words stopped him as he was about to leave the room. 'As soon as you tell me where she's gone.'

'Eighth Street.' He disappeared into the hallway with its painted walls, and from there up the stairway. 'Marie Gradeau's on Eighth Street, of course. It is where all the artists go to be seen.'

* * *

Damien was right. All creation seemed to be at Marie Gradeau's elegant townhouse and I suppose it was just as well. There was such a crush at the door, no one questioned if I had been invited.

I slipped in behind a woman in a gown of ivory and a man whose mustache was so long it curled along the sides of his cheeks and, once inside, I hoped no one would notice that I was still in my daytime clothing. Around me, the soft light of the overhead chandeliers winked and blinked against satin and silk in pastel shades of pink and blue and yellow. Here and there, those young people who considered themselves Bohemians strolled through, drinks and cigarettes in hand, wrapped in Persian robes and draped with paisley shawls, doing their best to prove how different and original they were. Though I had no knowledge of Marie Gradeau, it was obvious she was a lover of art, for the walls of her home were covered with paintings. There were portraits and landscapes and still lifes of high quality, and when I made my way through the crowd and into the parlor, I saw there was one large painting against the wall, covered with a cloth. What had Damien said? That the Walker painting would be unveiled that night? It looked as if he was right.

Marie Gradeau herself must have been the silvery-haired dowager holding court from the pink brocade chair in the corner. I did not introduce myself as doing so would have necessitated an explanation for why I was there. Instead, I watched our hostess extend her hand to guest after guest, sip her champagne, and laugh with so much abandon the diamonds at her throat sparkled.

What I did not see was any sign of Clarice.

I did two turns around the room and even stepped into the garden as it was a fine evening and there were guests there as well, all of them eager – if their conversations were to be believed – to see the newest work by Walker.

'I hear Walker's in the house,' one woman purred. 'I wish he'd violate his own rule against meeting with his admirers and join us for a drink.'

'He's a genius,' the man she was with reminded her. 'Geniuses do not mix with ordinary folk.'

Perhaps he was right, because by the time another twenty minutes had passed, all I heard around me was talk of the great artist. Walker was there! He was going to make an appearance! The great man was about to reveal his latest work!

Still searching for Clarice, I went back into the parlor and, from there, followed the crowd when it snaked into the front foyer. There, a stairway led up to the second floor of the residence and all eyes were on it. One minute melted into two, and two became three, and around me I felt the crowd buzz with barely controlled excitement. Then, from somewhere in the upstairs hallway, we heard the sound of a door closing and the crowd held its collective breath.

A man stepped up to the second-floor railing and, when he waved, the crowd sent up a round of applause. I had seen Walker's work, both at Clarice's and at Sebastian Richter's, and I was certainly impressed by his talent. I cannot say the same for the man himself. I am not sure what I expected. Extraordinary. Dramatic. Striking.

Hardly.

He was as a middle-sized fellow dressed completely in black. Just as Damien had mentioned in the poem I had been forced to listen to, Walker had a hat upon his head, it covered his hair completely and was pushed far enough down on his forehead to shade his eyes. Just as I had done on Sunday night to conceal my identity there on Water Street, he wore a muffler wound around his neck all the way up to his chin.

Before I had a chance to consider why the thought struck me as important, Walker lifted a hand toward the parlor and everyone turned to watch two men whisk the cloth away from his farmyard painting.

Everyone but me.

Even as the crowd oohed and ahhed with delight and unbridled admiration and moved back into the parlor for a better look at the astonishing painting, I headed in the other direction, excusing myself around those avid art fanciers who were eager to get closer to the picture. The wound in my side reminded me that taking the stairs two at a time was not wise, but I paid it no mind. When I got to the second floor, Walker was nowhere to be seen, but I heard a door close to my right. I strode down the hallway and, without a word, stepped into the room just in time to see Walker, who had been facing the room's only window, spin toward the sound of his unexpected guest.

'Hello, Clarice.'

FOURTEEN

The great artist did not say a word, simply walked past me and locked the door I'd just come in, then turned to me.
'How did you know?' Clarice asked.

'I didn't. Not until I came here tonight and saw you.'

'Then you think anyone might—'

'No,' I assured her and she let go a breath of relief. 'It was something Damien said. Renaissance man and miss. He recited his new poem to me when I went to find you in Chelsea. And then there's the muffler around your face, of course. You see, I've used the same ruse myself just recently.'

Clarice unwound the scarf to reveal a smile. 'Then it seems I am not the only one putting on a false face to the world.'

If only she knew!

I shook off the thought. I had more important things to worry about than the face I showed the world. For one, I could not afford to be taken in by the friendship offered in Clarice's smile and forget that it might very well hide the heart of a killer.

The thought firmly in mind, I strolled to the windows overlooking the street. It was dark now, and here and there along the avenue lights flickered from the windows of townhouses and shops. A horse and carriage clattered by, a couple strolled arm in arm. 'My disguise was in aid of looking into Andrew's murder,' I said, then glanced at her over my shoulder. 'Yours . . .'

Clarice pulled the black hat from her head and tossed it on a nearby chair. She shrugged out of William Kobieta Walker's cape and cast that aside as well, then peeled off her leather gloves.

'I have been told I have good hands,' she said, examining them in the light of the lamp that burned on the table beside her. 'Do you know what that means, Evie? When an artist is told he . . . she . . . has good hands, it is meant to be a compliment. It means you have talent. That you have an eye for your work and the skill and the gift to bring it to life on the canvas.'

'It's true. I saw your portrait of the man in your studio. You have a remarkable talent, indeed.'

'Portraits. Yes. Women are meant to paint portraits.'

I am no artist and have little knowledge of their world, and Clarice knew it. That would explain why, when she went on, sarcasm soured her voice. 'It is common knowledge among artists. The accepted wisdom. Women may paint, but they are meant to confine their talents to portraits.'

'Because?'

Her shrug told me she was as baffled as I. 'Because that's the way it's always been. Because it is what is accepted. Because going out into the fields and onto the farms and to horse fairs . . . well, that is simply something a woman shouldn't do. No more than she should paint what she sees in front of her, no matter how begrimed or pitiable or sweaty or real it might be. Heavens! Doing something like that would be as scandalous as a woman working at a museum, don't you think?'

'The prejudice against me isn't nearly as tangible.'

'Only because you have your brother to shield you from it. No one would dare criticize what you do, not at the risk of offending the great P.T. Barnum! Those of us who do not have so strong a person to stand against any who might criticize us need to find other means to express ourselves.'

'And so the creation of William Kobieta Walker.'

Clarice's grin was wicked, and if she noticed that I did not smile in return, that I stood there, my back rigid and my head high, ready to challenge her and eager for the truth, she didn't show it. In fact, she laughed.

'It was a brilliant plan, don't you think?' she asked. 'The moment I first caught wind of the sorts of paintings some of the young artists are doing in France, I knew I had found my true passion. You see, Evie, they do not sit in the studio and draw flowers and vases and fruit, dead things on a table. They do not recreate classic vistas or – heaven forbid! – religious scenes. They take their easels and their canvases out into the air, they paint what is real and alive and vigorous.'

'Walker certainly does. His . . . your . . . paintings are marvelous.'

'And they would never sell, not if word got out that they

were painted by a woman. Do you know, I am a member of the National Academy, my fellow artists allow that. But while the men may take classes in life drawing using live models right there in front of them, women cannot gain admittance. My goodness, if they knew I was not only painting from life but painting farm animals, bulls! There would be nothing but scandal, and my work would surely be dismissed. Packed away. Ignored. Or worse, destroyed.'

'I'm sorry.' It was all I could say. 'Perhaps it will all change some day. Women will paint what they desire to paint.'

'Women will work in museums. And perhaps even investigate murders.' Her grin melted. 'For now, I suspect that if he knew, even your brother would find your penchant for mystery shocking.'

'He does know,' I told her and I steeled myself for what I knew I must ask her. 'He is not shocked, but he is concerned. You see—'

There was a knock on the door. 'Mr Walker,' a voice called. 'If I might have a word.'

Clarice and I exchanged looks. While she grabbed her hat and cloak and the scarf that had provided me with a clue to the artist's real identity, I went to the door. I unlocked it and opened it but a hair's breadth to look out into the hallway.

When the man who stood outside stepped back in surprise at seeing me, I took the opportunity to slip into the hallway and close the door behind me.

'May I be of assistance?' I asked him.

He looked at the closed door uncertainly. 'I thought . . . that is, I imagined Mr Walker would be . . . what I mean is, I thought him to be alone.'

'We are old friends,' I assured him. 'And I stopped by to offer him my congratulations on his newest work. It is remarkable, don't you think?'

'Yes. Quite.' The man had hair peppered with gray and a rheumy left eye that caused him to look at me with his head tilted at an angle that made his jowls sag and sway. 'I had thought to speak with him about the painting.'

'He will be delighted to hear it. You are interested in purchasing it?'

I doubt the man expected me to be so candid. He tilted his

head in the other direction and when he was forced to squint, cocked his head again to the left. 'And you are . . .'

'As I told you. A long-time friend of Mr Walker's, and a sort of broker for his work. The painting downstairs . . .' I pretended to consider it. 'I do believe if you were willing to pay him five thousand dollars—'

'Five thousand!' His hand flew to his heart. 'That is a life's fortune.'

'And worth every penny, wouldn't you say?'

'Well, yes. Of course. But—'

'Thank you for asking about the painting.' I stepped back toward the door, a signal to him that our conversation had ended. 'You should know we've had any number of other inquiries. If you don't decide quickly, I'm afraid the painting will be sold to someone else very soon. Good evening, sir.'

'Good . . . good evening,' he said, and went back downstairs.

'Oh, that was delicious!' Clarice greeted me at the door, her face wreathed in a smile, the hat and cloak back on in case I allowed the man from the hallway into the room. 'Thank you for not giving away my secret.'

'I had no intention of doing that,' I told her.

'And for naming that asking price!' She clapped her hands together. 'If I could earn as much as that for a Walker painting I would be a happy woman, indeed.'

'And I would be just as happy. But first . . .' When I pulled in a breath, I was reminded of the wound in my side and the real reason for my visit. 'I need the truth, Clarice. About Andrew.'

'I told you—'

'You told me he wanted to marry you and you were not interested. But I have learned otherwise. When you left him at Delmonico's, you were angry at Andrew.'

She clutched her hands at her waist and stood a little too straight, a little too still. 'That may be true, but—'

'And are you so desperate to hide your guilt that you tried to kill me, too?'

Her mouth fell open. 'No. Evie, you can't possibly think—'

'I know I've been attacked, and I know the last attempt on my life left me with a vital clue, the scent of roses and lavender. Your scent, Clarice.'

She threw her hands in the air and let them slap back down against the black unmentionables that were part of her Walker disguise. 'A lot of women's scent! Oh, please, Evie, you can't possibly think I would do a thing like that. We are friends.'

'I would like to think so. I don't want to think you'd wish me harm, but I must. I was attacked on Sunday and my attacker . . .' Tears clogged my voice. 'My attacker killed a friend who did his best to protect me. I will not stand by and not see justice done for him, just as I will not stop looking into the matter of Andrew's death. You were angry with him at Delmonico's and still angry when you returned home.'

She thought about this for a moment. 'Damien. He told you.'

'Yes. Now you must tell me the truth.'

'The truth is . . .' She took off the scarf and tossed it away. 'Yes, I was angry at Andrew. But more angry at myself. You see, all this time I've lived the Bohemian life and preached its dogma. We are young! We are free to do what we like and love whoever we want, whenever we want. I am an artist, after all.' The tremor in her voice told me she had to convince not just me but herself. She breathed in deep and let the breath out slowly.

'Then I met Andrew. And I fell in love with him, Evie. Yes, I know. It sounds so plebeian, so ordinary. And, oh, how I try not to be ordinary! I had a picture in my mind of quite the happy family. Andrew working at the newspaper and me at home, painting when I could, spending time with the children I prayed we would have. When we met that evening at Delmonico's and Andrew told me he could no longer see me, I should have been happy. That was what I wanted, wasn't it? To be free. Unencumbered. And yet . . .' There was a chair nearby and she sank into it.

'I had to be angry,' she said. 'It was all I could do not to reveal that he'd broken my heart.'

'Were you angry enough to kill him?'

She looked up at me. 'Yes. But I didn't. I could not have. I couldn't tell you before, not without revealing the secret you have so skillfully uncovered tonight. But ask anyone here, Evie. They will surely tell you. The night Andrew was killed, there was a salon here at Marie's, and William Kobieta Walker was very much in attendance.'

William Kobieta Walker and I left Marie Gradeau's by the kitchen door, which was his habit, or so I was told once Clarice and I were settled in my carriage.

She waited until we were far from Eighth Street to remove her muffler and hat. 'He is terribly secretive.'

'That is, no doubt, one of the reasons his paintings are so popular. The more mysterious a thing, the more likely it is that people will pay money for it. I've learned that much in the time I've worked with my brother.'

We went to Chelsea and, once Clarice was changed out of her disguise, we drove to Castle Garden for a late supper. It was a fine night and we ate outside amid the flickering candles and the climbing vines that grew on trellises around each table and offered guests a bit of privacy.

Clarice finished the last of her oyster pie and smiled. 'Are you satisfied now that I am not a murderer?'

'I would certainly like to believe you are not, but have no doubt, I will return to Marie Gradeau's and ask about William Walker's presence there on the night of Andrew's death.'

She threw back her head and laughed loud enough for the people around us to stop what they were doing and look our way, including the pinch-faced man who'd been at the museum that morning. I only hoped my brother was paying him enough to cover the cost of his dinner. 'You are the most determined woman I know, Evie. The most determined person.'

I sipped my mint julep. 'Whatever I am doing, I am doing it for Andrew. You see, I feel I owe it to him.' I collected my thoughts. 'Did Andrew ever say anything to you about Madeline?'

'His sister? He told me he held her dear. He said that since the deaths of their parents he was responsible for her well-being, and he certainly thought that included making sure she married well.'

'But he never told you she was here in New York?'

Her head tilted to one side, Clarice sat back and considered my question. 'Is she? I wonder he never mentioned it. You would think he would have introduced us.'

'So he never said he was looking for her? That he was concerned about her?'

'Are you telling me she was here in the city and he didn't know where? That seems unlikely. They were very close.'

I schooled my voice so as not to betray my emotions. 'She was here with a man.'

A tiny smile played along Clarice's lips. 'Good for her!'

'No, it wasn't good for her, Clarice.' I did not mean to snap at her, but at least when I did, Clarice stopped grinning. I pulled in a steadying breath. 'His name is James Crockett and they were seen leaving Bethel together. James . . . Mr Crockett, has been known to seduce, and then abandon, women.'

'And you think Madeline—'

'I am sure of it. And so was Andrew. It is the reason he came to see me that day. To ask for my help. I think he wanted me to talk to Madeline, to talk some sense into her.'

'Then you know this James Crockett, too.'

I did not answer. I did not need to. We exchanged looks, and Clarice knew full well that I was speaking from experience.

She touched her napkin to her lips. 'Do you believe Andrew may have been killed by this James Crockett?'

Honestly, in all the time I'd considered the mystery, in all the ways I'd worked through how it might make sense and what it all might mean, that was one event I had not even imagined.

'James . . . he . . . He is a good many things,' I said and, try as I might, I could not keep myself from stumbling over the words. 'But . . . I . . . I cannot think him a murderer.'

'Yet if Andrew resented Madeline's relationship with this man—'

I interrupted her with a curt shake of my head. 'By the time Andrew knew enough to close in on them, James had already thrown Madeline over.'

Clarice folded her hands on the table in front of her. 'Andrew was an honorable man.'

'And you think—'

'That if he thought his sister had been done wrong – and according to what you tell me, she had been – Andrew might have confronted this James Crockett. There may have been ugly words exchanged and accusations. There could have been a fight.'

I thought back to the nearly pristine scene I'd found in front of the Feejee Mermaid that terrible night. 'I don't think so.'

'Or you don't want to think so.' Clarice did not give me a chance to speak. She knew I would dispute the theory. She knew – somehow, she knew – that she could present me with the evidence and I would still not see the truth. But then, I had always been blind when it came to James.

She went right on: 'What you're telling me, though, is that you believe Andrew's search for Madeline might have had something to do with—' Clarice's word caught on a gurgle of emotion and her eyes suddenly shone with tears. 'You don't think . . . It cannot be . . .' She took a handkerchief from her reticule and dabbed her eyes. 'Oh, Evie, I'm afraid I made a terrible mistake.'

'In regards to?'

'To Andrew, of course. Poor, dear Andrew. That last night we met at Delmonico's . . .' Her voice clogged and she took a minute to school it. 'The last time we were together, Andrew said he had something very important to do and it meant that he could not see me. As I told you, Evie, I got angry. I'm afraid I often act before I think, and that is exactly what I did that night. I assumed he was looking for a way to be done with our relationship. I thought he no longer cared. And now . . .'

'He may have just been trying to tell you that with his worries about Madeline—'

'He could not see me for a while.' She hung her head. 'I didn't give him the chance to explain. I erupted like Etna and never gave him a chance to speak. Oh, Evie, he died thinking me angry at him and I never had a chance . . .' Overcome, she hung her head.

'No doubt Andrew thought there would be time to speak to you again, to explain.'

'But there isn't.' She lifted her head, and the tears streaking her cheeks glistened in the candle glow. 'There wasn't. If only he'd told me—'

'He would have. I'm certain of it. He would most certainly have told you, just as he tried to tell me. I'm afraid we both let him down.'

She pulled in a stuttering breath. 'Then we both must surely do something to remedy the problem. Do you suppose Madeline's disappearance has something to do with Andrew's death?'

'I don't know for certain. I wish I did. If we could find Madeline perhaps we might learn the full truth.'

'You needn't tell me, I know you've looked. You are nothing if not thorough.'

'I have asked where I might. It has done me little good.'

Clarice wiped her eyes one last time and tucked away her handkerchief. 'Madeline has not returned home to Bethel?'

'I don't think she would. I don't think she can. The people of Bethel know she came to New York with a man who was not her husband.'

'Yes, I understand.' She did, and for that I was grateful. 'There are places here, missions of a sort that help women in need.'

I nodded and thought of the note from Sebastian Richter that had arrived that day at the museum and of its dispiriting contents. 'There is no trace of Madeline at any of the missions.'

'Then there must be something else we can do to find her.'

Though we were discussing things no less weighty than murder and the disappearance of a young woman, I couldn't help but smile. 'We?'

Clarice had a glass of sherry in front of her and she sipped and considered me over the rim of the glass. 'Do you think it could be dangerous for you to inquire further?'

'It is already dangerous. As I have told you—'

'Did someone really try to kill you?' As if the very thought was impossible to conceive, she wrinkled her nose. 'I thought you told me that simply to get me to pay attention.'

'Someone tried to kill me.' A shiver shot up my spine. 'Not once but three times.'

Though the very thought still made my insides fill with ice, it distracted Clarice from her regrets. She sat up and braced her elbows on the table. 'That is exciting! Like something out of a novel by Charles Dickens!'

'It is not exciting. Not when it's happening to you,' I told her.

She slapped the table. 'Then we must stop it from happening. How?'

It wasn't as if I hadn't considered the question myself dozens of time. But talking through the problem made the path before me somehow clearer. 'I must find the murderer. And I must determine what happened to Madeline. With those two mysteries solved, the threat to me should vanish.'

'And you know I am not the murderer.'

'I know I hope you are not, but I will not know the truth—'

'Until you ask at Marie Gradeau's.' Clarice waved away the problem with one hand. 'Let us just take that on faith for now, shall we? So if I didn't kill Andrew, and you are sure it is not this Crockett fellow . . .' She gave me time to say otherwise and when I did not, she went right on. 'Who else might have done it?'

I thought about all I'd been through in the days since I'd come across Andrew there at the museum. 'It was not Jeffrey Hollister,' I told her. 'He himself told me he didn't do it.'

'Very well. Then who else had reason?'

'Well, there is Frederick Withnower.' I told her the story of Frederick's father, Maynard, and how he had been ruined by a newspaper article written by Andrew's father. 'Frederick himself is destroyed,' I added. 'I saw it for myself. He is here in New York and, in fact, was in the city on the night of the murder, and he is in such reduced circumstances, he is forced to live at St John's House of Hospitality.'

Clarice pursed her lips. 'I have heard of the place. It is for the poorest of the poor. If he is so debased—'

'Then he has reason to be bitter.'

'And if he is bitter—'

'He might very well have murdered Andrew.'

FIFTEEN

*E*nter here and find comfort and hope.

The sign outside the door of St John's House of Hospitality did not so much cheer me as send a frisson of fear up my spine.

If I had hope here of finding the man who murdered Andrew Emerson, I might very well be about to confront the person who had also been trying to kill me.

As for comfort . . .

I twitched away the ice that built between my shoulder blades and raised my hand to knock on the door.

There would be no comfort – not for me and certainly not for Madeline if I ever found her – until I discovered who killed Andrew, and why.

When I rapped at the door, I was grateful no one was around to realize the sound echoed that of my knees knocking together. As grateful as I was that I had thought to tell Mercer to wait with my carriage and instructed him that if I was not back outside in just a few minutes, he must come in and look for me. It was the day after the salon at Marie Gradeau's and broad daylight, yet I found it nearly as impossible to banish my misgivings as I did to cast out the questions that had been plaguing my mind since the night of Andrew's murder.

When the door opened, I forgot my misgivings in a rush and found myself face to face with—

'Frederick Withnower!'

He didn't so much smile at me as angle me a careful look. 'I am afraid you have me at a disadvantage, ma'am.' Frederick was wearing a white shirt but no jacket. His sleeves were rolled above his elbows to reveal muscular arms and the tattoo of a cross. Though he saw me study the tattoo – amazed for I had never seen another tattoo except those upon Jimmy O'Connell – he did not push down his sleeves. Instead, he ran a hand through his salt-and-pepper hair. 'You surely know who I am, yet I do not believe we've met.'

If it was genuine, I was grateful for at least this bit of anonymity. Though the Withnowers were residents of Bethel, Frederick was years older than me, and our families had never socialized. Then again, if he was, indeed, the man who had dogged my steps these last weeks, who had started a fire outside my office and attacked me on Water Street . . .

I sucked in a breath for courage. 'My name is Evangeline,' I told him, leaving off the surname. If it was true and he did not know me, I didn't want to influence his opinion. And if it wasn't true, I might catch him up in a lie. 'I am here to—' The words refused to come and while I sought the best way to approach the subject, Frederick moved back so as to allow me inside.

'You don't have to explain,' he said. 'We ask no questions here. You are welcome.'

Because I didn't know what else to do, I stepped into St John's and Frederick closed the door behind me. I found myself in a long passageway, paneled walls and ceiling with dark wood. There was an open door on my right and it led into an anteroom of the church next door. Ahead of me lay a stairway. To the left of it, the hallway continued on and, here and there in it, men and women in tattered clothes sat on benches against the wall, some of them chatting and others with their heads back and their eyes closed as if they were afraid to face whatever they might see should they open them.

Though he did his best to do it discreetly, I couldn't help but notice that Frederick studied me with as much interest as I did my surroundings. My clothes were surely of a better cut than those of the people I saw there in the passageway and were neither soiled nor frayed. My boots were clean and polished.

'I am sorry to stare.' He glanced away. 'We are not used to women of your class—'

It was on the tip of my tongue to tell him that though my brother was as rich as Croesus, we were of no class at all except the working class. Until I realized that was not what Frederick meant at all.

'You believe me to be an adventuress!'

His cheeks flushed. 'Your clothing tells me you are not a laborer and surely no farm worker. To be so well dressed, I must believe you sell your body on the streets. But have no fear, it is not my place to judge.'

'Nor would I expect you to. But you are certainly wrong about me. I am not—'

He turned a gentle smile on me. 'We are all brothers and sisters here. What we did – what we do – outside these doors is of no consequence. Inside, we ask no questions and we need no excuses. All are welcome. You are welcome.'

I wasn't so sure he'd still believe that if he knew why I was really there.

Before I could say another word, he asked, 'Would you like to pray with me?'

'I would rather talk,' I told him.

'Yes, young women are so often in need of unburdening themselves. Unlike the men who come to us. Most of them would rather keep their pasts and their sins between themselves and their Maker. Women are more open, more inclined to want to tell their stories. We can sit.' He waved me toward the first doorway on the left. 'I will be most happy to listen to whatever you wish to tell me.'

'You?' I did not mean to sound so much the skeptic, yet I could hardly help myself. That day, Frederick was wearing clothes that drooped and were faded, and though he was surely clean enough, his hair combed, and his manner pleasant, there was an air of shabbiness about him that matched that of the people who sat there in the hallway.

'I do beg your pardon,' I said when I realized how impolite I'd sounded. 'I simply thought . . . that is, I expected there might be a minister or a priest or—'

To my surprise, he laughed. 'You think me one of the residents here!' He waved me toward the doorway he'd pointed out earlier and, because I had no choice and refused to leave without all my questions answered, I walked that way. I found myself in a small but neat room that contained bookshelves and a desk with two chairs in front of it. When I sat in one of the chairs, Frederick took the other.

'I am neither minister nor priest, but I am employed here,' he said quite simply. 'To help the unfortunates who find their way to us. If there is anything you need to talk about, Miss Evangeline, then I am most willing to listen.'

It was more of an opportunity than I could have asked for, and I knew I had to take it.

'I have come about Andrew Emerson,' I said. Before he could speak, I added, 'You didn't like him.'

His hands on his knees, Frederick went very still, and the light that seeped from the single window behind the desk threw shadows along his face like broad strokes of black ink. His features were large and strong and, in this light, his face looked to be carved from stone, like a death's head on a grave marker.

'What do you know about Andrew Emerson?' he asked.

'I know you were at his funeral. Just as I know you disrespected his final resting place.'

He had the good grace to blush a color that reminded me of the red ribbon pinned to my cloak. 'I thought it a private moment.'

'And so it would have been if I hadn't been there, anonymous in the crowd, much as you were. I understand your animosity toward the Emerson family.'

His gaze shot to mine. 'Do you? Then there should be no question as to why I did what I did after the service.'

'It was Andrew's father who did your family wrong, not Andrew himself.'

He waved away this particular bit of reasoning with one, square-fingered hand. 'Bah! What difference does it make? The Emersons always thought themselves better than everyone else in Bethel.'

'Yet your anger seems to go deeper than that.'

Frederick pushed himself off his chair and stalked as far as the door. The room was not large and he came back my way in a moment, fire in his eyes and his hands curled into fists, and I could not help it, my heart bumped against my ribs and I wondered if I'd made a mistake being alone with him.

He stopped two feet in front of me and, grateful, I let go a stuttering breath. Still, the anger in his voice shivered through the air and froze my blood. 'I could not forgive him! I went to talk to him, you see, when I learned that his father was interested in my good father's business dealings. I talked to Andrew, I told him I knew what his father had planned. I told him the information they were going to publish was false, that I had the proof, but . . .' He threw his hands in the air. 'Andrew wouldn't listen, no more than his father would when I tried to speak to him. They were interested only in creating a sensation.'

'And you have been angry about it for a long time.'

'Wouldn't you feel the same way?' Frederick's question pinged against the walls which were paneled in the same dark wood as the hallway. 'They killed my father. They ruined my family.'

'And so Andrew Emerson's murder, it was justified. It was surely divine retribution.'

As if he had never thought of Andrew's death that way – or as if he had and did not want to admit it – Frederick stood frozen, his mouth open and his breath suspended. The next second, he dropped back into his seat and hung his head.

'Forgive me,' he whispered, and I knew he wasn't talking to me. 'Forgive me for my weakness, Father. For my failings. I have surely sinned.'

I, too, held my breath for a few moments before I felt ready to ease my way toward the truth. 'On the night Andrew was murdered, you were here in New York,' I said.

Frederick's head shot up. 'Of course I was. I live here in the city now. But how on earth would you know that?'

'Because you had an appointment at the American Museum to discuss employment with Mr P.T. Barnum.'

His face went ashen and Frederick leapt again from his chair and went to the door. He closed it then turned to me, his back to the door. 'Who told you?'

'It hardly matters. I know it's true.'

'And no one here can know it.' He came back toward me so quickly, I fell back in my chair before I even realized it was a sign of weakness I could not afford to show him. I forced myself to sit up, to sit tall, my shoulders steady.

'If they know . . .' He cast a glance toward the now-closed door. 'If they know I am seeking employment in another place, they might ask me to leave here.'

'And you cannot. Yes, I understand. Because of what Andrew's father did to your family, you are destitute.'

'No, no, don't you see? I told you, I am not an inmate here.

I am not so destitute as I am desperate! Certainly it would help to have more coins in my own pocket. But I don't want the money for me. There is much we need at St John's and many we serve. The immigrant ships come to port every day and our population grows with them. The poor arrive from the countryside, displaced by new machinery that does the work they once performed by hand. There are those who find it impossible to turn away from alcohol, those who are abused, those with no hope.'

'And you want the money for them?'

The briefest of smiles touched his lips. 'Yes, of course. But I cannot let Father William and Father Axtel know. If they think I am frivolous, that I desire work out in the world beyond St John's, they might send me away, and if they do that, then I cannot complete my penance and prove my contrition.'

My insides went cold. 'Penance. Because you are the one who killed Andrew. Did you . . .' I ran my tongue across my lips. 'Have you tried also to silence me?'

Frederick's dark brows dipped over his eyes. 'Are you saying—'

I was, but I could not do it sitting so close to the man. I got up and paced to the door. 'I have been attacked, Mr Withnower, and I believe it is because I am investigating the murder of Andrew Emerson. It is only natural that the man who killed him would want to stop me from exposing him.'

'And you think I am that man?'

'I think you have every reason to hate the Emerson family.'

'Yes, I have admitted that much. Just as I admit that holding onto that hate is a sin, and for that sin, I must atone. I have tried.' His voice broke and his shoulders rose and fell. 'I have tried to make peace with my father's death. I have done everything I can think to make myself a better man. But there are times, I admit, when the anger still overpowers me as it did at Emerson's funeral. I went there, you see, to test myself, to show the world and the Lord that I had conquered the demons that snatched at my soul. I failed. You saw it for yourself. I failed, and I have prayed mightily to be forgiven for my sins.'

'Then you did not kill Andrew?'

I think he would have laughed if he had not been so burdened by emotion. Frederick simply shook his head. 'Emerson, he was killed the night I visited Mr Barnum at the museum?'

I nodded.

'A Friday, then.'

I nodded again.

'Yes, I was at the museum on Friday but did nothing more than talk with Mr Barnum there. I left immediately. You can ask him yourself if you'd ever dare converse with a man so famous! We talked, then he walked me to the door.'

And was still home for dinner. I knew as much because when I found Andrew's body, the attendant needed to go to Fifth Avenue to tell Phin the news.

'Still, I can understand how you might not believe me. Come with me, Miss Evangeline. You'll see.' He got up and, when he opened the door and started down the hallway, I followed along, nodding briefly to Mercer who I saw now inside, standing like a sentinel at the doorway, his eyes on me. At the end of the passageway we found ourselves in a large room where row upon row of tables were set and, against the far wall, two men in clerical garb were readying pots of soup they would soon dole out to the poor folk who waited in the passageway.

'Father Axtel.' Frederick approached a man with a receding hairline and doughy features. 'This is Miss Evangeline, and she has some questions for you.'

The priest wore spectacles, and when he set down the pot of soup he was carrying and looked at me, the lenses were befogged. 'What can I do for you?'

Actually, I wasn't sure. 'I am here to inquire about an unfortunate incident that happened two weeks ago,' I told him. 'A friend of mine was killed.'

Perhaps it was because of the place he lived, the kind of work he did, and the poor unfortunates who came to him for help that the priest looked not the least bit surprised.

'It was a Friday. Two weeks ago,' I explained.

'And?' Father Axtel looked to Frederick for clarification.

'This young lady thinks I might have done it,' Frederick told him.

'Done it? The murder?' Behind his glasses, Father Axtel's

eyes were wide. 'You cannot really believe that?' he asked me. 'Mr Withnower is a man of impeccable character.'

'As was the man who was killed,' I told him. 'Which is why I must get to the truth.'

'The truth, yes.' Father Axtel stepped away from the table. 'You did not tell her?' he asked Frederick.

'I doubted she would believe me,' he replied.

'Then I will tell you.' The priest turned my way. 'That Friday like every Monday, Wednesday and Friday evening, Mr Withnower conducts classes for our residents. He teaches them to read and write. He was out early in the evening, I remember that much. But then he was here. Oh, yes, he was most assuredly here. I remember it clearly, for we had a disruption with one of our residents that evening, and Mr Withnower helped me calm her.'

I didn't know if I should feel gratitude or disappointment or relief that I had chanced an encounter with a man who might have wanted me dead and come through it unscathed. I turned to Frederick. 'I must apologize, sir. I thought—'

'Your apology isn't necessary,' he told me. 'I see that you are a sincere and serious young woman, and you seek to learn the truth. You surely cannot be faulted for that.' He glanced toward the door Father William had gone to open so as to allow the people in the hallway in. 'We'll be serving luncheon soon. If you'd care to join us, you are most welcome.'

I declined. Not because I was uneasy sharing a meal with those who found nourishment at St John's but because I did not wish to take away a portion of their food. When I told Frederick as much and pressed a few coins into his hand to help defray the cost of the next meal, he thanked me for the kindness and walked me to the door.

We were almost there, our paths crossing with those who were eager for a place at St John's table, and just at the stairway I'd seen when I walked into the building, when out of the corner of my eye I saw a flash of red streak down the steps. The next thing I knew, the air filled with a high-pitched scream like the wail of a lost soul and a woman – short and thin and with her mouth twisted in fury – darted in front of me and punched me in the stomach.

The air rushed out of me along with a gurgle of pain, but that did not stop the woman. 'Took her! Took her!' she screamed, all the while she battered me about the head and body with her fists.

Caught off guard, I reacted reflexively, covering my face with my arms. I staggered backward and lost my footing and, before I could right myself, I tumbled to the floor and the screaming, wailing woman saw her advantage and jumped on top of me.

She was rail-thin with hair the color of carrots, and it flowed over her shoulders like lava from a volcano. Her eyes were wild.

I squirmed, and when her knee connected with the wound on my side I let out a yelp, all the while slapping at her, scrambling to fight back as much as I was able. She was remarkably strong. The woman grasped a white handkerchief in one hand, and the fabric trailed from her clenched fist. It fluttered against my face as soft as a butterfly's kiss, in strange counterpoint to the clap of her knuckles when they connected with my nose.

I kicked and twisted and, over the woman's shoulders, I saw Frederick Withnower and the ever-faithful Mercer wrestle to get a good hold of her so they might pull her away from me.

'No! Lucine, no!' Frederick did his best to overpower the woman but whatever madness fueled her also gave her impossible strength. He called for more help and one of the men who'd been waiting for a meal rushed to his side. Mercer caught Lucine around the waist, but she had her knees on either side of my ribs and did not budge when he pulled at her, and when she stopped punching and wrapped her hands around my neck, the other man did his best to release them. For his troubles, Lucine snapped at him and bit his arm and when she turned her full attention to me, her mouth twisted and her eyes wild, there was blood on her lips.

'Beer. Beer and the horse and mare. The green door. The green door!' Lucine tightened her hold, slowly cutting off the air to my windpipe, and I struggled to pry her fingers away. My heart raced and then I swear it stopped altogether and Lucine's pale face faded in and out of my vision. Stars burst behind my eyes and—

'Lucine!' Frederick's voice boomed through the hallway and brought me again to awareness just in time to see him catch up a handful of Lucine's crimson hair and yank as hard as he could. She screamed and thrashed and loosened her hold on me, and with Mercer's help, Frederick dragged her off me.

I cannot say how long I laid there fighting for air, my own rough breaths nothing compared to Lucine's vicious curses.

While Frederick struggled to keep his hold on her, Father Axtel raced into the hallway, his face red. Mercer was already at my side, his face creased with worry and his cheeks stained with tears, and the priest knelt beside him and took my hand.

'Breathe,' Father Axtel instructed, and I did not have the strength to tell him that though I was trying it was mightily painful. He called for water and duly administered it and, though it felt like fire going down my throat, I forced myself to drink then raised myself on my elbows and pushed over to the wall so I could prop myself against it.

'Oh, dear.' In the scuffle, my cloak had fallen open and Mercer's gaze went to my torso. When I looked there, too, I saw a stain of blood upon my blue gown. 'She has a knife!' His face paled and he called out to Frederick. 'Be careful! Lucine has a knife!'

'No. No!' The words rasped out of me and I held out a hand and waved it back and forth to try to better communicate. 'It is . . . an old wound.' I pressed a hand to my midsection. There was blood but not much. 'I'm . . .' I would have liked to tell him I was fine but that seemed a fantasy. Instead, I pulled myself to my feet and somehow stood, though my knees felt as if they were made of wet plaster. I braced a hand against the stairway bannister and looked over to where Frederick still had his arms around Lucine.

Though held fast, she still spat and kicked. She somehow managed to free an arm from Frederick's grip and, when she did, she pointed a trembling finger at me.

'Took her! You took her!' she screamed, and that handkerchief dangled from her fingers like a signal to all the world of my supposed guilt. 'The hell-bitch took her in the night. Wants to take me, too. No! No! Damn her to hell, she will not. She cannot make me go.'

Though I knew she could no longer harm me, I kept my distance. 'Who is she?' I asked Father Axtel. 'And why—'

A woeful shake of his head spoke volumes and, when Father William joined us in the hallway carrying a small, dark vial and a glass of water, Father Axtel nodded. Father William poured from the vial and took the cup to Lucine.

She cursed him and threw her head side to side, doing all she could to keep the cup from her lips, but Father William persisted, and though she surely spit out more of the concoction than she swallowed, swallow she did, and after a minute some of the stiffness went out of Lucine. Another few sips and her screams melted into low grunts.

'Horse and mare,' she mumbled. 'Mare and the green door.' Her gaze caught mine and her eyes flared. 'Beer and the green door!' she wailed then went limp in Frederick's arms.

I knew the danger was over, yet when Frederick scooped her into his arms and carried her up the stairs, I kept far back. That is, until that handkerchief fell from her limp hand and fluttered to the floor.

I bent to retrieve it.

'Sticky,' I mumbled to myself, my fingers playing over the fabric, sticky with something that felt and looked like honey.

SIXTEEN

'She must have thought you were someone else.'

Frederick Withnower set a cup of tea on the small table he pulled between the two chairs in the office where I'd conducted my interview of him a mere hour earlier. My head still muddled by the unexpected attack in the passageway, I stared into the depths of the steaming liquid while he went to the other chair and sat down.

'It's the only thing that might explain why it happened,' he said. 'Lucine must have thought you were someone else.'

Still too upended by all that had transpired to think my way through the incident, I took a careful sip of tea. The heat of the liquid felt heavenly on my injured throat.

'Unless you know our Lulu and you are for some reason her mortal enemy!'

Surprised by the comment, I looked up to find Frederick with a smile on his face that transformed his features from fierce to ruggedly handsome. His brown eyes brimmed with so much kindness, I could not help myself, I smiled back.

'You are teasing,' I said.

'Yes, I am.' He drank from his own cup. 'I thought to relieve some of your worry.'

'I am not . . .' I twitched away the sensation that made me feel as if there were cold hands against my back and slipped my cloak from the back of the chair and over my shoulders. 'I am not so much worried as I am grateful,' I told him. 'If you weren't there—'

'But I was and so was your brave carriage driver, Mr Mercer. It was the Lord's plan.'

Luncheon was being served, and the hallway outside the office was empty, but I cast a glance in that direction nonetheless, thinking of all that just happened. Try as I might, I could not banish the image of Lucine's wild eyes from my mind.

'Is it the Lord's plan to allow people to suffer so inside their heads that they act the way that poor woman does?' I asked him.

Frederick shook his head. 'I do not understand it. No one does. There are so many poor unfortunates.'

I thought back to what Father Axtel had told me earlier. 'She's the one who caused the disruption in your reading and writing lesson on the night Andrew Emerson was killed.'

He nodded. 'I'm afraid Lulu has caused many a disruption since she's been here. I have tried to work with her, yet the poor woman . . .' He finished his tea and set down his cup. 'She came to us not long ago. If you can imagine it, she was even more anguished then than she is now.'

I could not imagine it. I did not want to try. 'What is her history?' I asked him.

'No one knows. I was walking late one night and heard a sound like mewling coming from an alleyway. I assumed it was a cat and thought to pass by, but something led me . . . I must say I do believe the hand of the Lord was in my actions. I knew I had to see for myself what was making the awful sound. In that, Miss Evangeline . . .' His cheeks shot through with color. 'I do believe we have something in common even if it just our curiosity.'

I knew acknowledging the compliment would only embarrass Frederick further, so I asked, 'It wasn't a cat, was it?'

'No. It was Lucine . . . Lulu as we call her. She had been in the alleyway foraging for food in the gutters, and when she heard my footfalls she folded herself behind a barrel so as not to be discovered. When I approached . . .' He hauled in a breath and let it out slowly. 'She was so frightened I thought the poor woman would die right before my eyes.'

'You brought her here.'

He nodded.

'And the curses she threw at me?'

His shoulders rose and fell. 'Words she says over and over. The horse and mare. The beer. The green door. You heard her. And yet . . .' Thinking, he cocked his head. 'It is mighty odd. She said something to you I've never heard her say before. She said she didn't want to be taken away as someone else was. As many hours as I've spent with Lulu, I've never heard her mention anything like that.'

'Then why say it to me?'

He shrugged.

'And who was she talking about?'

Another shrug. 'If we knew, we might begin to understand the demons that plague poor Lulu day and night. And if we could only get her to stop worrying about this horse and the mare and the green door, perhaps we could get her to tell us more about herself. Then we might able to help her, or at least to help find her family, if she does, indeed, have one. The way it is, we do what we are able for her, but because she is so peculiar the other residents fear her. She has disrupted my reading and writing class. She's raced into the refectory screaming and interrupted dinner. She's even stood up and started dancing during Mass. You can imagine how that upset everyone! But she's never been violent before. Not until . . .' As if gauging how I might react, Frederick slid me a look. 'Not until she saw you.'

I did not know what to make of it, so I sloughed it off. 'As you said, she must have thought I was someone else.'

As if he was grateful I understood, he let go a long breath. 'She has little hold on reality. And that handkerchief, she had it with her when I found her, and she clutches it as if it is her lifeblood.'

It was the first I remembered I had scooped the handkerchief off the floor, and I offered it to Frederick. 'Then she must surely have this back. It is . . .' After I handed it to him, I scraped my hand against the skirt of my gown, but still, my fingers felt slightly sticky and it made me wonder. 'Father William gave Lulu laudanum to calm her, didn't he? I have had it myself recently because of an injury and I remember a sweetness on my lips after. Did he add honey to the dose as my physician did?'

Frederick frowned. 'No, I am sure of it. We use the concoction frequently here, for the people who come to us are sometimes injured and often ill. I have suggested we add honey to mask the bitter taste of the laudanum but Father William insists we should not make the dose so much a delicacy for those who need it as we must make it a reminder for them to curb their behaviors.' He gave me a conspiratorial look, but not before he glanced toward the open door and the hallway to be sure no one was about. 'I do not know about you, Miss Evangeline, but I do not believe Lulu is capable of curbing her behaviors.'

I was afraid I had to agree. 'It is a pity. But perhaps . . .' I bit back my suggestion; Frederick and the priests there at St John's surely knew more about the people who came to their door than I ever would.

Frederick grinned. 'There's no need to be shy about your opinions. You are most obviously a woman who is intent on finding answers. What is your advice when it comes to Lulu? For I'll admit, we have done everything we can think to do for the poor woman and nothing helps.'

I had never been shy about stating my opinion, yet somehow offering it to Frederick caused heat to flare in my cheeks. 'I thought perhaps we could talk to her. Now that she has had the laudanum she should be calmer and, if she is awake, if we could speak to Lulu, there might be a chance we can find the root of her fears. If she's relieved of the burden of her worries, there is a chance she might be less of a problem.'

'We have tried talking to her, of course. But now that you mention it . . .' Frederick rose and waved me toward the door. 'We have not had a woman talk to her. I wonder if that might make a difference.'

We looked into the refractory and found Mercer just finishing up luncheon and regaling the residents there with talk of horses and carriages. I insisted he sit and enjoy, left my cloak with him so that I was unencumbered and followed behind Frederick to the second floor of St John's where the men were housed and then on to the third floor where the women slept in two large and airy dormitory rooms. Lulu was not one of them and it was no mystery why. As Frederick had mentioned, she was as peculiar in her head as our oddities back at the museum were in their physical bodies; the others there at St John's feared her and, as our oddities proved, fear often led to hatred and violence. Lulu was alone in a room at the end of the hallway, for the safety of the other residents as well as for her own.

It was a tiny room with no windows and little light and Frederick must have known I was thinking just that when he opened the door to allow me inside and lowered his voice.

'We would rather she was with the other women but the windows in the other rooms proved a danger. More than once, Lulu has tried to leave by way of them.'

She was half-awake on a small bed pushed into the corner and could not have failed to hear. As I had told Frederick downstairs, I had no experience in these things, and yet I knew somehow that his comment provided me the opportunity to set my plan into action.

Considering how recently the woman in the bed had attacked me and how my throat still ached from the pressure of her fingers around it, I am not certain how I found the courage to approach her bed. Perhaps it was because, in the feeble light of the single lamp next to the bed, Lulu looked so pale against the white blankets, so small and so forlorn. Indeed, the only color in the room seemed to be the splash of her fiery hair against the pillow and, looking at it, I couldn't help but be reminded of Madeline. Madeline, too, had flaming hair. Both women were slim and fine-boned with features that made for a face that wasn't as pretty as it was delicate. Both . . . a stab of sadness ate at my insides . . . both Lulu and Madeline were lost souls, each in her own way.

Considering it all made Lulu seem suddenly more human to me and less a threat than a pity and, thinking it, the tightness in my chest eased and my quick, sharp breaths settled. When I crossed the room I found I was able to offer my attacker a soft smile.

'Mr Withnower tells me you do not like it here, Lulu, and that you are anxious to leave.'

Like an animal, as wary as it is cunning, she had watched us when we came into the room but now she closed her eyes and turned her head away. 'Beer and the green door,' she murmured.

'Yes, that is exactly what I wish to speak to you about. Beer and the green door.'

She turned again to look at me, a smile playing over her thin lips that had not so much to do with her mood or her thoughts as it did with the dose of laudanum she'd been forced to swallow. 'They'll take you, too,' was all she said.

'That is exactly what I'm afraid of.' With a look at Frederick to make sure he thought it was all right, I sat on the edge of Lulu's bed and, when Lulu did not come at me, when she did nothing more than lie there, the hatred in her eyes replaced by an empty stare, I relaxed even more. 'Can you tell me, Lulu, how do you know they will take me?'

'Will.' She nodded and pushed herself up on her elbows, the better to face me as we talked and even that bit of exertion caused a hitch in her breath. She slid a glance toward Frederick, leaned forward and whispered, 'They take them all.'

'All?'

'All the pretty maids. Taken in the night. Oh, yes. *Si, si.* Taken. *Adios.*'

I had dealt with enough shippers and suppliers, with enough ships' captains at the docks when I supervised the arrival of museum goods that I was familiar with the Spanish words, but it surprised me that Lulu was. A questioning look over my shoulder brought no answers from Frederick, so I returned my attention to the woman in the bed.

'These pretty maids, where do they go?' I asked her.

Her besotted smile faded and a deep V creased her brow. 'They don't come back. They don't come back.' She slammed a fist against the bed. 'They never come back. She didn't. She told me she would stay, but she didn't come back.'

'Who?' I asked her.

'Elizabetha Dorothy Jemima Arbower.' As if she was proud of remembering all the syllables of so complicated a name, Lulu bobbed her head. 'Pretty golden hair. Like sunshine. They thought I was sleeping.' She gave me a slow, exaggerated wink that might have been comical had I not known that the laudanum muddled her senses and weakened her ability to control her movements.

'Almost closed, almost closed.' She squeezed her eyes nearly shut and looked at me through the tiniest of slits. 'They thought I was asleep. And they came into the room and . . .' The familiar and terrifying flash of madness flared in her blue eyes and I did not dare wait to see if the laudanum would control it. If I fled, I would get no further answers from Lulu. And I wanted to hear more.

I pressed her hand in mine.

As if she did not recognize the touch of another human being, she froze, her words and her breath suspended while she slid a look down to where our hands were together on the bed. When she looked back to me, Lulu's eyes filled with tears.

'They told her it was time to wake up, but it wasn't. It was time . . .' Whatever thoughts played through Lulu's head, they were obviously dark enough to eclipse even the effects of the laudanum. Her spine collapsed. Her shoulders dropped. Her voice was so low I wondered I heard it at all. 'Time for sweetness and sleep.'

'Sweetness?' The word brought to mind the handkerchief. I held it out to her and, instantly, Lulu grabbed for it. Even then, I did not let go but held on so tight to the fabric she could not steal the handkerchief away. I looked her in the eye. 'It was honey, wasn't it? Did they give Elizabetha Dorothy Jemima Arbower laudanum and honey? Is that why she fell asleep?'

'Took her in the night. Far, far away.'

'And you found the handkerchief when she was gone and you kept it as a memory of your friend?'

Lulu did not answer and I could not so cruelly tease her any longer. I let go of the handkerchief and she gathered it up in her palm, closed her fingers over it and nestled it against her cheek. She did not so much lie back down as melt into the blankets.

'Beer and the green door.' Her eyes drifted shut. 'Far, far away. Goodbye. *Adios.*'

The weight of my encounter with Lulu sat heavy upon my shoulders. By this, I do not mean the after-effects of her attack. By the time I collected Mercer and left St John's, I had sloughed off the tremors of fear that had started up a rough rhythm inside me when Lulu had come at me and the wound in my side bled but a little. Though my throat ached, I knew it was nothing that time, hot tea and perhaps a glass or two of sherry could not fix.

It was the impact of my conversation with her that saddened me. Her desperation. Her isolation. Whatever it was that made Lulu attack me – whether it was my appearance, which made her think I was someone else, as Frederick had suggested, or simply the sickness inside her brain – I was sorry for the woman. Sorry and intrigued by all she had told me.

Who was the mysterious Elizabetha Dorothy Jemima Arbower? And where had she been taken?

Goodbye. *Adios.*

Where had Elizabetha gone? And why was Lulu terrified to think she might be next to leave?

The questions played over and over again in my mind as we traveled back to the museum. They were especially troublesome because I knew I would find no answers. My solution to the ensuing frustration was simple: it was still early in the day and there was much work to be done there at the corner of Broadway and Ann Street. That work would help rid my mind of the miasma that had settled in it at St John's.

Once I arrived, I hoped to slip up the stairs and to my office unnoticed, but I might have known my plan would be thwarted. Yes, I know circumstances do not always play into my expectations, for the world does not work according to the wishes of mortals.

Unless that mortal is P.T. Barnum.

Somehow, he knew I had arrived and had already rushed out of his office, kissed my cheek and handed off my cloak to an attendant when he stepped back and gave me a searching look.

'Good heavens, Evie! What's happened to you?'

I touched a hand to my hair and only then realized it was half undone, around my shoulders on the right and caught up in neat fashion on my left.

'It's windy out,' I told him.

He pressed his lips together. 'It is not.'

'Then raining.'

'No, and even if it were, that would not account for your dishevelment. Can you . . .' Though Phin is not usually either interested or worried about things like a woman's hair, he wiggled his fingers, indicating that I should do my best to get mine under control. 'There is someone waiting in my office to see you,' he said when I did not move fast enough to pin up my hair. 'Perhaps you should go upstairs for a minute and get yourself in order, then come back down.'

Even though his office door was closed, I looked at it over his shoulder. 'Who?'

'Don't you like surprises?' His eyes twinkled.

'No, I do not. Who?'

'Go on, Evie!' He put a hand to my shoulder and nudged

me toward the stairs. 'Hurry. I promise you will not be disappointed.'

I was not convinced, but as I apparently had no choice, I went upstairs as instructed and did as much as I could to make myself presentable. It was not so easy considering I had not realized the sleeve of my green gown had been torn in my confrontation with Lulu. After I was done pinning up my hair and splashing my face with water, I nudged up my collar so as to conceal the red marks of Lulu's fingers on my neck and tossed a shawl over my shoulders, the better to hide the damage to my dress. As presentable as I was likely to be after so eventful a morning, I was outside Phin's office in less than ten minutes.

I knocked at the door, and I couldn't have been more surprised when it was opened for me by none other than Sebastian Richter.

'Good afternoon, Miss Barnum.' As always, he looked elegant, and his manner was charming when he bowed slightly at the waist. He stepped back to allow me into the office. 'We've been waiting for you.'

'Have you?' Phin was seated behind his desk and, since he made no response to my searching look, I turned my attention back to our visitor. 'How may I help you?'

'Your brother has already done that,' Richter informed me with a smile. 'As for why we requested your presence—'

'Ah! Is it that time already?' Before Richter could finish whatever he was about to say, Phin popped out of his chair and scampered around me and to the door. 'I must meet with the sculptor who is delivering a new bust for an exhibit. Shakespeare! What do you think? That ought to impress our visitors, eh?' As if picturing the display, he put out both hands, thumbs and forefingers squared. 'We'll put ol' Will right there beside Lafayette and Franklin. Or should he be between Socrates and Cicero?' Thus working through the problem, Phin left the office and closed the door behind him.

'Ah, finally!'

The exclamation from Richter brought me spinning from the door to face him. His response was a smile.

'You and my brother have obviously shared a secret,' I said. 'Am I to be told what's going on?'

'You are, indeed, my dear Miss Barnum, for it involves you directly.'

I am hardly purblind. Nor am I some prim young miss who is apt to play coy. Ignoring the fast-paced tattoo that started behind my ribs, I raised my chin. 'I do believe you have something to ask me, sir?'

'I do, Miss Barnum . . . Evie!' Richter closed in on me, took my hand and folded his fingers over mine, and his voice was as soft and as affectionate as his touch. 'I have come here today to ask your brother's permission and he has given it wholeheartedly. I suppose I might have waited to speak to you some moonlit evening or in some spot like a garden that might be more conducive to the mood, but to tell the truth, I cannot wait. I am too excited by the prospect of all I hope. I would ask you—'

'What?'

Was my voice that breathless?

It was difficult to tell while my blood whooshed in my ears.

Richter's hand tightened over mine. 'I would be honored, Evie, if you would be my wife.'

There is a time in every girl's life when she dreams of such a moment, and in years gone by I was no different from all the other starry-eyed misses. In those dreams, I saw exactly how I would respond to the handsome man who stood before me, a smile tickling his lips and his heart on his sleeve.

I would stammer, but not too much.

I would blush if I was able.

I would smile in response to his loving expression and dip my head so as to enjoy the feelings that flashed through me just a little longer, savoring the warmth, treasuring the moment and committing it ever to memory.

But that was before I met James Crockett.

The thought intruded and the warmth inside me turned to ice and, little by little, I felt my smile fade. 'There is much you don't know about me,' I told Richter.

'I know you are intelligent, kind, and that you would love my children as if they were your own. I would hope . . .' He stepped nearer and bent his head just enough so that our lips might touch if either of us moved another inch. 'I would hope you would come to love me, too.'

I could not equivocate, not at such a moment. 'I would,' I confessed, 'for I already hold you in great esteem.'

A smile flashed through his eyes, sending out sapphire sparks that heated me through. 'Then we are on equal footing, for each time I've seen you, my admiration has grown.'

'But . . .' I swallowed down my misgivings. 'If you knew—'

He put a finger to my lips. 'Whatever it is, it doesn't matter.'

'But it does.'

'Then that is decided.' He backed away and for one terrible moment I thought my hesitation had sealed my fate. I could not give him my answer and he could not wait. If I had any hope of happiness with Sebastian Richter, my vacillation had shattered it.

'You will think about it,' he said instead, and I released the breath I was holding. 'And then you will give me your answer.'

Relief swept through me and that alone told me that though my head might not be clear on the subject, my heart knew what it wanted.

'You don't mind waiting?' I asked.

He had already reached for his hat and his silver-tipped walking stick, and he paused with them in his hands. 'I had hoped we might seal our agreement with a kiss. I do mind waiting for that.'

So did I, and there seemed only one way to tell him. Before he could move another inch toward the door, I closed in on Sebastian Richter and kissed him.

His arm went around me, his mouth closed over mine and again my heart reminded me that I knew what I wanted – I only had to speak the words.

And yet I could not.

By the time he released me from his grasp and I'd gathered my senses enough to step back, I was breathing hard. Sebastian didn't hold it against me; his breaths were ragged, too.

'I will let you know,' I told him. 'Very soon.'

He clapped his hat on his head. 'Very soon. For in all honesty, Evie . . .' he slipped a hand over my chin and caressed my cheek, '. . . I cannot wait much longer.'

SEVENTEEN

I would like to say that after Sebastian left I returned to my museum duties and accomplished a great deal.

But I have never been a very good liar.

Once Richter was gone, I first had to deal with my brother, who did not understand why I hadn't accepted the marriage proposal on the spot.

'He needs to know.' Thinking we would celebrate, Phin had come back to his office wearing a smile, and I faced him across his desk and watched his expression melt little by little. 'He needs the truth about me, Phin.'

His shoulders fell and the look Phin gave me was not so much a scowl as it was a reflection of his honest concern. 'And if he rejects you?'

Ah, if he rejected me . . .

Even hours later, the words swirled through my head, one moment daring me to remain firm, be brave, and speak the truth, and the next taunting me with the scene that would play out if I told Sebastian the terrible truth and he walked away from me because of it.

I am ashamed to admit that though it would wound me and destroy what I hoped would be a happy, loving – and passionate – relationship with Sebastian, I had an even bigger worry about telling him of all that had happened back in Bethel.

If Richter rejected me, I would never have the opportunity to be a mother to his children.

And if he put the word about that Miss Evangeline Barnum was a wanton woman with a sordid past and a bastard child and no man would have me because of it? Then I might never have the chance to have another child of my own.

That day and all the next morning I wrestled with the decision, and by noon, when I should have been tallying the morning's receipts, I had made up my mind. Yes, I was nervous. The next hours would determine my future. Yes, I questioned my own judgement and the words I knew I had to speak. Still, I called for Mercer and asked him to take me to Sebastian Richter's brewery.

To Mercer's eternal credit, he did not question my request nor did he comment on the fact that I was edgy and preoccupied the entire journey, even when we were hindered by a logjam of buggy and cart traffic and he turned from his high seat at the front of the carriage and tried to make conversation through the open window.

I am afraid my blank stare and disordered responses to his pleasant questions were not what he expected, and the poor man finally gave up and concentrated on driving.

By the time we arrived in that area of the Bowery known as *Kleindeutschland* or *Little Germany*, the scent of hops and malt filled the air. My heart clattered every bit as loudly as the beer wagons that drove away from the brewery, their wooden wheels clumping out a rough tempo against the paving stones, one after another, packed with fat barrels filled with beer. I couldn't help but watch all the activity in awestruck wonder. Workers scurried about. Horses whinnied. And all those carts and all the barrels of beer on them were headed to satisfy a thirst the likes of which this country had not seen before.

Richter's brewery was as much a wonder of industry as my brother's museum was of imagination, a red-brick building that took up an entire city block. The building itself was as solid and as firm as Sebastian's character, its flat roof corniced all around with blocks of stone like dragon's teeth so the brewery looked like a castle from a Germanic tale. I have enough of a head for business to know this was more than just a tribute to Sebastian's homeland. It was a reminder to all that he'd come to these shores with little and made a name – and a fortune – for himself. It was notice to all who arrived as strangers, as Sebastian had, that they, too, could build lives and futures that made the voyage over thousands of miles of water worthwhile. And it was an advertisement of sorts every bit as bold as my brother's blatant promotions – *we are immigrants together*. I could just about hear the words spoken in Sebastian's tantalizing accent. *You must buy my beer!*

I could hardly fault him for this.

The city of New York and, indeed, the country itself was changing. Over the last years, the population of immigrants – most of them from the Germanic-speaking states of Europe and from Ireland – had exploded. Those people had brought with them their traditions, and for those from places like Wurttemberg, Baden, and Bavaria, one of their most honored customs was that of making – and drinking – beer. With the introduction of railroads and the marvelous canal systems being built throughout the country, breweries such as Sebastian's were more easily able to deliver that beer, and people from here on the eastern seaboard to the faraway states of Ohio, Illinois, Missouri, and beyond had acquired a taste for it.

When I closed in on the building, I saw that there were cherubs carved into the stone around the door and a brewer's star I knew was called a *bierstern*, on the roof. According to what I'd heard about it, the six points of the star represented those things necessary for the making of beer: water, hops, grain, malt, yeast, and the brewer himself.

Inside in the wide lobby with gleaming floors and workers who bustled back and forth, barrels were etched into the wooden stair posts, and the place buzzed with diligence and excitement.

At a front desk elaborately carved with hops and sheaves of wheat, I asked after the owner of the establishment and was looked at so askance by the man there, I was tempted to tell him I was practically Sebastian Richter's wife and he'd best be careful for, in no time at all, I would have power over his employment. I am happy to report that (at least at that moment) I was not feeling either small-minded nor mean. Instead, I told the man I was sure Mr Richter would want to see me and waited when he walked away (not too quickly). He was back in ten minutes and accompanied by another, older man, with a sour expression and small, dark eyes.

'You're asking after Mr Richter.'

'Yes.' My answer was as smooth as my smile. 'I am eager to speak to him. I am Evangeline Barnum.'

I cannot say which worked the magic, knowing who I was or just hearing the fabled Barnum name. I only know the older man's face shot through with color.

'Miss Barnum! Of course.' He sent a look to the other man

who was back behind the front desk. 'Why didn't you tell me Miss Barnum was here, Mr Switzer? She certainly must not be kept waiting.'

Grateful, I sailed to his side. 'You can take me to Mr Richter?'

'I can. That is . . .' He wrung hands that were small and fine for a man's. 'He is not here at the moment. He's gone to pay a call at the ministry that was so much a part of his late wife's life.'

I touched a hand to the ribbon pinned to my cloak. 'Succor?'

He was relieved he needn't explain. 'Mr Richter always goes to the office there at this time on Thursday,' he explained. 'He will be back in an hour or two.'

And I could not wait that long.

I thanked the man, ignored Mr Switzer and was back in my carriage in no time at all. A short while later we were outside the building where Succor had its offices.

'I won't be long,' I assured Mercer, and before he could remind me that was exactly what I'd said when I'd visited St John's and been attacked by Lulu, I hurried inside.

I was greeted by Matron, who advised me that Mr Richter was not there.

'Are you sure?' I was so anxious to talk to Sebastian I was not thinking straight and asked her pardon immediately for questioning her. 'You see, I was told he was always here at this time and—'

Matron had been seated behind her desk, an open book in front of her, and she unclipped the spectacles from the bridge of her nose and stood to face me before I could finish my protest. I am a tall woman; Matron was taller still and she looked down her long, pointed nose at me. There was but a single lamp lit on the desk and the afternoon was gray. In the thin light, her eyes were bottomless black pits.

'I would certainly know if Mr Richter was on the premises,' she said, and before I could tell her that of course she was right, she stepped away from her desk. 'But if it will placate you, Miss Barnum, and convince you that I am neither duplicitous nor forgetful, I will check his office.'

'No, really, you don't have to—'

But before I could apologize yet again and tell her not to

inconvenience herself, she disappeared into the short hallway that led to Sebastian's office.

I cannot say I held it against her for taking her time to come back. Questioning her reply to my simple request had been rude and I am not usually ill-mannered. I blamed my behavior on nerves, vowed I wouldn't let them get the best of me and waited for her to return so I could explain as much without, of course, mentioning that she must forgive me for I had no experience preparing my answer to a man's proposal of marriage.

One minute of waiting turned to two and, too edgy to keep still, I glanced at the book open on Matron's desk. It was a ledger similar to the one I'd looked through the first night I had visited Succor and inquired after Madeline Emerson. A list of names, some signed, some printed out, some scrawled – women who had arrived at Succor seeking help and, hopefully, a reunion with those who would love and care for them.

Betty Smallwood.

Sarah Jane Smiley.

Elizabetha Dorothy Jemima Arbower.

My heart squeezed so that my chest ached, and I put a fist to it and read the name again below my breath, sure that my eyes must be playing tricks on me.

'Elizabetha Dorothy Jemima Arbower.'

'Is there something you need help with, Miss Barnum?'

Matron's voice crackled through the silence and, startled, I winced and looked up to find her watching me from the doorway.

'There are . . .' Since it was obvious I'd been looking at the ledger, there was no use lying about it. I pointed that way in what I hoped was an airy, unconcerned gesture. 'There are so many women listed in your book. I was thinking how terribly sad it is. It must be especially difficult for you, for surely you know more about these women than most. For instance, this one, this Elizabetha Dorothy Jemima Arbower . . .' I pretended I had to read the name carefully. 'What an unusual name! What is her story? Why is she listed here in Succor's book?'

As solid and impressive as the USS *Constellation* itself, Matron inched back her shoulders, clasped her hands together at her waist and closed in on me, the desk and the book where the name was so tantalizingly written.

'She is no longer here.' With a snap, Matron closed the book and Elizabetha Dorothy Jemima Arbower was gone.

Goodbye. *Adios.*

With a cough, I cleared away the tight ball of emotion that suddenly blocked my breathing. 'Gone? I suppose that is good news. Has she gone far away?'

'Back to her family,' Matron said quite smoothly.

'That's . . .' I pulled in a breath and reminded myself that, until I knew more, there was little I could say and nothing I could do. 'That's wonderful. A wonderful success story for you and for Succor.'

'And for Mr Richter.'

'Yes, for Mr Richter. Yes, of course.'

Having no choice, and no notion of Sebastian's whereabouts, I waited until that evening and sent a message across the street to his home.

I should have been pleased that he waited but a few minutes to show up on Phin's front doorstep.

Had we been meeting to discuss nothing more out of the ordinary than a marriage proposal, I would have been.

The way it was, I cast a glance at Charity, who'd been sitting in the parlor when Sebastian arrived and, as I expected she would, she understood our need for privacy. Or perhaps the small smile playing across her thin lips when she left the room spoke less about thoughtfulness and more about how eager she was to see me gone and out of the Barnum household for good.

'Dear Evie!' Sebastian closed in on me as soon as the door shut behind my sister-in-law. He took my hand in his and smiled down at me, his expression so tender it clutched at my heart. 'I cannot tell you how anxious I have been, like a boy waiting for the first day of spring! You have been thinking about my offer?'

'Of little else,' I admitted. 'In fact, I came to see you this afternoon to discuss it.'

It took him a moment to catch my meaning. 'Came to see me? But I was not at home.'

'I did not go to your home.'

Another few seconds passed while he considered this. 'You do not mean . . . you cannot mean you went to the brewery.'

'They told me there that you spend each Thursday afternoon at Succor.'

'As I do.'

'And yet, you were not there, either.'

Sebastian's expression did not so much still as it froze, and for the space of a dozen heartbeats, neither of us took a breath. At least not until his grip tightened around my fingers.

'Have you been tracking me?' he asked.

'Hardly.' I was afraid this was exactly what he might say, exactly what he might think, and finally hearing the word and confirming my fears made them seem nothing more than what I knew they were, figments of my imagination. I smiled up at him. 'I was eager to speak to you.'

'And you think that gives you leave to follow me?'

His question was too sharp, the words too accusatory. I pulled my hand from his grasp.

'I did not follow you. I went where the man at the brewery told me you might be.'

'The man at the brewery . . .' His golden brows low over his eyes, he grumbled the words. 'I have no doubt it was Mr Gruber. He should know better.'

'Better than to answer a simple question?'

Sebastian's lips thinned. 'Better than to decide who should know my whereabouts and who should not.'

'And yet . . .' We were at cross-purposes, and for the life of me I could not figure out why. Still, a tingle skittered over my skin and though I shook my shoulders to rid myself of it, I could not banish the feeling of apprehension. 'If I am to be your wife—'

'Are you?'

There it was – the question, pure and simple, without flowery promises, without the mention of children and all that meant, both to me and to Sebastian.

'I had come to the brewery to tell you my decision,' I said. 'And when you were not on the premises I went to Succor so that I might speak to you there.'

I do believe it was the first he realized my voice was every bit as sharp as his. He pulled in a rough breath and let it out slowly. 'Yes. Of course.' As if a cloth had wiped it away, his stony expression melted. There was not so much tenderness in his smile as there was tolerance, though whether that was meant for me (the very thought caused me to bristle) or for himself and what was surely a failing for making assumptions too quickly, I could not tell.

'You must forgive me, dear Evie,' he finally said. 'It has been a long day and I have been able to think of little other than seeing you again. I am afraid it has overstrung my nerves.'

Ah, an admission the fault was his! I should have been pleased.

Except the way it was, with the weight of all I needed to discuss with him pressing against me like a physical thing, I could find no joy in his confession. 'I know how you feel,' I told him, going to the other side of the table to allow myself some space and what felt like more room to breathe. 'I have been having much the same sort of day.'

We offered each other a tentative smile across the width of Charity's new table, both our thoughts, I believe, already on the future and all we might mean to each other, all we might accomplish together. Only . . .

I lifted my chin. 'Who is Elizabetha Dorothy Jemima Arbower?' I asked him.

It was not a figment of my imagination nor a trick of the light. Sebastian really did wince, and he really did seek to cover up his reaction with a shake of his shoulders. 'I have no idea who you're talking about.'

'Perhaps you do not seeing as how you are not involved in the day-to-day operations of Succor. But I do believe Matron knows. Or perhaps your cousin, Sonya, may be able to help me with more information, for Sonya is certainly personally involved in Succor's important work.'

'Yet Sonya hardly knows every woman who comes through the door.'

'Did I say Elizabetha Dorothy Jemima Arbower ever came through the door?' I fought to keep my voice from betraying the sudden panic that built inside me. 'I said nothing of her being the recipient of Succor's charity.'

'Aha! But you did . . .' Like a schoolmaster instructing an especially doltish student who would not otherwise see the light, he waved a finger at me and tipped his head in what might have been a playful gesture if I was feeling less terrified, less worried, more charitable.

'You did mention this Elizabetha Dorothy . . .' He fumbled over the rest of the name, muttered 'damn,' below his breath so that I was not supposed to hear it and sailed right on. 'It is an impossible name and I cannot remember it! You did mention the woman's name in the same breath as you talked of Succor. Naturally, I made the connection.'

'As well you should. Elizabetha Dorothy Jemima Arbower came to Succor for help. Her name is in the ledger.'

His laugh was a little too hearty. 'I am glad of it. The more women who come, the more we are able to help, and the more we are able to help the more word will spread that there is hope to be found inside our walls.'

'Yet I do not think Elizabetha feels so much hope. You see, she has disappeared.'

It was neither a scowl nor a frown that turned Sebastian's face to stone. This was something colder and less forgiving and, realizing it, a sharp, fierce tension built inside me.

'What are you saying, Evie?' he wanted to know.

'I am saying only that I'm curious, that I'm wondering what might have happened to the woman.'

'And I am saying I haven't even the smallest idea of who she is, why she might have come to Succor or where she might have gone. If she did, indeed, come to us for help and now she is gone, that must mean we were able to provide her with assistance. Perhaps we reunited her with her family. Perhaps we worked to find her employment somewhere in the west and she's gone there to begin a new life. Perhaps – because it does happen and I will not insult either your intelligence or my own by pretending it doesn't – she decided that she did not want our help. Some women do. They prefer life on the streets or in the cathouses. I do not understand why. Rather than accept our charity, they would rather forage in the gutters.'

As Lulu had done.

Ice settled in my stomach and howled through my veins and it was that, perhaps, that made it impossible for me to move, even when Sebastian closed in on me.

The hand he settled on my arm was warm, but there was a

chill in the depths of his blue eyes. 'Do you know this woman?' he asked.

'I saw her name. In Matron's book. When I stopped at Succor this very afternoon. I thought it such an odd name and it gave me pause.'

'A name. Really? Perhaps we should inform your brother, dear Evie, that you have talents of mind reading that he might display in his museum. You saw but a name in a book and you surmised not only that the woman is gone from Succor but that she has somehow mysteriously disappeared. You are gifted, indeed.'

Did I manage an airy laugh? I am not sure how, or even why, I thought I had to. 'It is nothing like that. It is simply because such an unusual name sparked my curiosity. I asked Matron, of course. She is the one who told me Elizabetha is gone.'

'But not that she'd disappeared.' He added a twist to the final word as I remembered Phin had once done when reading Irving's *The Legend of Sleepy Hollow* to Charlotte as he sought to add a mysterious eeriness to every word.

'No,' I told him. 'Matron did not use such a word.'

'Of course not.' As quickly as he'd grabbed me, Sebastian let go of my arm and marched across the room, taking his hat from the table as he went. 'I suppose I should be grateful to have seen this side of you now, Evie, before things go further with us. Have you always been prone to such imaginings?'

'It is simply curiosity.'

'And I am simply not amused.' He clapped his hat on his head and turned his back to me. He was already at the door when he stopped, and I saw his shoulders rise and fall. He spun to face me. 'I am sorry. As I told you, it has been a long day and I am hungry and tired. I fear neither of us is at our best this evening. We will talk tomorrow.' It wasn't a question. 'Perhaps by then you will have abandoned these imaginings of yours and made up your mind about what really matters between us.'

He left before I could tell him I already had.

I called for Mercer and left for St John's immediately.

EIGHTEEN

'It is very late, Miss Evangeline.' Frederick Withnower blinked back his surprise at seeing me. Or perhaps he had already been asleep by the time I pounded on the door of St John's House of Hospitality and he was trying to wake up so he might make sense of my sudden appearance. 'I am certain Lulu is already in her room.'

'Yes, I was counting on it.' I brushed past him and made for the stairway. 'I must speak to her.'

'Are you sure?' I had already ascended two steps when Frederick's question rang out and I stopped and looked down to where he stood at the bottom of the stairway. 'The last time you spoke to Lulu, she had just been given a dose of laudanum, so she was calm. This evening, you will not have the same advantage. When she last saw you here in the hallway . . .'

'Yes. I well remember it.' With all the thoughts swirling through my head, I wasn't sure how I managed a smile, but I supposed it was worth a try, to reassure Frederick as well as myself. 'I do believe I may have discovered what agitated her so.' I unpinned the Succor ribbon from my cloak and tucked it in my reticule. 'Perhaps she will feel more kindly toward me this time and, even if she does not . . .' I pulled in a stuttering breath. 'I must speak to her. It is very important.'

He inclined his head and followed me up the stairs when I made my way to the dormitories where the women stayed and, from there, down the passageway to Lulu's tiny room.

'Lulu.' When I made to rush into the room, Frederick stayed me with one hand and rapped his knuckles on the door. 'Lulu, you have a visitor.'

'Don't want the mare and the horse. Stay away from the green door!'

Frederick and I exchanged looks, and he must have read the determination in my eyes; without a word, he stepped back to allow me into the room.

Though she was still dressed in the dark gown she must have worn that day, Lulu was on the bed, her shoes still on, her knees pulled up to her chest, her fiery hair around her shoulders like the skewed halo of an unlikely saint.

I wasted no words. 'Lulu,' I told her. 'I need your help.'

She wrinkled her nose and studied me for a minute. 'Don't know you,' she mumbled and, as if to prove it meant she could not trust me, she scooted farther away and tucked herself in the corner where the bed met the wall.

That was fine with me; it gave me room enough to sit on the bed with her. 'You're right. You don't know me. My name is Evangeline Barnum, and I need you to leave St John's for a short while and come with me.'

Her eyes darted to Frederick, who I do believe might have given her some assurance if he had known what I was talking about. Then again, if he'd known what I was talking about, I doubt he would have approved.

'She's a friend,' he told Lulu. 'And you don't have to do what she asks, but you must listen to her.'

'Must.' Lulu wrapped her arms around her knees. 'Won't leave. Won't go.'

'You don't have to go far away. Not like Elizabetha did,' I told her. 'You only have to come with me for a short ride.'

When she shook her head, her hair shivered around her shoulder. 'Won't go. Can't take me. Won't go.'

'But you must.' I had already put a hand on Lulu's arm when I realized it was probably the wrong thing to do. I tensed, waiting for her to come at me but, much to my relief, she did not move and she did not speak. Her eyes, though, grew wide, and her bottom lip trembled.

I pulled my hand back to my side. 'I'm sorry,' I told her. 'I did not mean to frighten you. I only need to make you see, Lulu, there is something terrible happening. I do believe you are the only one who can help me stop it.'

She was not convinced. I didn't think she would be for I, myself, was not at all confident that I knew what I was talking about. The only thing I was sure of was that my words were as unintelligible to her as her mad rantings were to me, and they made as much sense. There was only one thing I could do to win her over.

Slowly, nerving myself for whatever might happen, I reached into my reticule, withdrew the Succor ribbon and held it out to Lulu.

Like an animal snared in a trap, she reared up on her knees and lunged for me, her arms out straight and her hands flat. When she slammed into me, I tumbled from the bed.

I landed with a grunt but little injury, and I was already back on my feet before Frederick could even come forward to help. When he did, I urged him to keep his place, fixing my gaze on Lulu. She had plucked the ribbon out of my hand when I fell, and now she held it between thumb and forefinger. In the light of the candle beside her bed, I saw tears well in her eyes.

'You went to Succor for help.' I dared to put words to all I was thinking.

Her gaze shot to mine. 'I won't go. They won't take me.'

I swallowed my fear and took a step closer. 'I won't let them take you, Lulu. I won't let them take anyone. But you are the only person who can help me, and you must begin by telling me what happened to you and how you ended up here at St John's. Did you have a family once? Are they now lost?'

When her breath caught, I knew I had touched upon a memory.

'You had a father and a mother, perhaps brothers and sisters.'

She shook her head, and when she spoke her voice was so hushed I wondered if I'd imagined the words. 'Husband. Son. Gone now. Dead.'

My heart squeezed and I dropped back on the bed, bending my head toward her and keeping my voice as low as hers so that Frederick could not hear. 'I had a son, too,' I told Lulu. 'He is gone like your son is.'

When Lulu made a move toward me, I braced myself for another attack, but instead of coming at me she took my hand and wound her fingers through mine. Her hand was delicate and very cold. 'I'm sorry,' she said.

We sat in silence for a long while, two mothers with broken hearts, until Frederick put a hand on my shoulders.

'Miss Evangeline,' he said, 'perhaps we might let Lulu rest?'

With a cough, I stripped the emotion from my voice. 'Soon,' I told him. 'But for now . . .'

After a squeeze that spoke my sympathy and my understanding, I untangled my hand from Lulu's and reminded myself that if I was to make sense of everything I'd seen at Succor, I must prod her further.

'You were alone,' I said, searching her expression for confirmation. 'You had no place else to turn. I do believe that is when you sought aid at the Society for the Relief and Succor of Needy Women.'

The light nearby reflected the tear that slipped down her cheek so that it looked like blood.

'Did you live there with the other women?' I asked her. 'I know they live above the Succor office and they are taught skills, and the good people there—'

Her gaze snapped to mine, so razor-sharp it cut my comment to shreds and I was forced to revise it.

'The people there help find employment for the women. And they locate their families, too, if it is possible.'

She nodded.

'But that is not what happened to you.'

This time, her nod was barely perceptible.

'Did they take you somewhere else to live, Lulu? Away from the Succor office and the rooms upstairs? Will you show me the way? The way from Succor to the green door?'

She started shaking her head slowly, and the motion gained speed little by little until it was as frenzied as the look in her eyes.

'Won't go!' Lulu wailed, as agitated as she had been calm only a moment before. 'Can't take me.'

'I can't,' I said, and I knew my voice was too loud but I feared she would not hear me otherwise. 'No one can take you. And no one can make you go. Not Mr Withnower and certainly not me. You must do this because you want to help, Lulu. You must make sure it doesn't happen again.'

'Goodbye. *Adios*,' Lulu mewled.

'Will you come with me, Lulu?' I held out a hand.

She batted it away.

'Really, Miss Evangeline . . .' Frederick stepped forward. 'You are asking for nothing more than ill-use and, when it is all over and you finally give up and leave, Lulu will be so troubled there will be nothing for it but for us to give her more laudanum to control her.'

I glanced over my shoulder at him. 'I have no intention of leaving. Not until Lulu comes with me.' I turned my attention back to her. 'Perhaps, with your help, I will be able to locate Elizabetha. Was she your friend?'

Lulu nodded. 'Came during the night. Thought I was asleep. But I saw. I saw it all.'

'Did they give Elizabetha laudanum so as to quiet her?'

That handkerchief Lulu had clutched in her hand when she attacked me was beside her on the bed and she glanced that way. 'Gone.' Tugging at her hair, Lulu wept quietly.

'We can search for her, Lulu. Perhaps we can find her.'

Lulu was quiet for so long, I thought she had either fallen asleep or that her mind had slipped to a place where the sadness did not sting so much. Finally, she sniffled and brushed her hands over her cheeks. 'You will come?'

'Yes.' I let to a shaky breath. 'I will come with you to the horse and the mare and the green door.'

'To help Elizabetha?' she asked.

'Yes. Please, please show me the way.'

She slid off the bed and raced for the door and I thought it was the last we'd see her, but Lulu stopped when she got there. 'I will find my coat,' she said and she darted into the hallway.

Frederick was sure to question my motives as well as my sanity, so I was not the least surprised when he stepped forward. 'What is happening? What do Lulu's ravings have to do with that ribbon you had pinned to your cloak?'

'I am not at all sure,' I told him. 'But I know that seeing the ribbon is what frightened her the afternoon I was here.'

'And finding Elizabetha?'

'Heaven help me, Mr Withnower, I did not wish to lie to Lulu, but I do not believe anyone will ever find Elizabetha.'

'And yet . . .'

I scrubbed my hands over my face. 'I don't know,' I admitted, doing my best to keep the desperation from my voice. 'I'm not sure. I only know that Lulu is the only one who can help. She's the only one who can lead me to the green door and from there . . .'

I could not speak the words and, for a long while, Frederick stood and I sat in silence in the gloom of Lulu's room. He, I was certain, was considering the possibility that I was every bit as mad as Lulu, and for this I could not fault him. In this matter, I questioned my sanity, too. I wondered if my quest for obtaining justice for Andrew, for locating Madeline, and now, for finding the answers to what – beside the unspeakable sadness at the loss of her family – had gripped Lulu with a fear that shaped her life, had also led me to a place where I could no longer see the world clearly or honestly.

Was I a fool, one who owed Sebastian Richter an apology along with an explanation for why I had questioned him so boldly earlier in the evening and why I had doubted his word?

Was I a meddlesome woman who could not control her flights of fancy, a marplot who should be ashamed to think good folk like Clarice and Frederick and Jeffrey might be capable of murder, that Sebastian, who certainly had committed no sin in having a missing woman's name in a book devoted to nothing more than charity, might somehow be involved in a sinister plot to do . . .

What?

The questions swirled inside my head, taunting me, shaming me. Perhaps like my brother, I had too much imagination. While his led to schemes and dreams, had mine led me in a darker direction? If there was even a chance it was true – if I'd seen guilt where there was none and formed suspicions that were false – then there was only one thing I could do. It was late, but I had to leave St John's. I had to go directly to Sebastian's and tell him how sorry I was to have caused the contention between us.

I had already slid off the bed and moved to the door when Frederick spoke.

'I'm coming with you,' he announced. 'Wherever it is you're going.'

I could not find the words to tell him I was going home to beg forgiveness from a man who, except for the wanderings of my errant imagination, was good and true and kind.

He stepped forward. 'If what you are about to do is dangerous, you will need prayers, surely, but you might also need a man at your side.'

'I am grateful for your assistance,' I told him. 'You are a generous man. When I came here, I thought if perhaps you could take us to the place you first found Lulu, she might be able to remember and lead us from there to the place she came from and then we might unravel the mystery. But truly, Mr Withnower, on considering my plan, I wonder if I have created something out of nothing. Perhaps poor Lulu is simply mad. Perhaps there is nothing more to it than that. Perhaps I've seen boogeymen where there are none and I am not—'

Lulu stepped back into the room and my words froze and my mouth hung open. In the time she'd been gone, she had not gotten her coat as she had promised to do, but she had found shears.

All my doubts were suddenly erased, replaced by a surprise that was palpable and a curiosity so overwhelming, I could not have fought against it if I tried.

'Your hair!' I stepped forward, my hand out to Lulu, who had hacked off her glorious red hair. It was so short that her scalp showed in places.

'No hair, no hair!' Lulu's eyes shone with tears but her smile was sly. 'They won't take me now!'

I did not understand what Lulu had done. I did not even try. Lulu, Frederick and I set out – as unlikely a trio as ever there was – back to the spot where Frederick had first discovered her rooting through the gutter. I told Mercer to wait. We disembarked from the carriage and, from there, we were under Lulu's guidance.

'Show me,' I told her, squeezing her hand in the hopes of giving – and getting – courage. 'Show me how you arrived at this spot. Had you been in the streets for days?'

She shook her head, glanced around and took off at a goodly pace. Frederick and I scrambled to catch up with her.

I do not know how long we walked or how much distance we covered as we trailed behind Lulu – I only know she was driven by a fire that was almost inhuman and by the time an hour had passed I was breathing hard. Still, I refused to lose her in the maze of streets we crossed, the parks we darted through or the alleyways where, time and again, we had to flatten ourselves against walls just so we might squeeze through.

We had just exited one such alley and stepped into the street when I lifted my head and breathed deep.

'Hops,' I said to Frederick and to Lulu now that she'd stopped to get her bearing. 'Hops and malt. We are near the breweries in the Bowery and Lulu spoke of beer. We should have known!'

Frederick shook his head. 'There is no way to ever know if a person such as Lulu speaks the truth or even what the truth might mean to her. I only know—'

What, he would have to wait to tell me, for Lulu caught sight of something she recognized and took off running.

We followed as best as we were able, dashing between the few carts and carriages still about at such a late hour, dodging do-nothings and drinkers and many a b'hoy, for we were well and truly in the Bowery now, and in the distance I could hear the sounds of a rollicking piano, of traffic and conversations.

At the next corner, Lulu came to a halt and looked both ways, and I knew when she saw what she was looking for. In spite of our recent exertion, her face paled. She had clapped a bonnet onto her head before we left St John's and now she pulled the ribbon tighter beneath her chin and tucked in those few wisps of hair she had remaining.

'Can't see my hair, can't see my hair,' she mumbled.

'They can't see it,' I assured her. 'Only tell me, Lulu. Who are they?'

She did not answer but lifted her arm and pointed a trembling finger to a building but two from the corner where we stood.

I could ask no more of her and, one hand on her arm, I handed Lulu off to Frederick.

'Oh, no!' Though he dutifully wound an arm through Lulu's to keep her from running away, Frederick would have none of it. 'I am not going to allow you to go there alone, Miss Evangeline. Can't you see Lulu is frightened? There may be danger.'

'And I intend to confront none of it,' I assured him. 'I only wish to see what the building might be and I will be less conspicuous walking alone than we would as a group. Besides . . .' Lulu had begun weeping quietly and I doubted she would hear, but I lowered my voice. 'Whatever happened in this place, you are right, there might be danger, and more of it should someone there recognize Lulu.'

He knew I was right.

'Here.' Frederick put a hand in his pocket, brought out something that glimmered in the meager light, and handed it to me. 'It is but a small knife,' he said, 'but it is something, at least.'

'I will be back shortly,' I assured him before I tucked the knife into my sleeve and turned toward the place that inspired such terror in Lulu.

It was a completely unremarkable brick building, the type of old Federal-style home that had once been common in this part of Manhattan with windows along the front in all four stories and a doorway with a simple brownstone arch around it and a fanlight above the door. A green door.

Unremarkable.

And yet remarkably lively for that time of the night.

Lights shone in every window and, against the light, I saw shadows scurry passed.

Curious, I was about to step nearer when a Conestoga wagon, like those that haul freight, lumbered onto the street. It slowed in front of the house I was watching and I stepped back into the shadows across the street, the better to see and not be seen.

Like all such wagons, this Conestoga was long and wide and had the distinctive curved floor that prevented its contents from tipping and a sturdy white canvas cover to keep its freight dry and protected. When it stopped directly outside the house, I could no longer see that green door, and I had no choice but to cross the street. There was a brick wall around the property no higher than my head and I stayed close to it, hoping that the shadows would hide my presence, and watched a man in laborer's clothes dismount from the horse on the left and closest to the wagon. He hitched up his unmentionables, clapped a wide-brimmed hat upon his head and knocked on the front door.

It opened with a spill of light that was blocked when a woman stepped through the doorway.

She was tall and thin, a silhouette against the light so that she looked as if she were cut from black paper. When she spoke to the man, her voice was crisp, but it wasn't until she turned slightly to wave an arm toward the back of the house that the light her touched her face.

Matron!

I had suspected some connection between the terrors that haunted Lulu and Succor yet it took a moment for me to make sense of what I was seeing.

'Bring the wagon around.' I snapped out of my surprise when Matron pointed to the street where Frederick and Lulu still waited, and from there directed the teamster to the back of the house. 'You can load the product from there.'

He tipped his hat, mounted the horse and the wagon rumbled around the corner.

I was determined to get to the back of the house before the Conestoga did, and as far as I could see there was only one way to do that. It took me a while to find a suitable foothold, but once I did, I hitched up my skirts, climbed the wall and dropped into the courtyard next to the house. There were no windows on this side of the building and for that I was grateful, for it allowed me the cover of darkness. Step by careful step, I made my way across the yard and to a gate that led me to the alley at the back of the house. There was no sign yet of the Conestoga but I could hear its iron-rimmed wheels against the paving stones as it neared, and from where I stood I could see the building across the way, a tavern called the Horse and Mare.

I could not allow myself the luxury of standing there, stunned. The wagon arrived and Matron opened the back door.

'You'll need more than one man to carry the barrels,' she barked, and the teamster did not argue with her. Another fellow jumped out of the back of the wagon and together they went into the house and came out hauling a barrel of the type I'd seen at Sebastian Richter's brewery. The load was heavy and awkward, and while the men struggled with it, I dared a step nearer.

I was just in time to see Matron bend her head to hear something from inside the house, call back, 'I'll be right there,' and disappear.

A few more steps and I was able to take a better look through the doorway and into the house.

There were four other barrels there waiting to be loaded and, as much as I would have liked to get a closer look at them, I never had the chance for I saw a flash of color like fire from the passageway and heard Matron's sharp voice.

'Get her back in here. It's not her time.'

Another woman appeared, her arm firmly around a short, slim woman with a glazed expression and the slow-motion movements of an automaton. My stomach swooped and suddenly, that bit of fiery color I'd seen made sense.

Hair.

Red hair.

Like Lulu's.

Only this wasn't Lulu. It was Madeline Emerson.

NINETEEN

S tunned, I hesitated, and it was a good thing I did. Again, Matron's voice rang out from somewhere in the house and, when it did, the woman who had hold of Madeline pushed her into a chair, told her not to move and left the room.

I saw my opportunity and dashed into the house, carefully and quietly making my way around the barrels and down one passageway crossed by another. There, I paused and tipped my head, listening, and when I saw no one and heard nothing, I closed in on the woman who sat, glassy-eyed, in a room crammed with packing crates and boxes.

'Madeline, it's me, Evie!' I took her arm and tugged her to her feet. Or at least I tried. Madeline did not move. She did not even look at me. 'We must leave here, Madeline. Right now!'

She blinked and shifted her gaze from the nothing it had been focused upon to me and the size of her pupils, like pinpoints, confirmed my worst fears. She'd been given laudanum and, from the slow, irregularity of her breathing, I would say she'd been given a good deal of it.

'Madeline!' My voice was a whisper but no less urgent because of it. 'Come with me. I'm going to take you home.'

'Home.' Her voice was as dreamy as the look in her eyes. Madeline's head bobbed to one side, and a slow smile brightened her expression. 'Home to James.'

I did not have time to let the name or the memories it called up clutch at me. I tightened my hold on Madeline's arm. 'Yes, home to James. But we must leave now.' Another tug, and this time she came to her feet.

It was at that exact moment that the two teamsters came back to the door for another of the barrels. Remembering the woman I'd seen with Madeline earlier, I braced an arm around her shoulders just as that woman had and, hoping they mistook me for the other woman, kept Madeline in place until the two men, grunting from their exertion, took the barrel to the wagon.

I knew we hadn't much time.

We didn't have far to go, and I would like to say we covered the distance easily but Madeline was like a man corned from too much whiskey. Her movements were loose and fluid, each of her steps exaggerated as if she couldn't judge how much distance there was between her feet and the floor, and time and again I needed to stop, get a better hold on her and urge her along. At the intersecting passageway, I once again stopped and held my breath, listening for any indication of noise that would alert me to where Matron and the other woman might be. Hearing nothing, I kept a firm hold on Madeline and led her across the darkened hallway.

That is when I felt her jerk to a stop.

I stopped, too, and spun and saw the woman I'd seen earlier with Madeline. She was behind Madeline and had both arms around Madeline's waist. She wasn't about to let go.

I tugged and pulled and poor Madeline, like a child's rag doll, flopped and would have collapsed if not for the hold the other woman had on her.

'You cannot keep her here!' I insisted, no longer whispering as I fought to drag Madeline away.

It was a pity I was so engaged in the effort that I paid little attention to my surroundings. I didn't realize anyone had come out of the dark passageway until an arm went around my neck and jerked back my head. Another hand pinched my nose and, while I struggled for breath, the first dose of laudanum poured down my throat.

I woke to the most comforting rocking motion, and for many minutes – my brain still addled and my senses befuddled – I did nothing but lie there on my back and enjoy the sensation while I stared at the unremarkable white ceiling.

Unremarkable.

Somewhere in the drug-muzzy recesses of my brain, the word sparked a memory.

Surely, the building where I had gone to search for the answers to Lulu's past, her fears and her connection to Succor . . . surely that building was unremarkable and, just as surely, it must be where I was at the moment.

And yet, drugged or not, I knew even unremarkable buildings did not sway.

Thinking through the conundrum and finding no answers, I drifted back into unconsciousness. The next time I opened my eyes, my head did not swim so and I dared to turn to see my surroundings. There was a cot beside mine and Madeline Emerson lay on it, her eyes closed, her breaths shallow.

Like a strike of lightning, the thought blew through me and I sat up. It was a mistake – the moment my stomach swooped and my throat clutched and my head spun, I knew it. Yet I forced myself not to collapse again upon the cot but rather kept my place and fought to get my bearings.

It would have been a damned sight easier if only the room would stop wobbling.

Wobble it did, back and forth in a gentle motion and, more fully awake now, I listened to the groan of boards, the whoosh of wind, the slap of water.

I was on a ship.

The words struck and my heart slammed my ribs, the terror so complete I could do nothing for a few long minutes but consider the implications and give in to the panic that filled my veins with ice.

Goodbye. *Adios.*

Far, far away.

Lulu's words did not so much mock me as send out a warning.

Too late, too late. I should have known. Si, si. Adios.

Lulu escaped because she knew – or at least she sensed – she was about to be sent away on a ship.

But where?

And why?

And . . .

My breath staggered. I swallowed the sour taste that filled my mouth and forced a breath that felt like fire. I held it deep in my lungs and let it out slowly. And I told myself to think.

There was no porthole in the tiny room, just our two cots and a small table between us, and I braced a hand against it and stood on legs that felt as if they'd been poured from hot candle wax. The boat rolled and I stumbled and nearly lost my footing, righted myself again and lurched a second time before I knew enough to stand with my legs slightly apart and my weight centered. With my sea legs finally under me, I went to Madeline's side.

I put a hand on her shoulder and shook her. 'Madeline, you must wake up!'

She moaned and turned her head and, encouraged, I shook her again.

Madeline's eyes fluttered open. 'Evie?' Her lips were caked with the honey that had been added to the doses of laudanum we'd both been forced to swallow. Her voice was rough, but I looked and saw no ewer and could not get her water. She hoisted herself up on her elbows. 'What are you doing—'

'There is no time to explain,' I told her. 'We must see if we can get off this ship.'

'Ship?' For a moment, I saw a flash of amusement light her eyes and was reminded of the Madeline I had known in Bethel, the lively girl with an easy laugh and a penchant for mischief. That is, before her eyes welled and her bottom lip trembled. 'Surely not!' She struggled to catch her breath. 'That cannot be, for the other women, they talked of such a thing, but I thought . . .'

'You thought it was no more than a story designed to frighten and entertain.'

Her nod was barely perceptible.

'And you heard this story at Succor, for that is where you went for help, didn't you, when James threw you over?'

Her tears flowed freely. 'He didn't mean it,' she insisted. 'We had words, and he spoke rashly, and I . . .' She gulped down the pain of the memory. 'I told him he didn't matter to me, but Evie . . .' Swaying from the movement of the ship and the cascade of emotion, Madeline sat up and swung her legs over the side of the cot. 'He matters more than my next breath! More than anyone or anything in all the world. I need to make him see.' She clutched both her hands around my arm. 'I must make him understand, then he will surely take me back and love me again.'

I feared not, for I knew James Crockett had no understanding of love, and surely no compassion. But this hardly seemed the time to mention it. We had more important matters to consider.

'When you went to Succor, Madeline, what did they tell you there? That they could help you?'

'Help?' Some of the confusion cleared from her expression. 'They hardly said anything at all,' she told me, 'and never asked a thing. They took one look at me and bundled me off to the building with the sturdy doors and the walled yard.' Her bottom lip trembled and I could not bear to watch her suffer so.

'I do believe it is your red hair,' I told her. 'For they lost a woman with red hair and they needed one to take her place.'

'Take her place for . . .'

I looked around the tiny cabin as my answer. 'They are shipping you someplace. And I do believe it is a place where Spanish is spoken.'

'*Si*, yes. *Adios*, goodbye.' She slid a hand down my arm and clutched my hand in desperate fingers. 'I did not understand the lessons. I had no idea. And now, you say we are aboard a ship, that we are being sent . . . where?' Her voice was reed thin and so filled with panic, it started up a stampede of fear inside me.

'Far away,' I whispered, the horror of it all only now slamming into me full force. 'Those barrels at the home where I found you . . . they did not contain freight, did they? Is that how they get the women onto the ships so no one notices?'

Madeline's ginger brows dipped over her eyes. 'I . . . I don't know. I only know I must find James. James will have the answers.'

'We will try,' I assured her at the same time I felt the lie burn through my insides. 'For now, I think it more important that we find a way out of here.'

Her eyes wide, Madeline considered all the word meant. 'If we are discovered . . .'

'Were other women discovered? Did others try to escape?'

She wrapped her arms around herself and grew silent.

It was just as well, for all I had to remember was the terror that haunted Lulu to know the answer.

'We must be very quiet and very brave,' I told Madeline and tugged her hand. 'Will you come with me?'

In answer, Madeline unleashed a fresh cascade of tears.

'We will find James.' I dangled the false promise and did not feel the least bit guilty when she stood at my side.

'Yes, James.' Madeline's smile was dreamy. 'We will find James and I will be happy again.'

I was not surprised to find the door to our cabin locked. I was surprised when I checked my sleeve and realized my captors had not searched me; the knife given me by Frederick Withnower was still there and I used it to strip away the wood surrounding the lock.

If it took minutes or an hour, I could not say. I only know by the time the lock gave way and the door swung open, my hands were slick with sweat and splotches of blood caused by many a sharp splinter, and Madeline was nearly prostrate with worry.

I reminded her to hush and led her into the passageway.

From the cabin across from ours I heard the sound of soft sobbing and, though my heart squeezed, my head told me to pay it no mind. It would be trouble enough to get one befuddled woman to safety; once that was taken care of I would worry about the rest. For I was sure there were others and wondered how many over the years. How many women had disappeared?

We crept down the passageway to stairs that led to another deck and still, no sign of crew or of Matron and the woman who'd help to capture us. At the top of the third stairway, I heard men's voices in rumbled conversation somewhere nearby. There were packing crates stacked below the stairway, and I tucked Madeline behind them, told her not to budge and not to make a sound, and moved toward the voices.

It was then I realized it was not so much a discussion as it was an argument.

Something about freight and missing shipments.

I flattened my back to the wall and dared a step closer to the room where the men spoke.

'The numbers don't tally,' one of the men said, and the voice was vaguely familiar though I could not place it with the cabin door shut. Then again, it was difficult to hear much over the pounding of my heart. 'I don't understand it. And if you don't, Captain—'

'I do. That is, I will, sir, if only you'll give me a chance to look into it.'

'So many barrels of beer equals so much profit. It is as simple as that. Only Captain . . .' the man's voice sank to a growl. 'I distinctly remember the order from Senor Martinez was for eighteen barrels of beer. And there are twenty-four barrels in the hold. I counted them myself. Six of those barrels are empty. Those six are listed here.' I heard the slap of his hand against paper. 'Just as the eighteen are. It makes no sense. If you are falsifying records, I will hear an explanation, and I will hear it now, or there will be hell to pay.'

'The barrels . . . they . . .' Even through the closed door, I heard the captain gulp. 'That is, sir, if you will give me but a little time, I will get the facts and figures in order.'

'I thought they had always been in order. Until now. I swear to you, sir, I will be going over every page of every manifest for every voyage you have captained on my behalf, and if my find-ings match my suspicions there will be hell to pay. We will not leave port until this matter is settled.'

Not leave port.

My heart skipped a beat.

We were still in New York. There was still a chance for escape!

I would tell Madeline and she would be greatly encouraged, and we would get to the topmost deck and yell and scream and attract attention, and then someone would come and save us.

Yes!

My spirit soared but my steps were not quick enough.

Just as I made to scuttle down the hallway, the door of the cabin where the men spoke swung open and a man stepped into the passageway. For the first time in two years, I found myself face-to-face with the father of my child.

James Crockett was surely as stunned as I was, for he stood as still as a statue, trying to make sense of the impossibility of my presence.

It did not take him long to recover. But then, if there was one thing I knew about James, it was that his mind is as quick as his heart is hard.

'Evie?' He bent forward, peering through the gloom to confirm what he must surely have thought was a trick of his eyes. 'What on earth are you doing—'

I put a finger to my lips and darted a look at the door of the captain's cabin and James – I could not help but bless him in spite of the emotions that cascaded through me – took me by the arm and led me into another of the cabins and closed the door behind us.

This cabin was considerably finer than the one where I'd woken next to Madeline. The walls were paneled with rich wood. The furnishings were heavy and lavish – mahogany chairs, a table big enough to seat four, a bed, heavily curtained, built into the hull.

A comfortable cabin.

An owner's cabin.

'We are on one of your own ships.' My voice was as hollow as my insides suddenly felt, and I cannot blame James for not responding, for surely he thought I was speaking the obvious. He shook his head and his hair – the color of a golden sunset – dipped over his forehead. He pushed it back with one well-shaped hand.

'How did you get here, Evie? What do you want?'

What I wanted was answers, and now that I looked into James's eyes I could not help but wonder if I would like them when I heard them.

'Women have been smuggled aboard this ship in barrels so that they are not discovered on the journey from the house that acts as a sort of holding place. Once they are aboard, they are released from the barrels, of course, or they would die. They are drugged and locked in cabins for the journey. All the way to South America, I suspect. They are being shanghaied,' I said, my voice so tight with fear I could barely get the words passed my lips. I had tucked Frederick's knife back into my sleeve and I touched a hand to it for courage. 'I swear to you, James Crockett, if you had knowledge of this scheme I will see you punished for such evil.'

'Shanghaied?' He had the temerity to laugh and I wondered that I'd once thought the sound as musical as church bells. 'Have you been drinking?'

'Yes. Laudanum.'

'Lau . . .' He threw his hands in the air. 'You are as much of an enigma as ever.'

'As much as Madeline Emerson?'

His mouth snapped shut, the better to bite through his words. 'What are you talking about?'

'I know she was in the city with you.'

'And that's what you've come here to confront me about? My friendship with Madeline?'

I sniggered. 'As much of a friendship as we two had together.'

'Evie, it is a little late for these sorts of discussion, don't you think? If you are feeling jealous—'

'Jealous!' I bit the word in half and spit it back at him. 'Is that what you think? Then you haven't been listening. I said there are women on this ship right now, women who have been taken against their will. Don't you see, that accounts for your empty barrels, for the manifest that doesn't tally with what you thought you were shipping.'

'What?'

The single word from him was as sharp-edged as a sword but I didn't let it stop me. Two years of anger and grief, two years of regrets, searing and painful, shot through me. I slapped his face.

'You heartless bastard! You are finding desperate women with nowhere else to turn and you are selling them. Damn you, James Crockett. Damn you to hell!'

I would have slapped him again if he hadn't seized my hand and twisted my arm behind my back. Pain cracked through my shoulder but I refused to cry out, not even when he pushed me into the nearest chair.

His breathing as rough as mine, he looked down at me. 'You heard what I told the captain. I don't know what you're talking about,' he said.

When I made to get up, he shoved me back. 'You own the ship.'

'And send shipments around the world for concerns all along the seaboard. Are you telling me . . .' His expression suddenly as flat as his eyes were empty, he dropped into the chair next to mine. 'They told me they were sending beer, and you tell me that they are really sending—'

'Women.' I spoke the word, but my mind was not on it so much as it was on what he'd said. 'Beer? These shipments are not for . . .' I could barely speak the words. 'For Sebastian—'

'Richter's brewery, yes.' James scrubbed his hands over his face. 'I never questioned it. I never thought . . . Are you sure, Evie?'

'I can prove it. There are women below deck. Madeline Emerson is one of them.'

Before I ever had a chance to interpret the frown that soured his expression, the air was rent with Madeline's screams.

TWENTY

I made it to the door of the cabin before James did, but he was bigger than me and faster, and he pushed me out of the way and took the steps two at a time, following the sounds of Madeline's desperate cries for help.

I stumbled up the steps behind him and, if I had paid any attention to the arm he threw out to keep me in my place, I would have stayed on the stairway. Instead, I ducked under his arm, scrambled up the last of the steps onto the deck and found myself as James did, in the sights of the silver revolving firearm held by Sebastian Richter.

To Sebastian's credit, he actually paled when he saw me.

'I see Matron does not keep you as informed as she should,' I said, somehow sounding as if my soul hadn't been ripped in two and my heart torn to pieces by the realization that he was involved in the shanghaiing scheme. 'You're surprised to see me.'

'I am disappointed to see you.' Richter's words were surely as sincere as the look he aimed down the barrel of the weapon was steady. 'I told you I would look into the matter of your missing friend. You should have listened and not gotten involved.' Ever so briefly, he glanced to the side where Matron had an arm around Madeline. It was a perilous situation, and yet Madeline's eyes were on James and her face glowed with a smile.

'James!' She would have darted forward if Matron released her hold. Instead, Matron held fast and, over Madeline's shoulders, I saw the restless chop of the East River and the lights of Brooklyn winking in the twilight.

'You have a good deal of explaining to do,' James told Richter. 'I thought you were using my fleet to ship beer.'

'As we are.' Sebastian laughed. 'The fact that we're sending a little more along with the beer is . . . how would you put it? A happy coincidence?'

'Hardly happy.' I shot the words at him. 'Women are being

held against their will, but not at the building where Succor has
its offices. You are too clever for that, aren't you?'

'Actually, I wasn't clever at all,' Sebastian admitted. 'I had
the germ of the scheme—'

'With Marta's blessings?' The words nearly choked me.

The very thought, it seemed, had the same effect on Sebastian.
His mouth pulled into a thin line. 'Marta had nothing to do with
this and I will thank you not to even suggest it. When Marta was
in charge, Succor was only what it was meant to be. A charity,
nothing more. But after she was gone . . .' For a second, his eyes
clouded with memory.

'You cannot understand, Evie, for you've obviously never loved
anyone the way I loved my Marta. After she was gone, I realized
there was nothing else that mattered in all this world except the
health and welfare of my children. When the opportunity came
along to provide more fully for them—'

'By selling women into slavery?' The words caught in my
throat.

'It is but a tiny piece of what we do. There is still the charity
work, the kind-hearted women who give of their time and their
talents to help those less fortunate than themselves. They, of
course, have no idea that we've devised a scheme to make the
best use of the others.'

'The others? You mean the ones they cannot connect with
family, the ones who have no one looking for them and no place
to go . . .' I thought of poor Lulu. 'Those you spirit away.'

'And no one ever misses them.' For Sebastian, it was as simple
as that.

'But someone did miss Lulu, am I right? She was special.
Because of the unique color of her hair.'

'Lulu was something of a special order. A fiery-haired woman,
that's what the man in Argentina wanted, and he was willing to
pay a princely sum for her. Once she ran off, yes, she had to be
replaced, so Miss Emerson coming to us . . . well, that was
something of a lucky coincidence. Really, Evie, you are a woman
of the world – I thought you would understand. I am sure Mr
Crockett does. His books tally and, to him, that is all that matters.
You can thank me for that,' Sebastian added with a little bow.
'Don't you see, Evie, this . . . it is simply business.'

'Business that enlarges your purse. You shanghai women and send them to other countries, Spanish-speaking countries. Are they servants there?' I demanded of Sebastian, moving to my left so that I might step closer to him. 'Or worse?'

Sebastian's smile was sleek. 'You have a marvelous imagination, dear Evie. It is just one of the things I admire about you. We still might make a formidable team.'

'You expect I will marry you? You think I will leave here and not tell the world—'

He turned ever so slightly so that the gun was aimed directly at me. 'If you plan to stay alive, you will keep your mouth shut.'

I raised my chin. 'You cannot make me.'

'Then perhaps I might begin by convincing you that I am deadly serious.' In one fluid motion, he turned and fired and a bullet that ripped into James.

Blood burst from the wound on James's shoulder and he fell to the deck, his mouth open in a circle of surprise.

Madeline screamed. I did not have the luxury of such a reaction.

Before he could recover and aim again, I threw myself at Richter and slammed into him with enough force to knock him off his feet. The gun flew from his hand and skittered across the deck, and I didn't dare wait for him to recover and make a grab for it. I slipped the knife from my sleeve and held it to his throat.

'Don't move,' I told Sebastian. 'And you . . .' I looked briefly at Matron. 'Let her go.'

She released Madeline, who flew to where James writhed in pain, the deck around him already slick with blood.

'You will come with me now, Mr Richter.' To prove I meant what I said, I nicked Sebastian's neck with the point of the knife so that a tiny drop of blood erupted at the spot. 'I do believe we need to see a constable.'

'I think not.'

The voice was a woman's and, surprised, I looked up to see Sonya at the top of the stairway. She stepped onto the deck and, in one swift move, retrieved the gun. She aimed it directly at me.

'The knife,' she said, and I had no choice. I dropped the blade on deck, and when Sebastian got to his feet he scooped it up and went to Sonya's side.

'I cannot say I am surprised that we find ourselves here,' she said. 'You are meddlesome, Miss Barnum. I told Sebastian as much from the start but he would not listen. He always was blind when it came to women, and you – he actually claimed to be falling in love with you. No matter!' She twitched the gun, ordering me to stand. 'What I couldn't accomplish before, I might be able to achieve now. You are remarkably resilient.'

I was already on my feet when the sense of what she said slammed into me. 'You! You are the one who shot at my carriage to frighten the horses! The one who started the fire outside my office!'

'What?' Sebastian's question cut through the air like cannon shot and he turned on his cousin. 'It isn't possible. Sonya, tell me it isn't possible. You know how I feel . . . how I felt . . . about Miss Barnum. How could you? Have you caused this mischief?'

Her laugh was shrill. 'Mischief! How simple and childish you make it sound. I did not wish to cause mischief; I wished to get rid of Miss Barnum once and for all.'

'You stabbed me,' I said. 'And you killed . . .' It was not the realization that I was staring down the barrel of a gun that caught in my throat but the memory of Jeffrey's bravery. 'When he tried to protect me, you killed Jeffrey Hollister. Did you kill Andrew Emerson, too?'

It was the first Madeline had heard of her brother's death and, at James's side, her head came up and her breath caught just as Sonya responded. 'He knew things he shouldn't have,' she told Sebastian. 'Things that would have ruined Succor.'

'You mean things that would have ruined Sebastian's scheme of selling women like cattle.' Though I knew I didn't stand a chance against the weapon she held, I dared to move a step closer to Sonya. 'Each time Andrew was in New York, he wrote dispatches for *The Intelligencer*, stories about his visits to the city. He was looking for Madeline when he was here. It was only natural that he would stumble upon the truth. And then . . .'

'And then I had no choice.' There was high color in Sonya's cheeks. 'I had to protect you, Sebastian. I followed Andrew

Emerson that night he went to the museum. There was no one around and a weapon close at hand. It was the perfect place.' She cocked her head and the feather at the side of her jaunty bonnet bobbed in the breeze. 'He was there to see you, wasn't he?' she asked me. 'Was he another of your lovers?'

'Andrew was a true friend,' I told her. 'He was a good man who wanted nothing more than to help his sister.'

Sonya's shoulders shot back. 'He had learned the truth of your dealings with South America, Sebastian. I don't know how. Andrew Emerson would have ruined everything for you. Just as Miss Barnum here would have ruined our chances at happiness together.'

'Our chances?' Sebastian's face twisted with confusion. 'But Sonya, we are nothing but business partners. I thought you understood that from the first day I took you into my confidence about our dealings with South America. It is Miss Barnum I love. Not as I did Marta, but perhaps, someday, my union with Evie would be as happy. Are you saying—'

'What you have always been too blind to see. I am the only one who could ever stand at your side. This woman will tell what you've done. No matter what she might promise to your face. She would never help you in this matter, not as I have. You can be sure of that. And if you let her leave now, she will surely report you to the authorities and then what will happen to you, Sebastian? What will happen to us? God help us, what will happen to dear Frida and Otto?'

When he looked at me, Sebastian's eyes misted. 'I thought you could be a mother to them and now . . .' It took him little time to make up his mind. Sebastian called Matron over. 'Bind her, and the other woman, too. We will see how much Miss Barnum has to say once she is in Argentina.'

I am not at all sure what made me angrier – Sebastian's pronouncement or the look of triumph on Sonya's face. My anger fueled my determination, and when Matron approached carrying a sturdy rope, I scuttled across the deck.

'Go ahead,' I challenged Sonya, 'shoot me, for I will not keep my peace about this, and I will not go quietly to Argentina or anywhere else.'

She leveled the pistol and aimed her sights down the barrel

and, though I refused to look away from her, I darted a glance around to see what I might use as cover. There were barrels – empty now – nearby and I had just judged the distance between them and myself and the chances that I could get behind them alive when a voice called out from the dock.

'Stop! You there! Stop now!' Constable Slater raced up the gangway as fast as a man of his age and size was able and, somehow, I wasn't surprised to see Phin right behind him.

'You there!' He landed on deck with a thud of sturdy brogans and pointed a walking stick at Sonya. 'Drop that gun. Right now!'

She did, and the fellows who'd raced onto the ship behind Slater and Phin surrounded Sonya and Sebastian.

'What is happening here? What is going on?' my brother wanted to know, but I silenced him with the wave of one hand.

'Sonya killed Andrew Emerson and Jeffrey Hollister,' I told the constable. 'As for Sebastian Richter . . . Send your men below deck. There you will find women who have been kidnapped by Mr Richter.'

I had never thought Slater to be especially bright, and I half expected him to question me but he did not. He did as he was told and, within fifteen minutes, Sebastian, Sonya and Matron had been shuffled off the boat and into a waiting carriage, their hands tied with the same sturdy rope Matron had thought to use to bind me for the journey to South America. Just a minute later, there was a commotion on the stairway and the first of the women walked up to the fresh air of the deck and freedom.

There were seven of them, all drugged enough to be glassy-eyed and confused, but none so dosed as to be insensible to what had nearly happened to them and how they had been saved.

'But how?' I asked Phin once the women were settled along the deck so that Slater might speak to them. 'How did you get here and how did you know—'

He pointed toward the dock where Frederick Withnower and Lulu waited.

'He's a good man,' Phin said. 'And bright enough to know there was something odd going on when that wagon appeared in the middle of the night at the home where the women were kept. He followed it, of course.'

'And went to you for assistance.' The sigh of relief I breathed shivered through my body. 'If it had not been for that—'

Phin put an arm around my shoulder and pulled me into a fierce hug. 'You are safe, as are these other young women. As for James Crockett . . .' His gaze traveled to where James was now propped against a stack of packing crates. His face was pale and his forehead would have been ringed with perspiration were it not for the fact that Madeline carefully dabbed it with her sleeve.

'It is his ship,' I told Phin. 'But I believe him when he says he knew nothing of the scheme. He needs a doctor.'

'Yes.' Phin bustled off. 'Mercer is here with me. I'll send him off to find a physician.'

I would just as well have waited there for Phin's return, where Constable Slater was speaking to the other women, but James held out a hand.

'Evie!' My name was punctuated by a stab of pain that clutched at his throat and twisted his handsome features. 'Evie, you're safe.' Something very much like a smile touched his lips. 'Come and tell me what's happening.'

I should have known better than to listen, but as always, James was lodestone and I nothing but a helpless piece of iron, powerless in his presence. I told myself it wasn't wise, but I went to him nonetheless.

He glanced at Madeline. 'Water, please,' he said, and she rose to her feet and went in search of it.

I took her place, kneeling at James's side.

'You've gotten yourself mixed up in some nonsense and that's sure enough.' The look he gave me carried the gleam of admiration. 'You were very brave.'

'And you should not be talking. There is a doctor coming to assist you.'

'Thank you, Evie.' I did not expect it so I hardly could have moved when he snatched up my hand in his. 'I do believe you saved the lives of all these women.'

'And my own,' I reminded him.

'And . . .' Another wave of anguish crossed his face and, this time, I knew it had nothing to do with the wound on his shoulder. 'What of our child, Evie? What has become of our child?'

It was a discussion I'd hoped to never have with him.

I coughed away my discomfort but I could not erase the pain of the words. 'Given up at birth. He is well and healthy.' His look was as gentle as the twilight quickly gathering around us. I sat back on my heels. 'You have no right to ask me any more.'

'I have . . .' He pressed his lips together. 'There is so much you don't know, so much I was never able to tell you. You think me a monster.'

Could I be strong in the face of the torment that wracked his soul?

I untangled my hand from his. 'I have seen your character with my own eyes. I know the kind of man you are.'

'But not the kind of man I would like to be. One who would treasure you and care for you, if only . . .'

My head was still too muzzy, my soul too deflated from all I'd seen. Exhaustion blanketed me, pressing against my shoulders and, in spite of it, I made to stand. 'I need none of your excuses and certainly none of your pity, sir. The doctor will be here soon and—'

He caught my hand in his. 'But I love you, Evie. I always have. There never has been another woman in my heart except you.'

I did not have a chance to be surprised at whatever words might have popped out of my mouth because from behind me came the sounds of breaking glass. I whirled and saw Madeline standing there, the glass of water she'd been carrying shattered around her feet.

'You told me . . .' Tears streamed down her cheeks. 'James, you said—'

'I never did,' he insisted. 'Madeline, you knew that from the start. You are lovely and charming and we had some good times together, did we not? But you are not—'

'Not Evie.' I knew she'd made a decision but I could not imagine what it might be. That is, until she turned and raced to the side of the ship. Too late, I saw her clutch the railing. Too late, I saw her lift a leg so that she might climb over.

'Madeline!' Too late, I screamed her name and was convinced she never would have stopped anyway.

Madeline Emerson took one last look at James and flung herself into the water.

Slater was nearby and he raced to the railing and called for help but, even so, we both knew it was already too late. The East River is vicious, the current bruising. It tugged Madeline under, then spit her up again, and she did not thrash and flail as so many would. She looked up to where James had dragged himself to the side of the ship, her hair around her shoulders like fire, and she smiled.

The current surged, the ship moaned and Madeline went under again.

The last we saw of her, her skirts were plastered against her hips and thighs yet flowing freely around her feet.

Like the tail of a mermaid.

TWENTY-ONE

I t was long past dark by the time we got home. My bonnet and cloak were long gone, back at the ship, I imagined, or perhaps left at the house with the green door, and though Portman looked at me in wonder for not having them, he never said a word.

'Sherry?' my brother asked. 'We have much to discuss.'

Yes, Sebastian Richter's vile and ugly scheme, Sonya's anger, Madeline's terrible, sad end. We might even discuss James who we'd left in the care of a physician on Nassau Street.

'I will be back down,' I assured my brother. My legs felt as if they were made of lead and my heart was just as heavy, but I knew what I had to do. I must unburden my heart and console my spirit, and there was only one way to do that. 'I'm going up to say goodnight to the children.'

'It's late.' Charity's voice called out from the parlor. 'The children are long in bed.'

Yes, I was sure of it.

I climbed the stairs, nevertheless, and went to the nursery to kiss my son goodnight.